DATE DUE		

MURDER by the TALE

MURDER
by the
TALE

Dell Shannon

WILLIAM MORROW AND COMPANY, INC. / NEW YORK

Library of Congress Cataloging-in-Publication Data

Shannon, Dell, 1921–
    Murder by the tale.
    1. Detective and mystery stories, American.
I. Title.
PS3562.I515M78   1987   813'.54   87-15419
ISBN 0-688-07538-X

Printed in the United States of America

First Edition

1 2 3 4 5 6 7 8 9 10

BOOK DESIGN BY MANUELA PAUL

Contents 〰

PART I

from the
MENDOZA
FILE

THE CLUE

Mendoza had just dealt the first hand round when the phone rang, and it was Hackett. "I suppose," said Hackett, "you'd just rung in the cold deck and were all set to go."

"This isn't funny," said Mendoza. "What in hell do you want?"

"You, *amigo*. In the office, right now."

"*¡Fuera!*" said Mendoza. "Unless the mayor's been murdered or war declared, you can go to hell."

"It's out of hours for me too, *chico*—if a cop ever does keep regular hours. But I think you'd better take a look, Luis—it's probably going to be what they call a *cause célèbre* and somebody over the rank of sergeant ought to handle it. It's Tommy Barron."

"Murdered? *¡Por Dios!* Then it could be somebody on the force did it—God knows he's got enough crooks away from us to annoy any peace officer but good."

"Not murdered, no. He's being held for one. Galeano and Matt went out on it. It looks awful damn open and shut, and he's got the thinnest story I ever heard. He asked for you—not that I hadn't decided to pass the buck myself, after Nick did to me—anyway, Barron's sitting here bleating for Lieutenant Mendoza like a lost lamb for its mama. Didn't know you knew him."

"I sat in with him at draw once," said Mendoza. Barron, of

· 9

course, was the lawyer you called in automatically if it was a serious charge on pretty good evidence—and you had the money. Or if you were somebody important in show business wanting a divorce or custody of the last-but-one spouse's kids. Nobody on the L.A.P.D., in uniform or out, liked Barron very much. Barron, on a homicide charge? "How very appropriate," said Mendoza. "I'll be there in twenty minutes." No good swearing. He apologized to the prosperous used-car dealer, the T.V. producer, the restaurateur and the man-about-town, left them in possession of his apartment, his cards, and his liquor (purchased especially for them: Mendoza never drank over cards), got out the new custom-built Facel-Vega and drove downtown to headquarters.

Sergeant Arthur Hackett met him outside his office. "It's the damndest setup, Luis. Looks as if he's got to be X, but would anybody with common sense do it that way?—let alone a smart boy like Barron? Here's this pro gambler, Jason Barker. Pro, *on* evidence collected. He was flush at the moment, by his room— Belvedere Arms Hotel on Wilshire. Somehow he gets into a game at a middling exclusive beach club with Barron and some friends of Barron's, and naturally they get took. So Barron— apparently—goes to see Barker at the hotel two hours ago and shoots him bang-bang with an old Colt .45. Which naturally brings everybody on that floor out of their rooms like scalded cats, so there's about a dozen can say they saw Barron hightailing it out of Barker's room. In fact, three men collared him on the run."

"That," said Mendoza, "sounds like any detective's fond dream of an easy case, Arturo. I see what you mean. Just a little too easy. Are those all the relevant facts you've got so far? Well, I'll see him before I hear any more."

Barron was sitting unhappily in Mendoza's office, a big bald stout man in good clothes, if not quite as dapper as the fastidious Mendoza's, or as expensive. For Mendoza, only grandson of a longtime miser, was a very wealthy man indeed, and still a police lieutenant only (as he said) because he'd never cured himself of earning an honest living; and he saw no reason he shouldn't enjoy his money. Barron jumped up and babbled at him, and Mendoza cut him off. "Let's just hear the story, Mr. Barron."

What it came down to, shorn of protestations that of course Mendoza as an honest and sensible fellow could evaluate it as the obvious truth at once, was about what Hackett had said. Plus a few nuances.

"How much did you lose to Barker?"

"Twelve hundred dollars. Now, obviously, Lieutenant—to be frank—none of us wanted publicity—" No, they wouldn't: the others, a bank vice-president, a wealthy local jeweler, a T.V. actor. Wouldn't want to show as suckers.

"Where did you meet him?"

"Er—Trevor" (the actor) "met him somewhere, I'm not sure—it was Trevor introduced him. He seemed a very good fellow, and quite well-off. But after this one evening of playing with him, well, we were sure he was crooked—I, er, remembered some of what you'd told me that time—"

Mendoza sighed. He had once sat in a game with Barron, indeed, and Barron was ripe for the taking. No card sense at all. Mendoza had mentioned to him, with purely altruistic motives, a few of the more common devices of the pro cheat.

"—But no sense in making it open, charging him. We, er, agreed on that. As it happened, I—well, not that I couldn't have written a check, but I thought cash preferable, and I had given him an I.O.U. I went to his hotel this evening to pay the debt in cash, and inform him that all of us had spotted him for a pro and it'd be as well for him to clear town." Of course, exactly what a cautious lawyer would do: nothing on paper. "That was all. I never *thought* of such a thing as— Really, Lieutenant, why should I? Twelve hundred dollars! I—"

Mendoza didn't see it himself. Barron wasn't a fool. Nor was he a dishonest lawyer: just damn smart at using the gimmicks and legal double-talk, and not particular about his clients. First rule of the con men: never try to take anybody at his own game. A lot of very smart boys were very dumb when it concerned somebody else's racket. "O.K., go on."

"He'd just let me in, and I gave him the money and began to

say all this, when the shot— I was really so startled, Lieutenant— he fell down, and I saw the blood, and then the gun fell on the floor beyond him—it was thrown from the bedroom door, I saw it in the air! It was somebody in the bedroom shot him. No, the bedroom was dark. I realized at once what an, er, invidious position I— Really, I was so startled and confused—"

"That you just bolted," said Mendoza. A thin story indeed: yet very human. Even for a lawyer, who was also human (despite some contrary evidence) and subject to losing his head. Barron had heard as thin stories from a lot of clients; and yes, he was a smart boy in the courtroom, but like most lawyers a sedentary man with small experience of real action.

He told Barron he'd look at the case personally, listened to some earnest and flattering gratitude, and saw him shepherded mournfully away. He collected Hackett and drove out to the Belvedere Arms. Barker had been in the money all right. A suite, living room and bedroom: low elegant modern furniture, a couple of cryptic abstract watercolors and a big ornate gilt-framed mirror. Mendoza straightened his tie absently, faced with the reflections of the slim dark dapper moustached man and the hulking sandy bulk of Hackett beside him.

"Here was where Barker fell." Chalk outline in the middle of the carpet, feet toward the bedroom door. "He got it in the back, right through the spine."

"*Vaya*," said Mendoza. "Turned away for a minute, when a man was inferentially threatening him? Not what an experienced pro would do."

"*Pues sí*," said Hackett, who found Mendoza handy to practice his Spanish on. "But did he turn away? No telling how he fell. He might have had his back to the bedroom door."

Mendoza went into the bedroom. "Prints finished in here? O.K.," and he switched on the light. A nice big bedroom, a walk-in closet. "Damn," he said, eyeing the other door. This suite was at the end of a wing, and there was an outside door in the opposite wall, to a cross hall.

Hackett read his mind accurately. "We'll never make the

charge stick," he agreed. "It *could* be that somebody else got in that door and shot him from here. It just *could* be."

"They have house service? As I thought. I want the maid, if she's still on duty." Mendoza found the phone.

"The manager's having kittens by the litter. This is a respectable place, so he says."

"Money is not," said Mendoza, "inevitably respectable. *Al contrario.*" He identified himself to the desk and issued polite commands.

"Some nice evidence of Barker's profession scattered around. Half a dozen decks of readers, all the best money can buy—edge work and concave strippers. Me, I always figured it as the hardest way to make a living there is. You got to have eyes like a hawk and a memory like God."

"You do. Too early to say about the gun, I suppose, or these other three easy marks."

"The gun, yes. They do float around. No telling, except that it's kind of a museum piece—about 1880, I'd say. Must have a kick like an army mule, it—"

"Never mind the gun, just trace it if possible." Mendoza wasn't much interested in guns, never carried one unless necessary; he was forced as an efficient police officer to take some notice of facts, but instinctively felt people to be more important.

"The other three, no, not too early. Under your stern training, boy? A little checking done already. They don't seem to be hard up, they all paid off Barker in checks which've been cleared, by all the evidence. You'll have noticed that Barker was about to clear out."

"Spare me the obvious comment." One suitcase shut and locked, one open on the bed, nearly packed. "I take it the boys put everything back as it was for me. O.K. He was clearing as soon as he had Barron's twelve hundred. I've often thought," added Mendoza, looking into the closet, peering under the bed, "how nice to be a detective in a detective story. They get clues left for them, and they get mixed up in such bizarre plots—

complex, you know—that there are inevitably only a couple of solutions, which any damned idiot could arrive at—"

"If he wasn't bein' distracted by blondes and bullets."

"As you say." Mendoza got up, dusted himself off, resettled his tie and went to answer the door. The girl in the hall was a pretty one, even if she hadn't any makeup on at all, and was dressed in a white cotton uniform, flat-heeled shoes. About twenty-eight: dark hair pulled back to a prim bun, downcast eyes.

"You asked for the maid this floor, sir. I already told the police what I know. I mean, I don't mind, sir, but I ought to be on duty."

"I'm surprised to find you here at such an hour." Mendoza, putting out his automatic charm with females, ushered her in, offered a chair, a cigarette; but she stood woodenly, hands clasped, looking past him.

"Miss Agnes Williams," said Hackett *sotto voce*.

"There's a maid on duty up to eleven each floor, sir. Part of the service. We're on a couple hours in the morning—more of us then, I mean—and then six to eleven. There's room service, and sometimes people want other things. Part of the service, sir."

"I see. Well, now, just a few questions." But he didn't get much out of her. Yes, she'd done Mr. Barker's room while he was here. No, she hadn't talked much with him; he wasn't always there, of course. No, she hadn't liked him; he was a bad man. "Bad?" said Mendoza. "Why do you think so, Miss Williams?"

"I don't know—just something about his looks," she said after hesitation.

"You come on duty at six, you said? Where were you when you heard the shot—you did hear it?"

"Oh, yes, sir. I was down at the end of the cross hall. I don't know what time exactly, but—"

"Ten past six or thereabouts," contributed Hackett, "by the other witnesses."

"I was in the linen closet there. I looked back where it seemed to come from, but there wasn't anybody there."

"You didn't see anyone come out the bedroom door of this suite?"

"Oh, no, sir. Besides, it'd be locked. . . . No, sir, the person renting it wouldn't have a key. It's a kind of service door but we don't use it anymore."

"Who would have a key?"

"I dunno, sir."

Mendoza let her go. "I suppose you knew all that."

"Nick had seen her, yes. You're always so hot on getting things yourself."

"You know me too well, Art." Mendoza wandered over to the bed, prodded thoughtfully at the middling-expensive clothes in the suitcase. "What was on him?"

"Four thousand two hundred and thirty bucks in a money belt, forty-odd in his wallet, a little change, handkerchief, two diamond rings, lighter. No keys—he traveled light like all that kind and kept his cash on him. Barron's twelve hundred was still in his hand when he fell—sixty twenties. Come on, have a hunch, Luis. Look into your crystal ball."

"Even Barron might lose his temper and pull such a damn fool stunt. He can afford the twelve hundred, sure, but it's one thing losing it honest and another having it cheated out of you. I'd like to know what those other three fellow-suckers were up to at ten past six."

Hackett lit a cigarette and said, "We can go ask one of 'em right now. I've got Bert and Higgins out chasing up the others, but the actor—Trevor Forsythe—lives two floors down, here. I expect that's how come he met Barker in the first place."

"You're going out of the way to be helpful tonight," said Mendoza, irritated.

"I had a date spoiled too. Not with a nice net profit out of an evening of draw, but with a blonde."

"You'd do better to stick to poker," said Mendoza, already on the way to the elevator. "Though you haven't much finesse at either."

"Not compared to the famous Mendoza," admitted Hackett, "granted. Two-oh-four's the apartment we want."

"These damn fools. Sitting in a nice friendly game with the pleasant stranger met at a bar. Why do we bother to protect them?"

Trevor Forsythe, whose original name had probably been something very different, was at home, wrapped in a carefully flamboyant silk dressing gown. He was cordial, regretful, and nicely under control: very sure, gentlemen, that all this would be straightened out and it would be shown that Mr. Barron had nothing whatever to do with it. After all, a man such as they suspected this Barker to have been undoubtedly would have had enemies among his own underworld acquaintances.

"Quite possible," agreed Mendoza.

"Can't I offer you a drink?"

"Thanks very much," said Mendoza absently, thereby surprising Hackett; and astonished him further by accepting and drinking a Scotch and water. Mendoza's drink was rye and very little of that; but he seemed mildly hypnotized by the mantel wall, on which was hung a fine collection of handguns. He gestured at it. "None of those missing, Mr. Forsythe?"

Forsythe turned a little pale and said with a forced laugh, "Good lord, no! They're purely decorative—I—most of 'em presents, actually. Since I've been doing this western thing, *Law Man,* you know . . . A C-Colt Forty-five? I really couldn't say, I'm afraid I—"

"Must be," said Hackett, looking, "in any respectable wild West collection. That's the gun, they tell me, that opened up the West. Yes, there's one. I don't suppose there'd've been two?"

"Look," said Forsythe, "what *is* this? I heard the story from the maid when I got in a few minutes ago, but I gathered Barron witnessed the murder—that—well, I mean—"

"You mean," said Mendoza, "that you were hoping like hell to stay clear of any publicity, whether Barron's guilty or not."

"Well, all right," said Forsythe angrily, "take it that way. I've got a reputation to lose. You trying to make out *I* killed that damn pro crook for nine hundred and fifty bucks?"

"I'd just like to know where you were," said Mendoza, "at six or six-fifteen."

"I was in the Copa bar," said Forsythe instantly, "with my agent and his wife, and we went on to dinner. I'll give you his name."

"Thanks very much," and Mendoza took it down and marched out with Hackett on his heels. They almost ran into the maid for this floor, who was passing with a stack of clean bedding. She sidestepped them neatly. She was a pretty redhead, and Mendoza turned and looked after her.

"You're supposed to be working," said Hackett, "and besides I think you've got a redhead in your collection."

"A much nicer one than that," agreed Mendoza. "Something just—oh, well, let it go, it'll come to me. This is wasting time. What did you haul me out for? This is underlings' work, checking out alibis and so on. All I've done is assure Barron of deluxe investigation. I don't give a damn whether Barron shot him or not, but I can't find any clues to say yes or no until all the evidence is in. I'm going home. We'll see what the boys turn up tomorrow."

"With every reporter in L.A. breathing down our necks."

"He's too smart to run if we let him loose—with a leash on him. His reputation—"

"Like Forsythe," and Hackett laughed. "That was funnier than any gag I ever heard on T.V. What?—oh, you wouldn't get it, not bein' so bourgeois to look at the stuff. Brother, *doesn't* the star of *Law Man* have a reputation to lose! He's cast as a demon poker player, and to have it come out in the *Times* he got took by a cheap pro—!"

"Mmh. Probably just as handy with a Colt as he is with the cards in real life. We'll send somebody to check that alibi. It's only ten o'clock."

At headquarters, he dispatched a man after Forsythe's agent, set the night staff to copy the various statements taken, sent a note to Ballistics demanding data on the gun at the earliest moment, and told Hackett to go back to his blonde. He went home himself, found the poker party still in possession, and in the next hour and a half took a net profit of a hundred and twelve dollars. When they'd gone, he cut up fresh liver for the sleek Abyssinian feline personage who lived with him, the green-eyed Bast, let her out and in again, and had a bath. And he thought, So, make it complicated: say Barron's too smart for such a thing. Anybody can lose his head. If he didn't, what do we have? Somebody in the bedroom who dissolved into thin air after the shot was fired. *¡Vaya historia!*

It wouldn't, however, do Barron any harm to spend the night in jail. Or even longer, he thought; and Bast purred in agreement.

There was just something—if he could only think what it was—some little nuance which had struck him as somehow significant. It had something to do with that redhaired maid outside Forsythe's apartment. Oh, well, sleep on it . . .

Forsythe's alibi checked out. The bank vice-president had been at home giving a dinner party. The jeweler had been entering a restaurant with his wife and mother-in-law. There was, of course, something in what Forsythe said: pro boys like Barker had undesirable acquaintances.

The faithful Higgins, Dwyer, and Landers turned up a few of them by that next afternoon. A couple of casuals who followed the ponies, the proprietor of a professional gambling house outside city limits, a small-time would-be pro not in miles of Barker's class: Mendoza placed them all as they came before him. He concentrated on Edwards, the small-timer (much to Edwards' uneasiness) because he seemed to have known Barker best. Which wasn't saying much.

"I dint know him real *good*, Lieutenant—honest—you know, just from seeing him around places" (gambling places, he meant) "and maybe Santa Anita once. You know how you just get talkin', but I dint *know* him really. . . . No, I dunno anybody mighta had it in for him. Gee, a real pro, was he? I dint know that. Honest, I dint." Which was a lie. "He seemed O.K., you know, just seeing him around like I did. I guess if he was, maybe a lot of guys mighta had it in for him, knowing they'd got took. I figured, when I saw the papers, it was a dame. I mean, it said about this big lawyer, but gee, a lawyer'd have more sense 'n to do it like that, like any cheap hood! Maybe not, I dunno. *I* never sat in a game with Barker, *I* wouldn't've had no reason—"

"Why'd you think it was a woman?" asked Mendoza.

"Well, see, he was an awful chaser, that I *do* know. Only

thing he ever thought about outside o' cards. You could tell by his talk—you know. Allus tellin' about all the dames he'd made—St. Louis, N'York, N'Orleans, Chicago *an'* points west like they say. He had ten stories about dames he'd laid for every town in the country. I just figured maybe one caught up to him.''

"And that could be," said Mendoza. He let Edwards go. The house proprietor said indifferently he'd never caught Barker cheating in his place; but anyway he hadn't come often. No, Barker would have angled for classier society groups where the stakes would be higher. Taken a nice little haul here, fifty-five hundred or so, and was moving on: voluntarily, as the gambler's restlessness urged him, or on the run from a threat? No saying.

So Barker had been a womanizer. Did that say anything?

Hackett came in and asked, "You want to see those two track followers again? O.K., I'll let 'em go. Here's Ballistics' report on the gun.''

Nice solid facts were always useful, and this one certainly was. Disregarding all the long-winded scientific officialese which proved the Colt to be indeed the gun which had fired the slug found in Barker, Mendoza skimmed down to the bottom of the page. As per requirements of state law for persons intending to carry firearms on the person or from one place to another in any vehicle, the gun was registered. Its license was held by Mr. Stanley William Burke, described as a salesman for a large engineering firm in San Francisco.

"Ah," said Mendoza, picked up the outside phone and got San Francisco, got the firm in question, identified himself, was put through to Personnel, and asked the whereabouts of Mr. Stanley Burke.

"Police," said the anxious male voice of Personnel. "Dear me, I do hope he's not in any trouble down there? One of our steadiest men—Well, of course, anything we can do to help, Lieutenant—Not an *accident*, is it? Oh, well. Let me see . . . Mr. Burke should have arrived in Los Angeles on the twelfth, and would be staying at the Belvedere Arms Hotel until the fifteenth. I do *trust* nothing unfortunate has—"

"Thank you very much," said Mendoza, and replaced the

phone, automatically lining it up nice and neat with the desk box and blotter. One of the reasons Luis Rodolfo Vicente Mendoza had a little reputation as a detective: the thing all untidy irritated him as much as the crooked picture or the wrinkle in the rug, and he had to get it all neatly straightened out. This looked like smoothing out some large wrinkles at once.

He took up his hat and drove the Facel-Vega uptown to the Belvedere Arms. The firm was a very wealthy one and its few salesmen could afford such places, of course. He asked for Mr. Burke: was he in? By a fortunate chance Mr. Burke was. Room 420.

"A *gun*," said Stanley Burke. "Why, yes, I have." He did not look perturbed, only curious. The consciously honest citizen, a big hefty man, good-humored-looking and prosperous. "You're a *police* lieutenant? Well, you'll find everything in order, I'm sure. See, I'm driving around a lot of miles, all day and every day, long night runs sometimes, and you never know what you'll run into. I figure it's only smart to pack a gun. Never had to use it—don't really expect to—but it's just as well. I've got a license—"

"I know you have," said Mendoza. "But why such a gun, Mr. Burke? A clumsy big thing like that Colt?"

Burke grinned. "Hell, maybe I'm cheap. I *had* it—it belonged to my grandfather. And you know, I carry it mostly for effect, to show if I get into some situation—know what I mean—and it looks a damn lot more impressive than these little automatics."

"I believe you," said Mendoza. "It's a lot of gun. May I see it?"

"Sure," and Burke went over to the bureau and opened the top right drawer. He was silent a moment and then said quietly, "Well, I guess you won't. It's gone."

"So it is," said Mendoza. "We've got it downtown. It killed a man last night."

"My good God above," said Burke, "you don't mean that fellow down the hall—that you're holding this lawyer for? But, my God—how could he have my gun? The door was locked, I was—"

"Where?" murmured Mendoza, lighting a new cigarette.

"My *God!*" said Burke. He fetched out a bottle of Scotch, mutely offered it, and at Mendoza's head shake poured a stiff drink for himself. "I never— I missed all the excitement, I was out with a client of the firm until eleven— What? No, I didn't come back here before dinner, I went straight from— I was out from nine in the morning. Heard about it when I got in—from the fellow in the next room, he was one of the ones stopped this lawyer when he ran, he'd been down at your headquarters making a statement. But *my* gun—"

"Room door locked, you said. When did you last see the gun, to know it was here?"

"My God, I've got to say it'd be when I unpacked two days ago. I don't take much notice of it as a rule—it's a habit—you know. Never had to use it. Loaded? Yes, sir, I'm afraid it is."

"It's still got five cartridges in it. Or had. Ballistics used a couple getting samples to compare. And of course," said Mendoza, smoking dreamily, "that's one thing about those old Colts. Anybody, even someone who's never handled a gun before, can see whether they're loaded or not—cartridges in plain sight in that open cylinder."

"That's so," agreed Burke numbly. "Look here, I can *prove* where I was when it happened. Carmody—fellow next door— said about six. Well, I was just meeting this client and his partner then, at a restaurant out on La Cienega, and we were there until ten o'clock—"

"Claro que sí," said Mendoza to himself, "no doubt. Everybody has alibis in this business. Good ones. Except Mr. Barron. Do you know Mr. Barron?"

"Never laid eyes on him," said Burke promptly. "Sure you won't have a drink? My God, this shakes me. *My* gun. But who—"

"Yes, who. How d'you know you never laid eyes on him, maybe under another name?" But that was reaching for it: it wasn't so difficult to get hold of a gun that anybody would go to all that trouble, and besides—

"Newspaper picture this morning," said Burke. "He's nobody I ever saw. I'd heard of him, of course. I thought at the time, it seems funny a smart lawyer'd do a murder that way, if he was going to."

"In spite of the fact that we don't love Mr. Barron very much, it seemed a little funny to us too," said Mendoza, and took out notebook and pen. "Let's have the names of your clients and the restaurant, please. Just to check—I wouldn't worry about it."

"My God," said Burke, and supplied them. "*My* gun. I can't get over it. Well, I guess if we knew the truth it's got other notches on it—baby as old as that. Tell you one thing, I'm damn glad you boys have got I.Q.s over a hundred these days—*and* that I've got a watertight alibi!"

"You should be," said Mendoza, and went downstairs to see the manager. And what did he get from that, that meant one damn thing?

A few suites had those second doors; they weren't used now. They had the same locks as the main doors. No, probably the maids (who had master keys, yes) wouldn't realize that: no occasion to know. No one else but the manager himself had a master. And the master keys the maids had fitted only the rooms on each maid's particular floor. No, of course, the manager had never known Mr. Barker personally: a transient guest, here for the first time. Really, Lieutenant—

"*¡Qué mono!* Isn't this pretty?" said Mendoza to himself behind the wheel of the Facel-Vega. It was after five. Time out to ruminate; and he might as well let his subconscious mind work on it in pleasant company. He stopped at the next public phone and called his redhead, Alison Weir, to invite her to dinner.

"*You!*" said Alison.

"What have I done, *chica*?"

"Not you, the phone. I was sitting here in absolute silence—you know how quiet this street is—putting on new lipstick, when the phone rang and I leaped three feet and ran the lipstick halfway down my chin. You should see—"

"*Lipstick,*" said Mendoza. "*Lipstick. ¡Ca!* Am I woolgathering? Is it a clue at last? . . . Listen, *querida,* I meant to say dinner tonight, but let's say tomorrow? I think after all I may be busy tonight. Six-thirty, O.K.'' He replaced the receiver and stared unseeingly at the pencil scrawls on the wall of the booth. *Lipstick.*

He drove back to the Belvedere Arms and met Hackett in the foyer. ''Finally tracked you down,'' said Hackett. ''For once I'm ahead of you. Bert turned up a fellow who'd sat in with Barker at that house, and I questioned him. He said he'd seen Barker with a tall thin blonde, and the last time he saw them together they were having an argument. He thinks Barker called her Betty—''

''Mary, Ann, Jean, what the hell,'' said Mendoza. ''I don't think it matters, on account of the gun. No.'' He went back to the manager's office, Hackett trailing him, and the manager sighed with ostentatious patience. ''Tell me, do you have any rules for the maids here, about their personal appearance? That they're not supposed to wear makeup?''

The manager stared. ''Good heavens, of course not. We'd never keep any maids, Lieutenant. Why?''

''I just wondered about Agnes Williams. The fourth-floor maid. I saw another one looking—mmh—quite the usual young woman, powder and lipstick, but the Williams girl, no. It's unusual.''

The manager unbent a trifle. ''It is. Miss Williams—she's, er, rather voluble about it if encouraged—is a member of one of these obscure militant-Puritan sects that preach plain unvarnished living, if you know what I mean. Very conscientious maid.''

''I see. I rather thought it might be something like that. This obnoxious so-called casual look—the rat-gnawed haircut and unmanicured toenails—they still stick to lipstick and mascara. Thanks very much. She's on duty? Yes, it's just six.'' Mendoza took Hackett down to the elevator, the manager's curious gaze after them.

''And what has Agnes Williams' unvarnished complexion got to do with Jason Barker down in the morgue?''

"Possibly quite a lot," said Mendoza. "Because, just as I said, practically all of them use *something*. And practically all of them—young women, say, under thirty-five—what's the casual pass? They know how to turn it down, get out of the situation— even a little compliment attached to it. They say in effect, No nonsense now, and that's that. *¿Y eso qué importa?*"

"Sure. So?"

"So, there are here and there a few young women it means more to. The very inexperienced, shy ones. And Barker was a casual womanizer. No snide remarks about my understanding the types because I'm the same kind! Degrees in these things. I read him—maybe in my crystal ball—the kind who automatically gave anything female the old routine. Mostly not meaning much by it. The careless hug, the casual hint and word. You know."

The elevator stopped and they got out on the fourth floor. The corridor was quiet, empty; and then Agnes Wiliams came round the corner from the cross hall, her master keys faintly jingling, and hesitated at the sight of them, and came on.

"I'd like you to answer just a few more questions, Miss Williams," said Mendoza.

"All right, sir." She stood stiff before him, hands clasped at her waist, not looking at him. She could have been a very pretty girl—the dark hair looser to frame her thin face, a little color on lip and cheek, a little tinted powder on the sallow skin; as it was, she was just a regular-featured young woman.

"How did you happen to notice Mr. Burke's gun?" asked Mendoza. "Or do you know his name? Room four-twenty. In the right top bureau drawer."

A long dragging second, and then she lifted her eyes to his. They were brown eyes, long-lashed and beautiful. "He left it open," she said dully. "I knew you'd find out. It's a judgment on me, I suppose. We aren't supposed to—to feel hate and want revenge. But I couldn't help it. He was a wicked, wicked man."

"You took the gun the last time you cleaned four-twenty?"

"For all I know," she said (hands still primly clasped before her), "he was the same one as—as *took* Elsie. My sister, sir. She was a good girl, saved in Christ like me, until *he* came along—whoever he was, I never knew. A tempter from the devil, he was—like this one here. And afterward Elsie hanged herself, because she'd sinned. I don't *know* he was the same one, but he was the same *kind*. Making up to me—calling me *darling* and *honey*. And trying to—to—to kiss me. He was a very wicked loose evil man. A fornicator like the minister calls it.''

"Yes," said Mendoza. "And you happened to notice the gun because the drawer was left open.''

"I could see it had bullets in it. I know—now—it was a wrong thing, in a kind of way," she said wretchedly, and for the first time her hands moved, twisted on each other. "He was a bad man, but I don't *know* he was the one—did that awful thing to Elsie. I just thought—for Elsie. So he couldn't ever make anyone *else* go to sinning.''

"Why just then, Miss Williams?" asked Mendoza gently. "When had he last approached you?"

"I'd thought about it—since—I saw the gun. Because he was a wicked bad man, a fornicator. Maybe—it's hard to know—it was really the devil tempting me. On account of Elsie. But I saw him come back to his room then—I'd just come on duty—and he walked like a—a big tiger. And I went to the linen closet to get the sheets for four-sixteen, only I kept *seeing* him, and feeling how—that morning—he touched me and said *darling*. A terrible evil man, he was. He'd maybe do the same sin to other good Christian girls like Elsie. I knew about the keys. . . . I don't mind telling about it now, it's like I always knew you'd find out, sir. . . . Absentminded like once, I tried my master in one of those bedroom doors, and it worked, so I knew. I don't know why I used that door then—I didn't know there was anybody with him. I just did. Maybe cause it was nearer. If whoever's in four-twenty had *been* there, I couldn't've taken the gun—but they weren't, and I did, and I went in the bedroom door of four-eleven and it was dark, but I saw him in the living room there ahead of me. I'd never fired a gun before but he wasn't so far away. But it was awful all the same, such a noise. I didn't go to steal the gun, so I left it. I threw it beside him. It's the Lord's retribution you found out, sir, and I'm willing and able to stand anything they do to me for it. But I can't say I'm sorry. He was a terrible wicked man.''

"And that," said Mendoza, "could be the truth. I must ask you to come with me now, Miss Williams."

"Yes, sir," she said submissively.

"That one you got out of your crystal ball all right," said Hackett.

"Not at all," said Mendoza, faintly irritated. "Purely common-sense reasoning, because of the gun. Despite all Tommy Barron's fulsome flattery. That man annoys me, Art. What odds do you take he defends that girl and gets her off on insanity, stashed away in Camarillo for five years and let loose?"

"No bets with you," said Hackett. "I wouldn't doubt. I won't like it either. But on the other hand, what loss was Barker?"

Mendoza looked even more annoyed. "You miss the point, Arturo. What a chance it was to get rid of Barron! How many guilty-as-charged felons will we arrest this next twenty years, and see Barron get them off? And we could have put him in San Quentin on this! But unfortunately—*¡un millón de diablos!*—unfortunately I'm an honest man.''

THE CAT

$\sim\!\!\mathcal{O}$ rdinarily Hackett would have handled it; but he took one look at this case and called Mendoza. And Mendoza dropped everything and pointed the Facel-Vega toward the Hollywood freeway within ten minutes. Not that it looked like a very difficult job: that was just it. But the obviously guilty party was a member of the force, and the L.A.P.D. as a crack police force with a reputation for integrity takes a poor view of having to charge one of its own men.

The house was a shabby middle-aged frame bungalow, on the same kind of street, in middle-class Hollywood. Mendoza got there while the headquarters boys were still busy, and the doctor. In the living room a big fair man sat alongside Sergeant Arthur Hackett on a lumpy couch; he looked half dazed.

"—For my uniform," he was saying. "Came back this morning for my uniform, I'm on eight to four shift, out of Hollenbeck precinct like you know. I got to call in, tell them—"

"It's been taken care of, Gibson," said Hackett, and sketched a shrug at Mendoza. Mendoza went on across a little dark hall to the front bedroom. Dr. Bainbridge was there, the boys from Prints, a photographer. There was also a dead woman. Very dead, sprawled gracelessly facedown on the floor beside the double bed. A lot of dark patches of dried blood on the shabby braided rug. The photographer was focusing on the left-hand footboard of the bed; there was a blinding flash as he exposed the plate.

"Well, when and how?" asked Mendoza of the surgeon.

Bainbridge said, "Morning, Luis. Not very nice. You can see for yourself. Beaten to death—partly fists, mostly that big solid walnut footboard—held and slammed down on it. At a guess, between eleven and two A.M. Maybe tell you nearer after the autopsy."

Mendoza stepped up closer as the photographer moved away, and then stopped, holding himself from involuntary recoil. He'd seen a lot of corpses, and he didn't mind this woman lying there bloody and ugly; but he did mind the cat, half under the bed. Also beaten, bloody, and dead. Mendoza was a cat person, one of the large company who understands and approves that old Persian king who cut off a piece of his robe rather than disturb his sleeping cat.

After a moment he knelt over the corpse and gently drew the dead cat out beside it. A handsome cat, it had been: a silver-gray almost-Persian with big green eyes. He smoothed the blood-stiffened long hair absently.

Hackett came in and said the morgue wagon was here. "O.K., they can have her," said Bainbridge.

"And the cat," said Mendoza. He stood up.

"I'm not a vet, Luis."

"I said and the cat. For dignified disposal." Mendoza looked around the room, lighting a cigarette. The Prints boys packed up and drifted off; the photographer had finished. Bainbridge shrugged and went out after him. "Let's hear the sad story."

"And it is," said Hackett. "He's got a good record. John Edward Gibson, eleven years on the force. One of our faithful workhorses—never made rank, still on traffic duty. No black marks at all. In fact, the only outstanding thing about him is that he finished among the finalists in the marksmanship competitions several years running. A good, honest, conscientious cop. Only he had a wife."

"It's a misfortune hits a lot of men," said Mendoza.

"They didn't get along very well, the ten years they've been married. No kids. By what a couple of neighbors say, she was

social-minded, liked to go out, give parties, and he didn't. A lot
more to it than that, of course. Anyway, they didn't get along,
that's common knowledge to everyone knew 'em. He didn't fight
back at her—one of the long-suffering kind—she just nagged at
him. That kind of thing. It can build up in a man.''

"*De veras,*" agreed Mendoza.

"So they have a real fight last night—him too—the neighbors
heard it, it bein' hot weather and windows open—and Gibson
slammed out of the house. About ten o'clock. Nobody heard or
saw him come back, and of course he says he didn't. Says he
went to his brother's place—out west of La Brea—and slept on
the sofa there. Came back at seven this morning to get his
uniform before going on duty, and found her. Only"—Hackett
sighed—"there aren't any signs of forcible entry. Whoever it
was had a key or was let in.''

"*¡Ya está!*" said Mendoza. "And he called the precinct like a
responsible citizen and reported it.''

"He did. He's put up a nice act, Luis. Dazed, shocked, and so
on. Must've been somebody broke in—a thief.'' Hackett swore
softly. "It doesn't happen often, but it happens. God knows
we're human like everybody else. And when it shows, the public
saying, Yah, look at the kind they hire for cops, thugs and
killers!''

"I don't like it either, boy," said Mendoza. "But let's not
jump to conclusions. It looks open and shut, but we'll work it
thorough as any other case, or more so. Who's here?—well, let
Landers take him downtown, and if possible let's keep this away
from the press boys, until I've had a chance to catch my breath.''
The ambulance men were taking out the body. Mendoza bent and
picked up the cat, very gently. He went out to the living room
behind the stretcher bearers, and his eyes went straight to Gibson.

Gibson, the unambitious harness-horse cop with a good
record, sitting hunched on the sofa. Gibson looked up slowly,
and winced away from the stretcher, and saw Mendoza; and he
lurched up to his feet.

"Lieutenant—" He recognized Mendoza, who had a little

reputation on this force. "Lieutenant—" And he saw what Mendoza carried, and said in a little gasp, "Oh, Queenie—they needn't have killed *Queenie*—oh, poor baby, Queenie, I'm so sorry—"

He was still standing there when Mendoza came back from the ambulance. But he'd got a better grip on himself. He said, "Lieutenant, I know how this looks. It's an awful thing— discredit the force, too, I know how it *looks*—but I didn't do it, sir! It's just like I told Sergeant Hackett, sir—I was out at Jim's all night, it must've been a burglar broke in or something. I can't say we got along—I *tried*, but we didn't. I might've walked out on her—it was in my mind last night—but, my God, why'd I want to kill her, like *that*? I wouldn't've. Even after the fight we had. I never did, sir."

Mendoza just stood and looked at him.

"It must've been burglars, or— But they needn't have killed Queenie too," said Gibson, bitter and hurt. Delayed reaction was on him; his eyes filled with tears and he sat down again heavily, knuckling his eyes like a child. Landers and Dwyer came in from the bedroom. "Ethel didn't like cats much," said Gibson numbly. "Queenie was *mine*, I'm the one who took care of her. They needn't've—"

Mendoza said softly to himself, *"¡Ca!"* And to Hackett, "Wait awhile, he can go downtown anytime. Ten minutes." He went out the front door and looked up and down the street. Neighbors probably watching avidly from windows: a knot of people a few houses down, talking excitedly. Patrol car still here, two uniformed men lounging beside it. He went to the house next door and rang the bell, and said to the eager-eyed fat matron who answered it, "Excuse me, have you a cat?"

"A *cat*!" She was taken aback. He produced his credentials, which increased the eagerness and bewilderment in her expression.

"Just to borrow for ten minutes, please."

"Well, *really*. I don't—there's the kitten, but what d'you *want* with it? S.'pose we got to oblige *police*, but if you figure *do* anything to it I really couldn't—Jeanie thinks the world 'n' all of that kitten, I—''

"It'll be quite all right," said Mendoza.

It was a pure alley-cat kitten, long-nosed and short-haired and striped black on gray: a vigorous and voluble tom kitten who struggled in his grasp. The housewife came out on her porch to keep a suspicious eye on him as he went back to the Gibson house. He got the kitten soothed down a little with judicious stroking; it began to purr rustily.

"Gibson," he said.

The man looked up; there were incongruous tears still clinging to his sandy beard-stubble. "Yes, sir," he said, "yes, sir?" And saw the kitten, and said dully, "What you doing with Butchie? Butchie doesn't like strangers much—" Mendoza handed him the kitten and he settled it on his knee, stroking it, automatic, gentle. The kitten's purr grew louder; it began to knead his trouser leg rhythmically. "Butchie belongs next door, he's Jeanie Sonderberg's kitten. He get in the back door, maybe?"

"O.K.," said Mendoza. "I'll take Butchie back home, Gibson. It's O.K., you go downtown and make a statement, and don't worry. We'll find out who did it. I'll have to hold you overnight at least, but don't worry."

"I've known your hunches sound pretty damn wild," said Hackett, "but this one must've hit you from outer space."

"Not a hunch at all," said Mendoza. "He didn't do it—he couldn't have done it, Art. He might have murdered his wife, most of us are capable of murder under the wrong conditions, but he'd never have killed the cat. He likes cats, and Queenie was his very own."

"If he was mad enough—these patient dumb fellows, when they *do* lose their tempers they go berserk. If the cat got in his way—"

"*Pues sí,* but he didn't go berserk. The neighbors saw him leave, you said. If he'd been going to lose his temper far enough to kill her, it'd have been right then. Any witnesses to her being alive after he left at ten? Well, we'll see. Bainbridge says she was killed at the earliest by eleven. But I don't care how far Gibson might lose his temper, then or later, he'd never have done *that* to his Queenie.''

"How can you be—''

"I know how cat people behave with cats. He's not putting on the sentimental act, Art. Now we'll get busy and find something to prove it.'' Mendoza wandered through the house. "She was a careless housekeeper—untidy.'' He found dust on the furniture, dirty dishes in the sink, litter of magazines and unironed laundry, and frowned at all of it disapprovingly. One of his sergeants had once expressed the opinion that if Mendoza found an uneven number of hairs in his precisely trimmed moustache, it worried him all day. The orderly mind, that was Mendoza. "She also had very bad taste. *Caray,* pink curtains and blue linoleum! But not really a motive to kill her, except to a purist. . . . And what have we here?''

"I said he'd taken a couple of medals as a marksman,'' said Hackett. This was the spare bedroom, rudely furnished as a study. A homemade guncase was built along the back wall, containing a couple of shotguns, a couple of rifles; a smaller open rack below it held three handguns, one the regulation .38 Gibson would carry when uniformed, the others a prewar Luger and a Browning automatic. Mendoza looked at them and then pulled out the top drawer of the old bureau nearby, handling it at the bottom edge to avoid the knobs.

"Nice supply of ammunition for the whole collection. You didn't send Prints in here, I see. Nowhere but the bedroom? Well, I think we'll have the boys take a look. I'm surprised at you, Art—you're better trained than that, at least since you've been working with me! Get them back, I want the whole house printed.''

"What fairy tale are you dreaming up, *chico*? I'd be just as happy as you to think he isn't X, but I think it's a waste of time.''

"*¡No me repliques*—don't answer back!'' said Mendoza. "I'm not intending to manufacture any evidence. Get on the phone, bring the boys back and do your homework over. I'm going to see if Gibson's brother can give him an alibi." He picked up his hat, started for the door, and turned to add, "Have a good look round the yard too, will you?—front *and* back."

"*Está muy pagado de sí*,—hasn't he the high opinion of himself," said Hackett to the seascape over the mantel. "O.K., and I'll keep my fingers crossed that you're right. Cats, yet!"

Gibson had bad luck. By that midafternoon most of the evidence was in, and what it would say to the grand jury was open and shut.

Gibson's brother was a little more ambitious; he owned an appliance store on Third, lived in a newish ranch-style on a manicured west-Hollywood street. He also had a wife. That was, maybe, bad luck for both Gibsons. Mendoza read her the first look, by the way her narrow mouth tightened when she looked at his badge. The house, the clothes, the manner and voice and makeup, all told him, the snob, the climber—money-crazy. And she took a second look at his suit, glanced at the Facel-Vega through the front picture window, and looked doubtful. He saw it in her mind, the bribes from gangsters: the corrupt cop.

He didn't feel called on to explain about his miserly grandfather and finding all those safe-deposit boxes after the funeral.

"Jim wasn't here when John came last night, he didn't get home until nearly midnight, he was bowling. He couldn't tell you anything. . . . I don't know what time it was when John came, I don't pay much notice to time. I thought he was being very silly, I told him to go home. . . . It might have been eleven when he came. It might have been later. I couldn't say."

Sure. She hadn't liked having a brother-in-law who was a common cop. No class—*or* money—to that. She'd like to keep herself and Jim clear of the whole business, and damn what she might do to John Gibson in the process. A muddy thinker: if she gave him a definite alibi, she must see he'd be out of it? So, an honest woman within certain limits: she couldn't provide one. Or did she have a grudge on him deep enough to withhold an alibi?

Just for being a common cop? People were funny, of course.

"You didn't hear him leave during the night, or return?"

"Our room's at the back. If he did, we needn't hear. It's a pretty big house. I couldn't say."

And wouldn't. Mendoza drove back downtown. He saw the afternoon headlines on the way, and swore: the press boys had got hold of it.

Hackett had just one lone thing for him. He gave out the bad news first. No prints anywhere in the house but those of the Gibsons, except for one set on a water glass in the kitchen, and those were almost certainly a woman's prints. "Do we tell a fairy tale about Gibson having a girlfriend who decided to put the wife out of the way?"

"Reno's much safer," said Mendoza. "I don't see Gibson inspiring such passion, somehow. And?"

"That's all. Except this. From the backyard, close up to the chain-link fence."

"*Vaya,* how pretty. Prints?—no, I suppose not." Mendoza picked it up. It had started life as an ordinary bread knife with a wooden handle, but the blade had been ground to a point like a hunting knife and the handle bound with friction tape. Some of that had come loose, and to the sticky side adhered a few fragments of soft leather. "Oh, this I like very much. You see him, don't you, Arturo? Plain as day. About sixteen, but not even starting to grow up—playing the bold swaggerer with the knife in his belt just like a real hood, the tough baby not to be fooled with. I can see him touching this up in shop class at school, feeling the hell of a fellow."

"I know you've got an overactive imagination," said Hackett. "Yeah, and I can also see that getting dropped there almost any time the last week, and in any case what's the connection? I'm not far behind you on smart deductions—and what I come up with is that that didn't belong to a real juvenile hood, because they can get easy money and buy the real thing, the bone-handled stainless steel, the tooled holster. That belonged to some kid just dreaming about it out of his comic books, and maybe snitching his mother's bread knife to fix up. And one like that I don't see beating a woman to death. Nor her letting him in."

"Take what clues show up and be grateful," said Mendoza. "I want to brood over this. . . . We are annoying Mrs. James Gibson considerably. She doesn't think it quite the thing to have a policeman in the family. Like the young squire marrying into trade, you know." Hackett said a rude word. "I haven't seen the brother, but it looks as if both Gibsons are long-suffering souls who put up with nagging wives. Me, I like women very much indeed, but not on the permanent basis—*¡Dios me libre*—God forbid!"

Hackett said sooner or later the most accomplished Casanovas got caught, and Mendoza laughed and told him to go away and have dinner. But he didn't feel very amused actually, thinking of the headlines and Gibson sitting in the county jail.

He wasn't hungry either, and he swiveled round in the desk chair to face the view out over the sprawling city—a bit smoggy, the line of hills just smudges eight miles away—and he brooded. He brooded so intently that Sergeant Lake, coming in half an hour later to ask for any instructions to the night staff, crept out again without opening his mouth.

At six-thirty Mendoza suddenly swiveled round again, took up his hat, went downstairs and drove out North Broadway to the jail. He found Gibson staring dispiritedly at the floor in his little cell, and without preliminary asked him, "Do you keep your car keys and house keys on separate rings?"

"What?" said Gibson. "Why—no, sir, I don't. All together. It's silly, keep keys in different places. All together, you know where they are."

"*¡Diez millón de demonios!*" said Mendoza. "So you wouldn't have been locked out, if you'd decided to come back last night—your wife wouldn't have noticed your house keys left behind, and left a door unlocked for you in case you came back?"

Gibson shook his head. "She wouldn't've done that anyway. I keep 'em all together, and I took the car, so of course I had the house-keys too. . . . I did lose the whole bunch awhile ago, don't know how. Damndest thing. I'm not that careless usually.''

Mendoza sat very still there beside him on the jail cot. ''You did? When and where?''

''I dunno *where*. About a week ago. It was my day off. Ethel was out somewhere, I was all alone in the house that day. All I can figure, they must've dropped out o' my pocket when I went down to Eddie's for a beer in the afternoon.'' He'd seized gratefully on the little inconsequentiality to talk about, off the worse subject. ''See, you just bang the front door to lock it, I wasn't even sure I *had* the bunch o' keys on me. I usually leave 'em on the bureau until I go out, and that day I left the back door open for the kid—case he wanted to use the bathroom or wanted a drink, you know.''

''The kid?''

''I don't like yard work, see, sir,'' said Gibson. ''I hire this neighborhood kid to cut the lawn and so on. Kind of an extra expense, and Ethel said I ought to do it myself, but—''

''What's the kid's name?''

''Bobby Ryder, he lives two doors down. I guess he could do a better job, you know kids, sir. But, time I get home off duty, I'm tired, I don't want to go out and sweat over a damn lawn. Ethel said I should've—save the two bucks.''

''I see,'' said Mendoza. ''O.K.'' They never stopped to think, the ones like Mrs. James Gibson, the hell of a thankless job: riding a squad all day, the faithful harness cops like this one, seeing the public safe on its daily ways. Such an unspectacular job. Such a tiresome job—he could remember—fraught with little picayune annoyances. ''When'd you find the keys again?''

''Not for about two days, it was the hell of a nuisance. Then Ethel found them, right along the sidewalk—just on the edge, like they'd fallen out, you know—halfway down the block. Funny nobody'd seen 'em before.''

''O.K.,'' said Mendoza. ''Now tell me if there's any woman, either in your neighborhood or elsewhere, who was friendly enough with your wife to drop in on her that late, after you'd left last night.''

"She had a lot of friends. I don't know though, that *would* be kind of late. But she liked to stay up all hours, and a couple of those were like her. Might have been one of the neighbors—Mrs. Pike, maybe. She knew her pretty well. Did you find somebody else *was* there, sir?"

"Oh, yes, somebody else was there. Thanks very much," and Mendoza got up.

"Sir—you *know* I didn't do it, don't you? I—"

"You might have killed your wife, but not Queenie," said Mendoza, "That's what I know. It wouldn't convince the D.A., so we'll just have to find something else to satisfy him."

It was seven o'clock. Housewives would be annoyed, interrupted in the middle of dinner dishes; and now he was hungry. He went home, to an affectionate greeting from his own sleek household ruler, Bast of the green eyes, and provided her with fresh liver before getting a meal for himself. She got up on his lap while he ate, and he apologized to disturb her when he was finished. . . . A hunch? Quite straightforward evidence, in any human sense.

He looked up the address—three houses down from Gibson's—and sought out Mrs. Pike. A little dark gamin of a woman, consciously coy. And anxious, uttering little cries of admiration for our wonderful police. "I should've *known* you'd find out, Lieutenant. I was going to call, honestly, but I've been just *prostrated* by this terrible thing—Ethel was one of my *dearest* friends, you know! I can't tell you what a shock—I had to call my doctor to give me something, I felt—"

Mendoza began to feel better. The luck turning, to strike the right one first shot? He sat down and offered her a cigarette. "You were there last night. What time?"

"I'll never be able to sleep, thinking of it—why, if I'd stayed, I might have been there when he came *back*! It was about eleven, I just ran in to give back a magazine she'd loaned me, I knew she'd still be up, she was a nighthawk like me. I would have stayed, but I'd been shopping all day, I was so tired I just chatted a few minutes and came home—"

"You had a glass of water."

"Why, however did you know that? Yes, I did, my throat was dry and I asked—"

"You left your prints on it," said Mendoza. "We'll have some comparison ones to check," and she gave a little scream. "No trouble, I'll send a man up tomorrow. Did Mrs. Gibson lock the door after you when you left?"

"Oh, yes—she always did. At night, I mean. Not that it's a dangerous neighborhood—goodness, no, quite respectable—but just as well, the awful things that happen. But of course he had a key—"

"Yes." Mendoza thanked her and got away; and sitting in the Facel-Vega debated his next move. This was all up in the air: just what Hackett called it, a fairy tale. In seventeen years on the force, he'd learned to watch his overactive imagination, but not always to control it. He hunted down the felons because it was his job, not always feeling any personal animosity toward them; but this one he wanted to find, and see him punished adequately. Not, God knew, for Ethel Gibson the nagging wife. No. For the pretty silver-gray almost-Persian Queenie, whom Gibson had loved. The innocent creature struck down with no motive but brutality.

The devil of it was—say there was something to his fairy tale—how to pin it down? Inevitably the analogy which occurred to him was, Here you are holding three of a kind; bluff it to look like a full house, will you get away with it? Can you? With how many draws to make? You might just make it; or next time round, somebody might turn up with a royal flush.

All that five-percent common stock and the property deeds, in those safe-deposit vaults, was the result of the gambling money; the old man had made his capital like that, maybe with the handy ace up his sleeve; and there was something in heredity, after all.

Mendoza grinned and switched on the ignition. He said to himself, *"Mañana será otro día*—tomorrow is also a day," and went home to bed.

The high-school principal looked at Mendoza warily. "I shouldn't like to think any of our students—"

"I don't know," said Mendoza. "I'm just checking. Just asking, Mr. Grove. This Bobby Ryder."

"Yes—well," the principal looked at the record card he'd had brought in. "A middling satisfactory pupil, Lieutenant. Not a— a delinquent by any means. Not a gifted student either. Normal, I'd say."

"IQ tests don't say much about personality. Now tell me, you do have a few real problem kids? Even in a school in what we call a fairly good section of town?"

The principal relaxed and sighed. "That we do indeed. This rapid expansion of population—various factors—you won't need any lecture, I dare say." He glanced sidewise at Mendoza. "Er—racial aspects, and others—"

"O.K., I know all the problems, sure. Me, luckily I went to school down the wrong side of Main where everybody was Gomez or Li-Chong or Fornisetti—or black. What I'm asking you is the names of boys you've got here, maybe seniors a couple of years older than Bobby Ryder, who might be—mmh—embryo or real hoods, *and* who know Bobby."

"Dear me, that's a tall order. Offhand, I— Well, let's see. There's Chuck Burdette," said the principal. "He is actually on probation, for petty theft and assault. A—between us, Lieutenant—a most obnoxious and stupid lout. And Kenny Wildman. He was found carrying a knife. And Jerry Johnson—he threatened a teacher, and was found not too long ago manufacturing a pair of—er—knuckle-busters in shop class. . . . This is a better school than most, you know." Suddenly he smacked his hand down on his desk blotter and said violently, "What's the answer, Lieutenant? Why? You said, the wrong side of Main—yet you didn't turn into a hood."

"A lot of answers, maybe. They give us some, the sociologists. Lack of religion—which is a laugh, because what the hell is more corrupt and hypocritical than any orthodox religion? T.V. Working mothers. I don't know the answers. Just, there it is. I want to see Bobby Ryder's curriculum, who he's in what class with."

Mr. Grove bowed his head and obliged. And maybe it didn't

mean anything, but Bobby Ryder had three classes with Chuck Burdette. Who was on probation for assault . . . Mendoza expressed gratitude, and came away.

It was Saturday. He drove up to the Ryder house. Bobby was, said pretty Mrs. Ryder, over at a friend's helping him with his car. A Chuck Burdette, on Emmett Street. Very nice. Mendoza thanked her, and felt sorry for her. Just momentarily.

Two healthy-looking suntanned kids, in the driveway of a nice house, over a twelve-year-old Chevy. Wholesome-looking American kids. He felt damned old, looking at them, for just a minute. He sized them up coldly: Burdette a great hulk over six feet, yes, and loutish-looking. He walked up the drive, and they turned and looked at him, and he said, "Mr. Robert Ryder?"

"I—that's me." Sallow acne-complexioned kid, seen near to, flushing at the formal address. "What d'you want?"

Mendoza reached into his breast pocket and took out the crude hunting-knife. "I think this belongs to you."

Bobby Ryder looked at it, and took a little breath, and said involuntarily, "Oh, no, that's Jerry's—I—"

And the Burdette kid said, "Son of a bitch—you *snitcher*! It's a cop—damn fool, can't you see—" And he swung wild on Mendoza. A very damn silly thing to do, but of course he was only a punk. Mendoza sidestepped him neatly and brought one up from the ground; it connected with Burdette's jaw, but only staggered him back a couple of steps; he was a good four inches over Mendoza's five ten. With no compunction at all Mendoza followed him up and sank a satisfactory knee into his groin.

Not for nagging Ethel Gibson. For the pretty silver-gray Queenie. They really needn't have killed Queenie.

"Crystal ball, hell," he said to Hackett. "Quite straight evidence. If you looked at it. Especially once I'd heard about Gibson losing his keys. Bobby Ryder had been going round with these two—the Johnson kid, and Burdette who was really a delinquent, not just a borderline case. Who played on the other two, had 'em looking up to him. Such a hell of a lot of fun, and an easy living, holding up the liquor stores, the supermarkets. Make fools of the damn stupid cops. *Vaya por Dios,* yes, what's the answer?—these kids! I don't know the answer, any more than Fowler down in Juvenile knows! Let it go. He'd worked on these two rather ordinary kids—immature kids, ready to go along with anything to be popular, the big wheels. And Ryder got two bucks a week for cutting the Gibsons' lawn. He knew Gibson was a cop, knew he had some guns—chances were he'd even seen them. It was the guns they were after, the guns and ammo. For holding up the liquor stores and supermarkets—the smart-boy big-time pro crooks—you need guns.''

"I still say you got it by radar.''

"*Pues no.* I knew it wasn't Gibson, so it had to be an outside motive. Once he told me about the keys, it was obvious. Bobby, under Burdette's coaching, got hold of the keys and they had the one to the house copied. And Mrs. Pike was part of the plot too, unwittingly, because they saw her leave the house and thought it was Mrs. Gibson—thought the house was empty. I'd bet Bobby, as living in the neighborhood, was posted to keep an eye out for that eventuality, and called up the others. In they go, via the key, expecting an empty house where they can take their time. And they run into a scared and voluble Ethel Gibson. It was Burdette did the killing, of course. The unteachable, unreachable lout. The insensitive. The brute. The primitive. No, he didn't mean to kill her—just shut her up. But it got out of hand.'' Mendoza lit a cigarette. "And then they were all three scared. Even Burdette's just a punk—yet. And he'd never admit it. They ran, without trying for the guns—scared somebody'd heard the noise. And Bobby lost his knife getting over the fence. . . . I wish Burdette had put up more of a fight. Pleasure to take him down. But of course they're always cowards, that kind.''

"They won't be so tough on the other two,'' said Hackett thoughtfully. "They're only sixteen.''

"No. But, the good God above be thanked—*excusar,* I'm a

rational agnostic—Burdette's over eighteen, not a minor, and subject to the gas chamber. Though unfortunately he won't get it, on a second-degree charge.''

''Vindictive, *chico*.''

Mendoza said, ''He needn't have killed Queenie.''

THE RING

Lieutenant Luis Mendoza took his lunch hour off to buy a Mother's Day gift. Not that he approved of this purely commercial sentimentality foisted on the public; but his grandmother, the only mother he had ever known, was conventional and would expect it. There was moreover only one place to buy it. Ever since the old man died and they'd found all those safe-deposit boxes, the old lady had been getting rid of quite a lot of income on the items of portable value. Just in *case*. Pieces of paper, *hijito*, she said, what are they? Diamonds one can always get something for. No good lecturing her.

So a quarter to one found him walking into the very exclusive black-glass-and-marble establishment of Shanrahan and Mac-Ready on Wilshire Boulevard. To his surprise it was empty. No bland impeccable Shanrahan: no clerks. Simply glass cases with gleaming contents. Even the watch-repair cubicle was empty.

After a few minutes of waiting for some response to the discreet electric chime announcing a customer's entrance, Mendoza reached the conclusion that there was something wrong, and walked round behind the glass cases at the rear to the door leading to the back premises and Shanrahan's office. In the little dark passages he stopped and cocked his head. Sounds from the office: muffled sounds.

"*Caray,*" he said to himself, "why must I be so affected as never to pack a gun? Very awkward." He opened the office door with great care to make no noise, and standing flat against it looked in.

A man in a dark hat and suit was rifling the office safe, tossing out boxes and papers furiously. A second man lay prone on the floor, very still, and Shanrahan was propped up in the corner behind his desk thoroughly bound and gagged. Even as Mendoza gathered himself for the silent rush across the room to tackle the thief, the man exclaimed in satisfaction and turned; he was wearing a black stocking mask over his entire face. He snatched out a gun and fired as Mendoza launched himself, and ran forward; they collided heavily, Mendoza swung on him and missed, and took a smart blow on the temple from the gun butt. He staggered back and fell over the prone man on the floor. The other man fled like a deer, banging the door behind him.

Mendoza picked himself up, found that the door had locked itself, said, *"¡Diez millón de demonios desde infierno!"* and went to the phone on the desk. Within a minute and a half he had a general call out and a patrol car on the way. He then untied Shanrahan, who spit out the gag and called down imprecations on him.

"You might have thought of that sooner—really, Mendoza! Well, yes, important to get after him immediately, but you have no idea how uncomfortable that gag— Really, this is too much of a good thing! We've never been burglarized in broad daylight before! One *expects* burglars in a jewelry shop—natural affinity, one might say—but at high noon! Don't you fellows do anything to earn your pay down at headquarters?"

"Burglary is not my department," said Mendoza. "You'd better check the safe and see what's missing."

"I know what's missing," said Shanrahan bitterly. "Didn't you see him tossing everything else aside? He wanted Miss Marvena Rayle's jewelry, and he got it."

After a moment Mendoza identified the name. One of the meteoric-risen new stars. Vaguely he remembered a newspaper cut: an improbably buxom gilt blonde. "I see," he said, and examined the man on the floor, who turned out to be very dead.

"Though why he should turn round and murder his accomplice I couldn't say," added Shanrahan, sitting down. He looked shaken. "Oh, yes, quite deliberate. That one came in yesterday at about the same time." The man was nondescript, but well dressed and eminently respectable-looking. "He bought a small brooch, a Mother's Day gift, he said. He chatted. Quite an ordinary customer. I realize now—my God, what happened to my natural caution I don't know, but he seemed all right—I must have let out somehow that I'm alone at present over the noon hour. MacReady's attending a convention in New York, and one of our regular clerks is on vacation. At any rate, they walked in here twenty minutes ago, and *that* one put a gun on me. The other one was hanging behind adjusting that damned mask—I never got a look at his face at all. He took the gun while this one tied me up, and then he turned on him cool as— My God, I never saw anything like it!—and clubbed him down from behind. He *is* dead? My God—"

"No further use for him," deduced Mendoza. "And he probably knew X fairly well, too." There were sounds of entry outside, and he hammered on the door until the patrolmen opened it. "Well, that puts it in my department after all."

Sometime later, with the clerk in charge outside and the men from headquarters gone, together with the body (naturally nothing had been found in the way of prints or clues), he joined Sergeant Arthur Hackett and Shanrahan in the office again. "But why only those things, of this obnoxious female's?"

"Miss Rayle is a very attractive young woman," said Shanrahan coldly.

"*Cómo no,* if you like the type. But obnoxious, like all rising young starlets—I won't say actresses, though the types overlap. The eternal egotists, the spoiled darlings."

"I gather she'll be more so," said Hackett. "Didn't I see something about her bein' engaged to some millionaire from back East?"

"Mr. Thomas Wentworth Horley the Third," said Shanrahan.

"Ah, money," said Mendoza. "So now we know why Mr.

Shanrahan was obliging and let her stash away her pretty baubles in his private safe.''

"Don't be silly, Mendoza. It was just to oblige her for a few days until she moves into this new Bel-Air house she's bought, which has a safe built in. Certainly she's a valued customer, we like to oblige—''

"I don't believe a word of it. She batted her eyes at you and you fell over yourself to offer it. She can afford a safe-deposit box, after all. However, the odd thing is that X passed up a lot more of value just to take her stuff. Why not increase the profit while he was at it? Was it a valuable collection?''

"Not at all," said Shanrahan. "Which makes it all the odder. Miss Rayle's only recently—er—come to the fore, so to speak, been in a position to acquire much good jewelry. I *had* a list, unless he took it too—no, here it is. Face value would be about ten thousand.''

"He wouldn't get a third of that from a fence," said Hackett.

"No. Let's see the list, Shanrahan. Diamond bracelet, diamond pendant, emerald ring, pearl and garnet ring, ruby pendant—''

"All quite ordinary stuff, really. Not a piece that cost over three to five hundred retail.''

"Oh, is that so? The odds and ends an enterprising girl might acquire piece by piece from generous boyfriends?''

"There's no need to be vulgar about it," said Shanrahan.

"Especially not to the future Mrs. Thomas W. Horley the Third. You forget, they might forsake Hollywood for New York.''

"What," said Hackett, "just as she's getting somewhere in pictures? Don't you believe it, *chico*.''

"Well, at any rate the store hasn't lost anything." Shanrahan sighed. "Er—what was it you came in for, Mendoza? Perhaps there's something I could show you now?—some very attractive new wedding-set designs in, if it *should* be—''

"Remove the rapacious stare," said Mendoza. "When you sell me one of those it'll be in your dreams, friend. I'll take this inventory, we'll see what turns up. I haven't time to haggle with you right now, but what's the asking price on that triple-linked bracelet with the emerald clasp in the window?"

Shanrahan told him. Mendoza said, *"Ay de mi—¿no le da vergüenza?*—no shame at all. I'll beat you down later. Come on, Art."

The dead man was one Edward Foster, and very little investigation showed him to have been the husband of Miss Marvena Rayle's current maid, Betty. Who wept over him and disclaimed any knowledge of his nefarious plans.

"There you are," said Mendoza. "That's how X knew where the stuff was. He was the mastermind, not Foster. He wanted that, only that, and he wanted it in a hurry. Why the hell?" All they knew about X was the meager glimpse Mendoza had had, confirmed by Shanrahan: a man about six feet tall and slender, age and coloring unknown.

This was one of those things where you waited to see what routine turned up. The first thing was that Foster had done time, a three-to-five for burglary and assault, ten years ago. The second thing was that he had recently been seen, in a bar near his current residence, in confidential talk with an unknown man about six feet tall and slender. That was a dead end, of course. They didn't like police much in that section of L.A., and if there was anything more to be got it wouldn't be handed out.

"It just could be," said Hackett, "I mean, considering that it wasn't much of a haul on face value—it just could be that he's going to hold it at ransom for its sentimental value. She might pay a lot more than a fence to get it back."

"I think it'll be some time before you rank lieutenant, Arturo. Disregarding the murder, because there might have been a personal grudge—females like La Rayle are never burdened with much sentiment. If it wasn't for two things, I'd say it was the old, old story—the fraud on the insurance company. But ten thousand isn't what she'd call big money, and also the homicide seems a little gratuitous—added to which, it'd have been easier for her to stage a burglary at home. That was a neat and daring little business, you know, in broad daylight on Wilshire Boulevard.''

"Which had occurred to me too. I've got Records looking up any pros who might have happened to be occupying San Quentin at the same time as Foster.''

"That's my boy,'' said Mendoza. "You may pass the lieutenants' exam some day after all.'' He got his hat and before he left examined himself critically in the washroom mirror. Not, God forbid, on La Rayle's account, but because he was still rather doubtful about this imported herringbone: just a trifle less discreet a shade than he liked. He made a mental note to wear only his very quietest ties with it henceforth—one could not throw three hundred bucks out the window—sought the custom-built Facel-Vega in the lot and drove out to Bel-Air.

When one came to think, it was surprising that the L.A.P.D. had usually little contact with these show-business people. Considering the kind most of them were.

It was a nightmare of a modern house, painted pink. There was, of course, a pool; it was there a white-coated houseboy conducted him, looking surprised to see a visitor clad in a suit, white shirt and necktie. These people. An oversized pool it was, with several females sitting about it artistically in the all-but-nude, and several males self-consciously displaying muscles and suntan on a diving board. Mendoza surveyed them disapprovingly. As an agnostic and something of a connoisseur of females, he felt no moral disapproval; only a social one. He was sufficiently old fashioned to believe that nudity should be reserved for bedrooms and doctor's offices.

One of the females came to him and cooed greetings. Our newest domestic star, Marvena Rayle. Naturally, he thought, that in-between hair neither brown nor blond, washed-out blue eyes; now made over into the latest version of platinum, with the newest shade of mascara, lipstick, and nail polish. She probably had to watch her weight: by the apparent bra size she'd turn hippy without a constant diet.

"But how intriguing,'' she said. "You policemen have been

marvelous. All so polite and obliging.'' They'd sent her to a voice teacher, a grammar teacher, but underneath he seemed to get an echo of Main Street. ''You're going to be *horribly* cross at me. Won't you have a drink?'' Her pale eyes were gauging the price per yard of the herringbone.

''No, thanks. Why?'' asked Mendoza.

''My dear man, it's all come back. In a cardboard box, wrapped in brown paper. This morning. I *knew* I should call and tell all you nice people about it, but I was rather exhausted—a party last night, you know—and then I had these people coming this afternoon. I was barely dressed when they came. I *was* going to call.''

''All the jewelry returned,'' said Mendoza. ''Isn't that nice. Why do you suppose the thief did that?''

''Remorse, I expect,'' said Miss Rayle, widening her eyes at him.

''I'd like to have the box and the wrapping.''

''Oh, goodness, I'm afraid that's past praying for. You don't know Andy—that's what I call the boy, he's Korean and his name's *quite* unpronounceable—the most damnably orderly mind, he can't stand clutter. You can *ask* him, but I expect he's cleared it all away. Are you sure you won't have a drink?''

''No, thanks.'' Mendoza retreated and asked Andy, who said, Sorry, sir, all burned in the new hygienic gas household incinerator. Of course . . .

He went back to the office and said to Hackett, ''Where do they come from? A breed apart, the *species* Hollywood. Under infinite artificial layers, perhaps a very small piece of real woman, but the veneer far more important! She has had her modest collection of jewels returned to her,'' and he told Hackett about that.

''Remorse,'' said Hackett, and laughed. ''That's a damn funny one, isn't it, Luis? Did you see the stuff?''

''I did. All very intimate, in her bedroom—*caray*, a symphony in pink and white—her being very earnest and honest with a representative of our wonderful police.''

''Especially,'' said Hackett, ''with our very obvious

man-about-town Luis, with his fetching Latin moustache and well-known way with the ladies.''

"Don't flatter me—I wasn't complimenting myself. That one, very well she knows what she's doing. The head, in effect, screwed on very damn tight. Yes, I saw the stuff.'' In self-defense, the old lady investing (as she fondly called it) in that kind of thing, he'd learned a little about it. And the haul for which X had passed up whatever new quality stuff was in stock at Shanrahan's, and killed a man, didn't add up to much. The diamond pendant, for instance, ten or twelve little stones totaling maybe a carat. The pearl and garnet ring, maybe seventy-five bucks retail new. Very odd.

If it hadn't been for that aspect of the matter, a routine pro business. Homicides get committed for the hell of a lot less than a split of, say, four thousand bucks. But there hadn't been even four thousand bucks. Just a dead man, and that modest haul of ordinary jewelry returned in plain wrapping.

Mendoza wasn't always a very orthodox policeman, but seventeen years on the force had necessarily conditioned him to routine, so that he felt unhappy about anything so wildly un-routine as this.

As was only to be expected, Records eventually turned up no fewer than forty-seven men of the same general conformation as X, who had been in San Quentin at the same time as Foster. And that had been nearly ten years ago; what did it say about today? Mendoza had men nosing around the area where Foster had lived, but nothing turned up there either.

A police officer had to have faith in routine, sure. Sooner or later they were bound to turn up some friends of Foster's, check on them, weed them out; in the end they might be pretty certain which of them might have been in on the deal—or masterminded it. That didn't say they'd be able to get nice legal evidence on him, and it didn't say why the deal had been pulled or Foster clubbed to death.

And damn the legal evidence for the grand jury, Mendoza always felt that the why was most important.

□ □ □

Routine hadn't come up with anything three nights later when he took his redhead Alison Weir out to dinner.

Over preliminary drinks he asked suddenly, "What d'you think of movie stars, *chica*?"

"*When* I think of them," said Alison, "I'm sorry for them."

"*¿Cómo es eso?*"

"Oh, you know—*tiene su pizca de gracia,* a sort of funny way to think really," said Alison, also bilingual from a childhood in Mexico. "All that running just to stay in the same place. Such—such an ephemeral thing. Not as if they had to be really good at anything, in spite of all the talk about drama lessons and so on. Far as I can gather, it's mostly a matter of the important contacts and good publicity. And docility."

"Docility? Elucidate."

"Didn't you get the implication? It seems quite horrible to me." In business hours Alison operated a charm school, painted her seascapes over weekends. "Once you're taken up, they make you all over. The pictorial gospel according to Hollywood. Whatever they decide, if you object, you're dead. Doesn't matter what type you are, if this year's model is the simpering blonde, the simpering blonde you've got to be. And maybe next year something else. I should think they'd all be schizophrenic."

"That is a thought," said Mendoza, finishing his rye.

"Or cases of multiple personality. Of course everything has to be subordinated to publicity. It reminds me," said Alison thoughtfully, "of eugenics."

"*¿Vaya por Dios, por qué?*"

"*Solamente un muy sensible,*" said Alison with a grin. "All the real emotional feeling left out—not to be admitted it's there."

"I have the feeling," said Mendoza, "that you have just said something significant, but at the moment I'm not sure what. . . . We will now cease to talk shop."

"Oh, have we been?"

He sat at his desk next morning (nothing new from routine on this business) and, feeling exasperated, got out all the records on it for reexamination.

Hackett came in and found him at it, and said, "Eventually we'll narrow it down."

"Don't comfort me," said Mendoza irritably. "I've missed the boat on this somehow, there's something I should have seen before. . . . Ah, *¡si será cierto!*" He stared at the paper in his hand.

"What's hit you?"

"Maybe nothing," said Mendoza slowly. He cast his mind back. Damn, you didn't stop being human because you were a cop, *or* a cynic. That silly amoral gilt blonde who was nine-tenths veneer was still quite a bit of female. "Hell!" he said, and carefully folded up Shanrahan's inventory of La Rayle's jewelry. He got up from his desk and said, "If anyone wants me I'll be in Goldberg's office."

Lieutenant Saul Goldberg of Burglary and Theft sneezed, groped for Kleenex, and said automatically, "Damn allergies. Now that one says something to me. Wait a minute. Let me think." Like most good cops, Goldberg had a long memory. "Yes. We'll check the files, but I'm pretty clear on it. Just let me hear the description again."

Shanrahan, bless his precise soul, had been thorough. "Emerald ring," read Mendoza from the list, "approximately two carats in weight, set in white gold, mounting a dimensional scaled serpent coiled about stone, two one-point emeralds in eyes."

"Yeah, it rings a bell," said Goldberg. "Kleinert. The Kleinert job. About eight years ago. He was a banker or something. Money, anyway. Jewelry stolen, along with bearer bonds and cash, some other stuff. West Hollywood, I seem to remember. Anyway, I remember the ring. We got most of the stuff back from pawnshops, but not that ring, and—oh, hell"—as he began to sneeze again—"Mrs. Kleinert raised a fuss, she had some sentimental attachment to it, you know. Far as I know they never did get it back. . . . We'll look at my files, glad to oblige."

□ □ □

So, he'd been careless: blame sex? Mendoza hated to think so. That obvious pin-up calendar female, God forbid. Nevertheless, he didn't remember seeing that emerald ring in the collection someone had so kindly sent back to her.

He read an evening paper, so Hackett was ahead of him for once that next morning. "Your friend Shanrahan'll be disappointed. Our newest domestic star has broken her engagement to the millionaire."

They'd made minor headlines of it, for God's sake, as if it ranked with important news. MARVENA RAYLE TO WED CHILDHOOD SWEETHEART, they said. JILTS EASTERN MILLIONAIRE AT LAST MINUTE.

"¿Pues y qué, so what?" said Mendoza. "These reporters."

"Don't be so damn fastidious," said Hackett. "You notice her new choice has a moustache. I figure myself she fell hopelessly in love with your well-known charm, and—"

"You go to hell," said Mendoza, looking at the cut of buxom gilt-blond Marvena and a smiling, moustached, slender man identified as Robert Follette, salesman. "This says something to me—what? First and foremost, that some very powerful emotion made La Rayle give up that millionaire for a salesman, so-called. De veras . . . I do just wonder."

Without any excuse at all he called on Miss Marvena Rayle again. She wore diamonds and rubies on hands and wrists—no emeralds—and she was soulful and welcoming. She held no animosity for the poor misguided man who had stolen her jewelry, and really hoped our wonderful police wouldn't waste time hunting him. Oh, well, she supposed they *had* to on account of this other poor man killed. No, of course she was keeping Betty on, it hadn't been Betty's fault.

In the foreground also was the aforementioned Robert Follette, smiling, moustached and suave; also a well-known columnist, the Rayle's agent and a rising juvenile male actor. Mendoza, who could outperform all that kind in conscious charm when he chose, was charming. He stayed half an hour. He drove straight back to headquarters and turned over his gold-plated cigarette case to

Prints. "I'd polished it beforehand, and this down in the left corner is me. I think what you want is the upper right-hand corner."

Prints ran the result through their inhumanly efficient machines and relayed the news to him half an hour later. One Robert James Fowler, nine arrests (four juvenile, under eighteen), two prison terms. Grand theft auto, burglary, burglary with aggravated assault, burglary (third count). Probation, reform school, a one-to-three, a three-to-five.

"Oh, yes, very nice," said Mendoza. "People more important, but there is a lot to be said for Records." Unprecedentedly he stuck a regulation .38 in his inside jacket pocket, and asked Hackett to accompany him. They drove out to Bel-Air in the Facel-Vega.

The pool as usual was in use. Hackett sketched a wolf whistle and Mendoza looked disapproving. The boy brought them, eventually, the gilt blonde and the fiancé.

"Mr. Robert Fowler," said Mendoza. "I believe you are still on parole, and have neglected to report in to your officer."

"What the *hell*—" said the fiancé. He looked stupefied.

"So surprising," said Mendoza, "how you people continue to underrate us. You were careless at Shanrahan's, you know—you left a print."

"That's a damn lie, I—"

"When you blew the safe. Really no finesse these days."

"What the *hell*—" Fowler was rattled largely because this had come on him out of the blue, he'd thought he was quite safe. He was so rattled that he broke past Mendoza and ran, and Mendoza and Hackett converged on him neatly and gathered him in.

"We'd like you to make a little statement, Mr. Fowler," said Mendoza tenderly; and about that time the blonde started to scream.

"Well, if there's money to hire the smart lawyer, he might get off," said Hackett.

"Somehow I don't think there will be," said Mendoza, and laughed. "In the vernacular, he had her over a barrel, and I doubt whether she'll feel like coming to his rescue. In fact, her best chance is somehow to convince the millionaire she's a poor misguided little girl who got led into bad company, and persuade him to take her back. I wonder if she'll try. We'll never prove it, but she'd been Jackie Mark's girlfriend, and he pulled that Kleinert job—Goldberg got him for it, a three-to-five, but Mark died in San Quentin in a knife fight. The operative factor was, that emerald ring was part of the Kleinert haul, and Mark gave it to her, and she'd kept it. I was a damn fool, don't tell me, not to check Shanrahan's inventory with what she showed me that day. She never got the ring back. The ring was what Fowler was after. He was in on that deal with Mark, but he wasn't dropped on for it—Goldberg knew that at the time, there just wasn't any evidence. Fowler knew the ring—such a distinctive piece, custom made, if not worth much—connected her with Mark and the theft, and it was nice blackmail material. You remember she's only had Betty the maid for a month or so. Fowler spotted Foster and somehow got Betty Foster into the household, but I'd lay a bet Betty refused to play, got cold feet. So when the stuff was out of the house, when La Rayle was moving into her new quarters, they pulled the job at Shanrahan's. Fowler needed a second with him on that job, but once Shanrahan was helpless, Foster had served his turn and out he went. He knew Fowler too well *and* what Fowler's game was. He was playing for high stakes, you know. He gave her the choice—marry me all open and aboveboard, cut me in on this nice deal you've got, or I'll blow it open—you were in the know on the Kleinert job and kept part of the loot. She and Mark and Fowler came from the same background, of course—wrong side of Main. She couldn't afford the risk. Not even when it meant jilting Thomas W. Horley the Third. On account of the publicity. The publicity agents are a little warier these days, you know. The big shots have to look a little more moral on the surface."

"There'd be lots of people who could swear the ring was hers, for some time back," agreed Hackett. "And he wouldn't be incriminating himself."

"*Pues no.* Goldberg hunted for evidence at the time and

couldn't get any. He could have picked up a description of the ring anywhere, as part of the loot on that job—he'd have had a good story ready if she'd tried to doublecross him. Well, we've got him now anyway.''

"And've spoiled our Marvena's chances at big stardom."

"*Por favor*, look at it straight. Not us. Our Marvena herself— or whatever her original name was."

"Well, I guess you're right there. If she hadn't kept that emerald ring—"

"*Vaya por Dios*," said Mendoza, "you remind me I have not yet got a Mother's Day gift. I must go and haggle with Shanrahan, that robber."

ACCIDENT

~~~~~~ And then there's this," said Hackett, handing over a thin sheaf of statements. "I guess that's all the new stuff for you today."

Mendoza glanced through the pages and raised his brows at his senior sergeant. "What's this doing on a lieutenant's desk?"

"I'd be obliged," said Hackett, "if you'd turn your second sight on it and tell me whether there's something funny about it or not. Smith down in Traffic gave it to me for the same reason. On the face of it, it's just an accident. Very sad and so on, but these things happen, ¿cómo no? But Smith isn't happy about it. Neither of us can point to anything definite, but—" he shrugged.

"Well, let's have a look," said Mendoza, and began to read the file with more attention.

The Reyes family lived on Whiteoak Avenue out beyond the railway yards. It wasn't a very classy neighborhood. Whiteoak Avenue ran right across the end of Pierce Street, which stopped there; and that end of Pierce Street consisted of a very steep hill rising from Whiteoak. The house the Reyes occupied was exactly opposite Pierce Street and the hill. Yesterday some new tenants had been moving into 187 Pierce Street, almost at the top of the hill. The truck had been parked at the curb. And at a few minutes after noon, the driver and his partner in the house shifting furniture, the truck had somehow slipped its brakes, rolled down that steep hill gathering speed as it went, smashed straight into the Reyes house and killed the only occupant, Carlotta Reyes, aged ten, who was in the living room. It was a big, heavy truck.

"As you say, these things happen," said Mendoza. "So what's funny about it?"

"I don't know that there's anything funny about it," said Hackett, sounding irritated. "There's nothing at all that says it isn't just an accident. But Smith looked at it twice and passed it to Homicide to look at on account of the driver. The truck driver. He's so very damn positive the truck couldn't have got away by itself. Says he's always careful about parking on a hill. There's also the truck. The company is a big national one—the people were moving here from Phoenix—and their insurance calls for a complete overhaul of their trucks fairly often. This truck had been gone over three days before and the brakes were O.K. then."

"So the driver was careless."

Hackett was silent and then he said, "I wish you'd see him, Luis. Maybe I've caught it from you, having hunches."

It was a very unimportant little affair, but Mendoza took ten minutes to go down the hall to an interrogation room and see the driver. And he saw why Smith of the Traffic Bureau and Hackett were a little unhappy. Fred Hansen, the truck driver, wasn't jumping up and down protesting excitedly that he had *too* left the truck parked safe, he ought to know! That would be the normal reaction, of course, of the man who had been careless, now trying to evade responsibility. But Fred Hansen looked like the kind who never got excited about anything. He was a big square middle-aged man with mild blue eyes and a bass voice. He just sat there, his workman's cap on his knee, and went on saying, "The truck was parked safe. Way I always do on a hill. Wheels turned in to the curb and the handbrake up tight."

"You're perfectly certain?" asked Mendoza.

Hansen looked very mildly annoyed. "Mister, I been saying it ever since the thing happened. Wouldn't say it if I wasn't sure. You can ask anybody knows me. Ask the firm. I'm always careful."

Hackett had asked the firm, of course. Hansen had worked for them for sixteen years and had an excellent record. No accidents. Cross-country truck drivers had to be pretty good; and a firm like this one had standards.

Mendoza looked at him. "Would you swear, Mr. Hansen, that you'd turned the wheels in to the curb?"

"Mister," said Hansen patiently, "you drive a car? Sure. It's second nature to anybody drives a car—you park on a hill, you cramp the wheels in. Back or front. Just like you automatic reach for the brake. Just like you don't have to stop 'n' think about shifting. Isn't that so?"

Of course, it was. Anybody can get careless once. But Hansen wasn't the ordinary private driver; he was, you might say, the professional.

"I see what you mean," said Mendoza to Hackett. "But if— ¡vaya historia!—somebody deliberately released the brake and headed the truck downhill, what was the point?"

"There's only one answer on that. Just random mischief. Which probably says, a kid."

"Yes. Well, you'd better take a look. Ask up and down the street—though if anybody had been looking out a window or walking past, and seen it, he'd have said so by now. Or—"

"You think so? Just maybe, in that end of town. People down there aren't any too crazy about cops."

"There is that," agreed Mendoza. Briefly he cast his mind back to Daggett Street twenty-three years ago: much the same kind of neighborhood. On any given block, in a street like that, there might not be one soul who had ever committed even a petty crime; but the social attitude, as it were, suspected Authority. You let me alone, I'll let you alone. People like that did not automatically call the cops in an emergency; they would answer questions a little grudgingly, seldom volunteer anything. . . . Because a lot of police business is always to do with people like that, his experience of having grown up among them often helped him on the job. These days, after they'd found all those safe-deposit boxes full of gilt-edged stock, when the old man died, Luis Mendoza drove a custom-built car and bought Sulka ties from his Wilshire Boulevard tailor; but there had been a time he'd been just another ragged little Mex kid running the slum streets.

He fingered the Sulka tie absently and said to Hackett, "Go and ask. Maybe something'll show up. If that's the way it was, the kid ought to be found, even if the law can't do much to him—involuntary homicide. Hansen and his partner were in the house, of course—likewise the new tenants—housewives around, probably in their kitchens, nobody to see. But it was a crazy chance to take—I'm with you there, it must have been just random impulse. *Vaya*, you look. Just in case."

He didn't do much thinking about it the rest of the day; he had a few really important cases on hand. But just before five-thirty something came up on the Briskow case that he wanted to see Hackett about. And Hackett had left.

Sergeant Lake said Art had said he was going to stop by Whiteoak Avenue, on that accident, see if Bert or Higgins had got anything yet. About twenty minutes ago.

"Damn," said Mendoza. But he might catch him still there; it would be only about a ten-minute drive from Headquarters. He sought the Facel-Vega in the lot and drove out there, through the shabby streets surrounding the proud modernity of the Civic Center.

It was indeed quite a little hill; and a heavy outsize moving van— The frame house at the bottom of the hill, facing Pierce Street, had sustained a good deal of damage. Its porch had been smashed in completely, and the front wall on the left side had disintegrated—just splinters of old lumber lying around, and a gaping hole where the truck had rammed through the house. The truck had been hauled away, which must have been a little job. There were several men standing around the yard in a disconsolate way, one of them such an obvious prey to gloom that Mendoza put him down as the landlord. Hackett's Ford was parked across the street a little way down, and he was leaning on the fender talking to Dwyer and Higgins.

Mendoza pulled up behind him and joined them. "Anything useful shown up?"

"*Nada*," said Hackett, looking annoyed.

"Never will," said Dwyer. "It's only natural. So O.K., some fool kid wandered by and thought what fun it'd be to send that truck down the hill, make a big smash. Even that kind of kid wouldn't do it if he knew there was a chance somebody was watching him. And while it was a little chance, he could be pretty sure. The truckers had just carried in the stove, it'd take them awhile to get it in—four-five minutes anyway. That hour, around noon, most women'd be in the kitchen at the back of the house, and he could see if there was anybody else on the street—which we can say there wasn't. It wouldn't take thirty seconds, you know. Climb up to the cab, release the brake and turn the wheels, and jump clear."

"And I think," said Hackett, "that's just about what happened, Luis. Because I'm sold on Mr. Hansen. I think he left it safe. And even around here, sure to God if anybody'd seen it they'd be talking now. When it was just a wanton piece of mischief that killed somebody. But how the hell do we start looking for the kid who did it? I ask you. . . . It makes you wonder sometimes, doesn't it? That poor kid, dead just because she was getting over the measles and still home from school. Damndest thing."

Mendoza looked at him, and lost interest in the Briskow case just momentarily. Hackett didn't seem to realize he'd said anything significant. "Have you," asked Mendoza, "seen the family?"

"What? No, not me, Smith did, of course. Why? Not very relevant, the family. It does make you wonder. She was alone in the house because her mother'd gone marketing and taken the baby along. Half an hour earlier, maybe the mother dead too—half an hour later, maybe the father as well, he comes home to lunch. It smashed right through to the kitchen, you know, and the poor kid—"

"*¡Bastante!* Kindly cease this maudlin moralizing, Arturo." Mendoza lit a cigarette, staring at the house. "How far away is the nearest school?"

They all stared at him. "*¡Qué lástima*—what a pity!" said Hackett. "Brilliant mind giving way at last. Why and what does it matter?"

"And you once passed the sergeants' exam. Just use a little ordinary common sense on it, *chico*. And find out about all the schools in this district. I'd like to know whether they all have cafeterias. In any other area, we wouldn't have to ask—practically all public schools do—but there might be one or two backward ones down here. *Aguardar*—a lot of Mexicans and Italians around here, aren't there? The kids whose parents can possibly squeeze out the money will be attending parochial schools—*qué ridículo,* but they will do it. So you'd better look at the parochial schools too."

"This I don't get, Lieutenant," said Higgins.

"Then you're all bigger fools than I ever took you for. And come to think, you should all have seen it before I did, because I'm older than any of you and consequently further away from my schooldays. Look, *estúpidos*. Yesterday was Wednesday, a weekday. It's November, and kids are in school on weekdays. The only reason Carlotta Reyes was absent from school was that she was sick. Most kids don't come home for lunch anymore. So, go and find which kids were loose. Kids who were also absent from school—or do come home for lunch—who might have been coming down Pierce Street about that time. And you might also ask if any schools around here are on half-day sessions, so that some kids would be out at noon."

For once Hackett forgot his role of the big tough cop and remembered his university degree. "*Mea culpa*—say it. Talk about elementary. That ought to narrow it down some, all right. . . . Though I wouldn't doubt that around here a lot of kids play hookey habitually and nobody thinks much of it. Kind of hard to keep track of. But we'll have a look."

"Do so. Oh, about that Briskow thing—"

And even then it didn't puzzle him or look important. Just one of those things that happened. If it had been a kid, not just Mr.

Hansen's carelessness, they ought to find him and do what they could about him. But just an involuntary homicide, no malicious intent of same.

The check on the schools was helpful. The Holy Family parochial school had had a visiting bishop and a little special program with the bishop awarding prizes for scholarship. There had been only three absentee pupils—Carlotta Reyes was one of them—all for reasons of illness. The other two were checked, and vouched for by their mothers as having been in bed.

"Though I will say the sister I talked to seemed kind of vague, it could be she's wrong. Maybe you—"

"*¡Nada de eso!* You don't get me in a mile of such a place. And you don't know them. Vague, hell. A very strict check kept."

Only the more affluent families around there could afford the tuition at the Holy Family. More than half the kids attended the local public schools. The nearest elementary school was nine blocks from Whiteoak; the nearest junior high almost two miles; the nearest high school almost four, out on Temple Street. All had cafeterias, the pupils were not supposed to leave the grounds, and none of them went home for lunch; special permission was needed for that. Those who didn't get lunch at the cafeterias (either by straight purchase or vouchers from county relief) carried their lunches.

"So," said Hackett, "I had another idea, and contacted the nearest corrective school. You know, where they send the backwards and incorrigibles. It's out on Macy. They keep an even stricter check there, of course. A cafeteria, yes. Five boys absent that morning—all of 'em because they had to make court appearances on misdemeanor charges. So far as we can check, unless the mothers are lying, all the kids from all the schools who were absent because they were sick, really were sick. And no others missing from the corrective school—"

"You don't tell me," said Mendoza, "that from all those schools there weren't any kids at all playing hookey?"

"I do not. None from the corrective school. Four from the

elementary, sixteen from the junior high, twelve from the high school.''

"*Vaya,* this is an improvement—I begin to have faith in progress. When I was in high school twenty years ago, the percentage was a lot higher.''

"Never, *naturalmente,* including Luis Mendoza.''

"Only once, to attend a cat show at the Biltmore. The admission was a dollar ten, hell of a lot of money those days, and I took it off Johnny Li-Chong at Spanish monte. You're looking at all these kids?''

"We are.''

"So let me know anything interesting you come up with.''

Hackett had not come up with anything two days later when Mendoza found an interesting paragraph in the evening paper. The Briskow business was settled, he had only the usual dull routine before him at the office. His current redhead, Alison Weir, who was a professional painter on weekends, operated a charm school during the week, had inconsiderately deserted him and gone off to La Jolla to paint a seascape. His grandmother was in Palm Springs. His club, where he might have repaired for an evening of poker, was closed for redecoration. He had nothing to do. He came home at six o'clock, was affectionately welcomed by the graceful Abyssinian feline who ruled his household, Bast of the green eyes, and cut up fresh liver for her before he got a meal for himself. Over his coffee he read the evening paper. It is undoubtedly difficult to read a newspaper in comfort with a cat on one's lap; he had necessarily mastered the technique.

And tucked away as a filler on a back page was a little item he read twice.

Emilia Gonzales, aged 10, was found dead in a vacant lot on Bishop Street, by a pedestrian, early this afternoon. Sergeant Edward Davies, who had earlier instigated a search for the child when she did not return home last night, believes that she was struck by a hit-and-run car, her body flung by impact into the lot. A piquant circumstance is that only three days ago Emilia's best friend, Carlotta Reyes, met her death in a freak accident when a truck slipped its brakes and crashed into the Reyes home.

Mendoza read it again; and then he stared unseeingly for a long while at the bookcases opposite his chair. And then he said to himself, "*¿Qué significa eso?* So what? Art and his philosophizing. But . . ."

Next morning he called Hackett in and demanded his latest news on Carlotta Reyes.

"Oh, that thing. It's a dead end, Luis—never get anywhere on it. Try to check all those kids! Sure, only fourteen of 'em are boys, and I think we can leave the girls out on this one—"

"*Conforme.* The kind of trouble girls make isn't so—mmh—straightforward."

"You should know. But what do we get? They wander, kids like that, and time means less than nothing. Joe says he was maybe in a Sixth Street pool hall about noon—if you can't get confirmation, it doesn't say he wasn't. Bill says he was in Pershing Square—who can say yes or no? It doesn't mean a damn."

"Difficult, I know. The Reyes family," said Mendoza. "Who are they? How many? What kind?"

"And why the hell?" asked Hackett.

"A little feeling up my spine," said Mendoza dreamily, flicking his lighter. "Bear with me. You know, you get dealt a damn low card and think, get rid of it—and then something says no, it might be worth something next time around. You can talk about the mysteries of fate all you please—me, I'm a rational agnostic, I like facts. And I see in the paper that Carlotta Reyes' best girlfriend has been killed—ostensibly a hit-and-run—and I wonder."

Hackett looked interested. "Is that a fact? I missed it. You wonder what?"

"See Sergeant Davies of Juvenile and get the details. . . . I'm not quite sure," said Mendoza, "yet. Get me details on the family. Have we got any of them in Records, maybe?"

Hackett looked at him and said, "What wild idea's occurred to you now? A deliberate homicide?" Because he'd worked with Mendoza a long time, and for all he looked something like a pro wrestler, he grasped nuances first time round, having majored in psychology at Berkeley.

Mendoza looked at his cigarette. "Also look, *por favor,* at any close family friends and local relatives. Me, I'm not given to the artless confidences, but a lot of people are—we're a simian race after all."

"What the *hell,*" said Hackett. "It's a damned long chance."

"*Eso cae de su paso*—maybe it'll pay off. Go and look."

Hackett did so. He took a day looking. Over lunch next day he said, "Nine in the Reyes family. Four younger than Carlotta, four older. Reyes works for a plumbing company—desk clerk—out on North Main. The oldest boy, Eduardo, is eighteen. Got a work permit at sixteen after a year of high school. He's held odd jobs—never long anywhere—and he's on probation for car theft eight months back."

"Oh, yes?"

"Nothing on any of the rest of 'em. Reyes has a good record. He's a naturalized citizen and so is his wife—both emigrated from Mexico City. No relatives this side of the border. Their closest family friends are the Cayados down the street and some people named Obrado a couple of blocks away. No record on any of them."

"Oh, yes?" said Mendoza. "What about Emilia Gonzales?"

"Well, what about her?" Hackett shrugged. "No line. I'm bound to say—which Traffic also says—it's a little funny that nobody saw or heard it. You'd think somebody would have heard the squeal of brakes, whatever time it was—it's a residential street, with this vacant lot on the corner. It may have been after dark, of course. She hadn't come home from school, but she didn't always, and it wasn't until after dark the family got worried. The cause of death, by the way, was extensive head injuries—no other marks on the body." He threw that off carelessly.

Mendoza, who had been smoking lazily over his coffee, opened his eyes and met Hackett's. *"Insubordinado,"* he said softly. "I like the casual tone. You don't tell me. I do wonder how Sergeant Davies earned his rank. A hit-and-run, causing only head injuries?"

"I once took a course in logic—which you don't need, of course. Sure. I went and saw the corpse. Here's the autopsy report. It doesn't say much, it could have happened—"

"The Detroit designers the idiots they are," said Mendoza, "and foreigners as well, can you name me a car less than twenty years old high enough to hit any human being above the neck? Even a kid? On first impact?"

"It could be. Say she'd dropped something and was bending over to pick it up—"

"No. Tell Traffic this is tied in to something we're working."

"You really think so?"

"I really think so. There's a proverb—*La ocasión hace el ladrón,* the chance creates the thief. But it's what one might call ephemeral. . . . Look at Emilia Gonzales' family too."

"You're making like Dr. Thorndyke or some other book detective," complained Hackett, "other people bring you the facts and you interpret 'em. So O.K., here you are. Emilia had just one brother, nearly ten years older. He looks like a perfectly respectable fellow—drives a bus for the Metropolitan company. Her father drives a city refuse truck."

"Mmh. What is Eduardo Reyes working at now?"

"He's a stock clerk at a men's shop on Olive Street."

"So. You will oblige me to put a tail on Eduardo Reyes, Emilia's brother, both fathers, and any habitual male visitors to both households."

"For God's *sake*!" said Hackett. "Ten or twelve men? We're too busy, I haven't got—"

"I want to find out about this," said Mendoza. "I'm getting interested."

□   □   □

Hackett said, a waste of time and men, but Mendoza was the boss. The men were put on. And four days later the day tail attached to Eduardo Reyes reported that his charge had met with one Joe Schlicker, in the Birdie Bar on First Street, and had a long talk with him; he thought money had changed hands. The tail happened to know Schlicker because he'd once picked him up for assault. Schlicker appeared in Records as a dope pusher; and just lately, probably as running a string of pushers, or so Narcotics thought. The familiar pitch: they're gonna buy it somewheres, why not you, easy money, you just need the contacts. No legal evidence, or Narco would have picked Schlicker up before now.

And what did it mean, if anything? It didn't say anything about a truck slipping its brakes and running away downhill. Or did it?

He wasn't really justified in keeping all these men busy on it. What could they ever get to constitute evidence? If what Mendoza had dreamed up—as Hackett said—really had happened, there'd be no evidence to find.

Or would there?

He took all those tails off the others, the relatives and friends, leaving just the one set on Eduardo Reyes. He went upstairs to Narcotics and laid before Lieutenant Callaghan what he had on Eduardo, who just might possibly be in Schlicker's string of pushers. "Get a search warrant, Patrick, and let me come along, *por favor*."

"This says nothing, he talked to Schlicker in a bar. So what? Schlicker talks to a lot of people who aren't pushers."

"Don't be difficult, *amigo*. You'd like to get something legal on Schlicker, wouldn't you? This Reyes is just a punk, he might talk if he was scared enough. He might also not have been smart enough to have wiped off whatever blunt instrument he used on Emilia. If he used one. I hope. The hell of a long chance, but it's the only one I see, and the lab men are so efficient these days."

"Well, we can give it a try," said Callaghan.

In Eduardo Reyes' room they found a nice present apiece.

About fifty made-up reefers for Callaghan, and a professional-looking leather sap for Mendoza. Who recommended to the tails that they keep a close eye on Eduardo, as he might be a little upset to hear about the search, and took the sap straight to the lab.

Fortunately Emilia's funeral had been delayed, so if the lab came up with something—

It did. No blood, of course—he'd wiped it off, but not very carefully; and stuck in a little crack in the leather they picked up three hairs. The lab men so very damned efficient these days; they matched them up with the body for sure.

Mendoza was pleased. He thought it was enough to bluff Eduardo with. He put the sap in his pocket and went to see Eduardo, who was, the tail had said recently, sitting in a pool hall down on Main.

He was still there. He looked uneasy when Mendoza introduced himself. And Mendoza didn't waste any time. "We've built it up, friend. On evidence. You're in Schlicker's string of pushers, on a commission basis. Your little sister Carlotta found out and threatened to tell unless you gave her a cut." It had to be that way, because if she'd meant just to tell, she'd have done it at once. "You paid her off a couple of times, but you didn't like it. You came up Pierce Street that day and when you saw that truck sitting there you had a sudden brainwave. You knew Carlotta was alone in the house—"

"What the hell you talkin' about? I never—" Eduardo sprang up, gray with panic, and tried to run. Mendoza hauled him down to the bench again and showed him the .38 he'd unprecedentedly brought along.

"*Paso a paso, amigo.* It was a long chance that she'd be killed, and it was a crazy thing to do—risky—but you took a look around and saw nobody, and you knew most housewives would be in their kitchens at that hour. You took off the brake, turned the wheels, jumped and got out of there in a hurry, round the corner at the top of Pierce Street, so you wouldn't be called as a witness. You even remembered to use your handkerchief to handle the wheel, in case we suspected something and looked for prints. And the crazy impulse paid off—your greedy little sister was put out of the way. Permanently. Only then you found out that she'd told her best friend about it—Emilia Gonzales—"

Eduardo began to swear. He stopped when Mendoza took out the sap and said, "You didn't clean it very well. We have some nice legal evidence that this was used on Emilia. I think you met her on the way home from school, and she approached you then. Poor Emilia, like poor Carlotta—with rosy dreams of endless dollars for movies, ice cream, and visits to Disneyland. You had to do something about Emilia too. Schlicker doesn't lay out a very high commission, and you wanted to keep it yourself. I think you told Emilia to meet you, say behind that big billboard in that lot, after dark. It was quite simple—just a kid. But—"

Eduardo began to cry then and between sobs begged for a priest to confess to. Mendoza, regarding him with contempt, phoned in for a warrant.

When the signed confession was on his desk, he read it through and said to Hackett, "So, on this I'd have missed the boat. Everybody would have. It illustrates the essential efficiency of the capitalistic system."

"And how do you make that out?"

"Competition," said Mendoza. "Here I am sitting at a lieutenant's desk, and all the rest of you resenting the fact that I'm naturally the hell of a lot smarter than you are. So—"

"*¡Egotista!*"

"Well, so I am. So Smith—and all the rest of you—are always trying to be just a little smarter. Keeps you all on your toes, you know. Which was a very good thing in this case. . . . We'll keep an eye on Smith, Arturo—he seems to have the makings of a reasonably good detective."

THE MOTIVE

*H*omicide in real life, unlike homicide in fiction, is seldom either interesting or mysterious. There is a depressing sameness about the types of corpses and the situations which caused them to become corpses.

Consequently Sergeant Arthur Hackett was somewhat intrigued to be handed a real mystery, and took it in to show his superior, Lieutenant Luis Rodolfo Vicente Mendoza.

"Nothing at all if he'd been a juvenile hood, out on Boyle Avenue or somewhere. But it's a very much upper-class section of Hollywood, and that private high school gets most of its kids from very much upper-class homes. No record of any vandalism around, principal says there's not a kid in school who's ever been in bad trouble, and there's no dope problem either. I checked with Callaghan's office. They picked up a pusher approaching kids there awhile back, but evidently right away, before he got to any of 'em."

"Get to the homicide," said Mendoza.

"Well, here's this senior boy, Edward Blake, shot dead in his own car outside the public library last night. Only reason it's our baby, the library is just within our beat. It was one of the weeknights a lot of the kids go to the library—homework. A couple of them who knew him found him when they came out at nine o'clock."

"Maybe the pusher'd got to him and he *was* mixed up with

some hoods.'' Mendoza took the reports Hackett handed over
and commenced to read them.

"Don't think so. He was, according to everybody, a nice quiet
studious boy. Top marks in all his classes. Didn't go around
much with any crowd—or with girls.''

Mendoza grunted over the statements taken. Which indeed
added up to something of a mystery. Blake senior was a
well-known physician; it was, as Hackett said, that kind of
neighborhood and school—most of the kids would have fathers
who were professional or white-collar men, comfortable homes
and so on. The tuition there was fairly high. Which didn't say a
great deal, because that kind too got into trouble these days. But
it seemed that neither Edward Blake nor any of his friends at
school had done so, by what showed.

Eddy, a nice quiet studious boy. Nice-looking boy, by his
picture—dark hair, regular features, glasses, a serious expression. He went around some (such was the gist of the statements)
with Bob Hilton, Jim Canaletti, Mark Light, Frank Hauser; you
could say they were about his closest friends. He took girls out
sometimes, but no special ones; awhile ago he'd dated Ursula
Marble a lot, but not lately. The ones he'd taken out lately were
Sue Wood and Alice May Smith.

"I saw 'em all,'' said Hackett. It was nearing five o'clock and
he'd been at this all day. "Nice clean wholesome American kids.
Not a smell of delinquency, to give it the fancy name. No
apparent reason for anybody wanting him out of the way. He was
an only son—there's a sister—and on his record, one of our more
satisfactory teenagers. But there he was, shot through the head.''

"*Cómo no*, a funny little problem,'' said Mendoza. "What did
it look like, a fight?''

"Anything but. I figure he'd just got behind the wheel, and
somebody got in the backseat, or was already there—it was an
old sedan—or leaned in the back window, and let him have it.
And something else funny, too. That's not the loneliest or darkest
street in town along there, and these kids—a flock of them—were
coming and going all the time. But nobody heard a shot or
backfire. He was last seen leaving the library at about a quarter

past eight, and he must have been killed as soon as he got to his car half a block away. These two who found him are out of it—they'd been together all the time in the library. They knew him and knew his car, see, and noticed it still there when they came past. Nothing in that. But how come nobody heard the shot? It was just crazy luck to get away with it like that—that street's never quite empty of people, on a warm spring night. The odds were that somebody'd hear the shot, and look, and see the killer walking away. Nobody did."

"Talk about my having wild ideas," said Mendoza. "Are you trying to say you think a silencer was used? *¡Qué disparate!*"

"I think just maybe," said Hackett.

"A bunch of nice nondelinquent high-school kids, and a private school at that. I ask you. Nothing among his possessions to give us a hint about the motive?"

"*Nada absolutamente.* Just the stuff any eighteen-year-old might have. Except that he was more serious than most. A lot of books, not much sports equipment. And he was dressy for that age, had a lot of good-quality clothes—but the father's in the money, of course. This is one you feel damn sorry about, you know, Luis. The father—he couldn't seem to take it in, just dazed. They're nice people."

"Yes, I see. This *is* a funny one, isn't it?"

"Why else did I bring it to you? Take a look in your crystal ball and tell me the answer, boy."

"You haven't looked deep enough, that's all," said Mendoza. "Only on it today. If there isn't something in the facts to point the answer, there'll be something about the people."

"That's what I said, your crystal ball."

"*¡Zape!*" said Mendoza. "I'll stand you a drink, Arturo, and hear every little thing you've collected on this business."

Because Mendoza was one of those irritating people who went around straightening pictures: the orderly mind. Untidiness of any kind annoyed him; confronted with the jigsaw pieces, he could not rest until he'd fitted them all together.

In this odd little business, which looked so pointless and so tragic, only one thing Hackett said struck him as a possible lead.

"Talking to all these kids, I got the feeling none of them was what you'd call a close friend of Eddy's. Hell, I don't know— kids—who knows what they're feeling? They're pretty good at covering up." Hackett laughed a little ruefully over his drink. "They make you feel damn old."

"Let's see, you hit thirty-three last July. About time to start the long white beard. Even these kids who're quoted as his best friends? They didn't act that way?"

"Just an impression. They said all the right things, who'd want to kill Eddy, isn't it awful—but— Oh, well, maybe I'm catching your habit of having hunches."

Mendoza let that simmer in his mind overnight, and the next morning—which happened to be Saturday—he did not go to his office at all, but headed the custom-built Facel-Vega for that section of Hollywood and spent most of the day seeing all the kids for himself. Hackett was going deeper into the tiresome routine, checking times.

Maybe the kids made Art feel old; they just made Mendoza abstractly happy to be the wiser side of thirty, with all that nice five-percent stock the old man had left—never again to be in the throes of late adolescence, but forever safe in maturity.

Bob Hilton. Sandy, ordinary, earnest. "Gee, it's just awful, I can't imagine who'd want to— Yes, I was at the library. I picked up Jim and Sue Wood, I've got my own car. Sure, I saw Eddy there but he left before us."

Yes. All the right things, but Mendoza got it too: not the way he'd talk about an intimate friend. And Jim Canaletti: "I just can't imagine who'd do a thing like— Well, gee, it's quite a thing, isn't it, Eddy murdered! . . . No, sir, I haven't got a gun. No, my father hasn't either. Well, what *for*? I mean, Dad's a C.P.A., and what's a C.P.A. want with a—"

Mark Light. That one a great big kid, didn't look very bright, and his room, where Mendoza talked to him, was cluttered with sports equipment. "It's just an awful thing, I don't know why anybody'd have it in for Eddy, he was a real good guy. . . .

Yeah, I was at the liberry, I saw him—not to talk to, he left pretty soon. . . . No, sir, I was drivin' my own car. . . . No, sir, I didn't have anybody with me, I went alone."

Qué demonio, get search warrants for the houses of every kid in school, to look for the gun? These upper-class parents would raise hell. Ballistics said the gun had been a .32, which was all they could say about it until the actual gun was forthcoming.

Frank Hauser. Another ordinary, clean-cut eighteen-year-old. Just an awful thing. And all the rest of it.

The girls. Females always better at covering up, if there was anything to be covered up. On the other hand, Mendoza was accomplished with females. In the ordinary way he kept his distance from very young inexperienced ones (much less interesting) but he exercised his charm patiently on these, and got very little for his efforts.

Or did he? At three in the afternoon he sat behind the wheel of the Facel-Vega on a quiet residential street, lit a thoughtful cigarette, and wondered about Ursula Marble.

She was a pretty girl, maybe seventeen. Dark hair in an unfashionable but becoming long bob, unmarred magnolia complexion, very round and innocent blue eyes, and a prim little-girl manner. And a well-developed and enticing figure, in a pink sundress.

"It's just *awful*," and her voice had trembled, her blue eyes filled with tears. "I just can't stand to think about it. Eddy was just a dear. . . . No, sir, I wasn't at the library. I'd been the night before. I was home all evening. . . . The l-last time I saw him was school that day, we had English Ten together at two o'clock. I n-never saw him again. Oh, I just can't stand to think—"

And about then her father had come in, asked suspicious questions of Mendoza, reluctantly admitted that a police officer had the right to talk to the girl, but stayed as a witness. Quite within his rights and what any father would do; but naturally, if she did know anything, she wouldn't be coaxed to tell it before him. He was a big dark man with shoulders like a prize bull, and he listened frowningly to Mendoza's questions and the girl's quite expectable answers; after five minutes he interrupted with heavy finality.

"You can see she can't tell you anything, Lieutenant. It's a bad business and I'm sorry for the boy's family, but my girl didn't know him well at all, only went out with him a few times and I didn't approve of that many, but that's water under the bridge and no matter now." The girl looked sullen. "Whatever bad business it was brought about his killing, my girl didn't have anything to do with it and can't tell you anything."

"You disapproved of Eddy Blake?" asked Mendoza. "Why? By all accounts he was a very satisfactory young man."

"So he may have been," said Marble. "I don't doubt it. I liked the boy well enough, daresay he was a good boy. But he was Protestant, and with us being Catholic it'd just lead to trouble."

Oh, hell, said Mendoza to himself. Nothing at all: no lead. The heavily paternal Mr. Marble, like everyone else, knew nothing to Eddy Blake's discredit.

But now his thoughts veered back to the girl Ursula. To those round innocent blue eyes. A bit too innocent. She wasn't the bucolic backward maiden: she couldn't be, with those looks and attending a big-city high school, even a private one. She might be and undoubtedly was a perfectly virtuous and respectable girl, but at seventeen she'd have learned how to cope with the pass, the obnoxiously amorous date. She was acting the sweet twelve-year-old (for the father's benefit? no, even before he came in) but she wasn't as unsophisticated as that.

Why? Grant that she was a lot smarter than she was acting, he didn't see pretty virtuous Ursula Marble using a gun on Eddy Blake. She wasn't, reflected Mendoza out of much experience, that kind of girl.

There wasn't a line to get hold of in the whole damned business. Except the little fact that Eddy had been a lone wolf. The kind of introverted, ultra-intelligent youngster other kids couldn't feel really close to: who didn't make many intimate friends. And that was natural with a boy of superior intelligence.

Look at them. That Light boy, a sports-mad lout. The others just ordinary kids a little brighter than Mark Light but not real brains. What would they have in common with Eddy Blake who got As in all his classes, read Proust when it wasn't required in school, and had an IQ of 140?

And that wasn't the typical picture of the boy who got mixed up with real hoods.

Mendoza said to himself, "*Qué molesto*—I do indeed need a crystal ball," and turned the ignition key. Such a simple little problem on the face of it, but no handle to grasp at all.

Like Hackett he was sorry for the parents. Nice people, yes: respectable people. Still dazed with the suddenness of tragedy striking out of the blue. The sister a pretty fifteen-year-old who looked at him under long dark lashes with the solemn unexpected maturity of the female at any age.

"You—you won't need to question Anne, will you? She really couldn't— Run along, dear. . . . I really don't know what else we can tell you, Lieutenant. The other man—he was very nice, I'm afraid we were both in rather a state at the time—you understand—I—I think both my husband and I'd like to say we appreciate how considerate you've all been. . . ."

"I'd like to know," said Mendoza, "how much allowance Eddy got." More or less at random, because there were two things practically always hooked up to homicide somehow— money and strong emotion. Sometimes both together. So you asked about them first.

"His allowance?" said Dr. Blake. "What on earth— Well, he had twenty-five dollars a week for his personal expenses. And what he could earn otherwise, if he wanted to." Fleetingly Mendoza remembered the low-stake Spanish monte bank he'd run in the back room of a Main Street restaurant, after school; if he was lucky, five or six bucks to take home to the old lady on Saturdays. *Vaya,* only chance how one was born, and now (the old man the miser he'd been) he could buy and sell Dr. Jonathan Blake seven times over and have money left. But Eddy Blake certainly, by his background, hadn't much reason to get into trouble. Plenty of money to run his car, indulgent but upright parents, probably not too strict discipline.

No handle at all. But a little something Hackett had said— "Did Eddy buy his own clothes, Mrs. Blake?"

"Why, mostly, yes. That is, I mean he'd pick them out. Underwear and things like that, I'd buy for him—but he liked to choose his own slacks and jackets and shirts. He—he was quite particular, we used to tease him a little about it. Not like the usual eighteen-year-old boy, you know. Why, just last week he bought a very expensive sports jacket, I happened to see the bill by accident—forty-nine fifty—I think he was a little ashamed, he rather snapped at me. . . ." Mrs. Blake contrived a tearful smile. "I suppose other boys laughed at him for it, liking clothes so much. He'd been saving up his allowance to get it. He was like that. A—a very mature boy for his age."

He asked more random questions, getting no faint clue, and thanked them. When he came out to the Facel-Vega at the curb, he found Anne Blake regarding its low-slung rakish lines seriously. "That's a pretty car," she said. She gave him a level long look. "You're the policeman looking for whoever killed Eddy. Are you the head one?"

"I suppose you could say so," said Mendoza.

She gave a little satisfied nod. "Parents are funny, you know. They keep on thinking you're just a baby. But I'm not, and I know two things about Eddy that might have something to do with it. They wouldn't let the other man ask me anything either, and I s'pose he thought I wouldn't know anything anyway. But I do. If I tell you, will you really listen and—and think about it?"

"I will indeed," said Mendoza.

She scuffed one sandal heel round in an aimless circle. "They wouldn't listen—Mother and Daddy. They said I couldn't be sure. But I am. See, it's just two kind of funny things about Eddy—and it was a funny thing, I mean a different thing, I mean a—an *unusual* thing—his getting killed like that. Wasn't it? So maybe it's got something to do with it. Eddy didn't save up the money for that new jacket out of his allowance. Because just the week before, he borrowed a dollar from me for gas, he said his allowance had *run out.* . . . But that was the week he got new seat covers for his car, twenty-eight dollars they cost, more than his allowance. And he gets his allowance on Saturdays, and he paid me back that Wednesday before, and I saw he had a lot of money—in bills, you know. So he got it somewhere else. . . . He sort of thought I was a baby too, or he'd have known I'd *notice.*"

"That's very interesting," said Mendoza.

And a sharp voice called from the front door, "Anne! Come in, dear, don't bother the lieutenant—"

She gave him a grave smile. "And he was going to marry that girl named Ursula. Sometime. They were *secretly engaged.* On account of her father not liking him. Mother and Daddy don't like her much either, I guess, and besides they said he was too young to get married. That was 'way last year, there was kind of a fuss about it. So Eddy didn't take her out anymore, he went out with other girls sometimes just to make people think they'd broken up. You know. But they hadn't. I heard him lots of times talking to her on the phone when Mother and Daddy weren't here. It was kind of *romantic.*"

"Anne! Come in—"

She turned suddenly shy and self-conscious, blushed furiously, and ran for the house. Mendoza got into the car and started back downtown.

Money, he thought. And here was the first hint. Because in his experience, while he didn't approve of homicide as a way of settling problems, generally the deceased had done a little something to provoke the homicide. Money. Eddy Blake (could one say on hearsay evidence?) had had more money than he should have had. Where had it come from and what had happened to it? All spent on clothes? No, the parents would have noticed. Would have noticed any new possessions costing more than they knew he could afford.

That girl Ursula. A secret engagement. Pair of romantic kids, planning an elopement. Anything there? Well, Eddy was a mature and serious boy; he'd look ahead and plan carefully. For an elopement you'd need money. Maybe quite a lot of money, to live on awhile until your parents could be persuaded to accept the situation. . . .

He found Hackett in the office. "What've you got?"

"Nothing. A great big blank," said Hackett.

"Cheer up. Come up to Federico's, I'll buy you a drink and dinner. Maybe I've got something. . . . I agree with you about the rest of the kids," Mendoza said when they were settled in a booth at Federico's. "Except for that Ursula girl. She really meant it. She was in love with him—mostly because her father disapproved of him, I'd say. They were planning to run away and get married."

"Then she'd hardly be the one killed him. Unless he'd got her in trouble and was maybe cooling off—"

"*Caray,* Art, you're the typical cop, not used to dealing with respectable people! The girl's virtuous as the day she was born, I'd lay money on it. But aside from her, all the others quoted as his intimate friends don't seem to have thought all that much of him. He was the lone wolf—natural, with his intelligence. They wouldn't have had much in common—"

"Oh, I don't know," said Hackett. "They were all the studious type. I thought there might be something in that myself, you know—I looked around to see what they all had in common, because those other boys didn't quite jibe with Eddy. I went and routed out the principal to look at school records, see if they belonged to the same clubs and so on. All I can figure now is, maybe that kind of kid, the very bright ones, just aren't demonstrative. Because they're all the kind Eddy was—top-ranking students. Honor society. A's in everything."

Mendoza set down his rye. "That lout Mark Light?" he asked incredulously. "An honor student? *¡No me diga!*"

"Well, that's what the records say. . . . *Could* he have got mixed up with dope pushers or something? You'd think there'd be something to point to—"

"There is. Not to that, but to something. He had more money

then he should have had," and Mendoza relayed Anne's news.

"For God's sake," was Hackett's comment. "Twenty-five bucks a week? When I was eighteen I got two bucks a week for doing the yard work, *and* I walked to school."

"Don't be snobbish, boy. It's a democratic country. The point is, the extra money above that. From where?"

"In that nice quiet respectable school, no dope problem, no—"

"Eminently superior teenagers," agreed Mendoza absently. And then he stared at his empty glass thoughtfully and said, "Or are they? Damn, too late to get on this tonight, but tomorrow— And there *is* something we can do tonight, at that. . . . This is a crazy idea, but it's the only thing occurs to me at the moment and we might as well check it out."

The Blakes were obliging, if bewildered. Mendoza and Hackett closeted themselves in Eddy Blake's room and examined every paper and notebook. Naturally, in his initial search, Hackett hadn't gone carefully through what was obviously schoolwork.

An hour later Hackett looked up from an English-literature essay and said, "You and your crystal ball."

"It looks like it, doesn't it?" said Mendoza. "It was really the only answer, once it occurred to me. He was such a brilliant student. . . . I'll lay you a hundred to one that girl knew all about it. He was saving up for that runaway marriage—she was probably the one person he trusted. And I'll also lay you that's where the money is. Eddy had a prying and curious little sister. . . . I'm sorry for the Blakes. But I can't say I regret that somebody put a period to this one, Art. That cold brilliant mind—he might have turned into a really dangerous pro. All the signs."

"*De veras,*" sighed Hackett. Eddy hadn't had a chance to get rid of this week's work, and it was all there. Nine different essays for English 10, twelve different pages of algebra problems neatly copied out, eight copies of the week's chemistry problems, and so on. Eddy had been selling the use of his superior intelligence to lesser brains, probably at a handsome fee. "Yes, all these kids would have generous allowances. . . . Damn it, you needn't look so pleased with yourself, Luis."

"Not with myself. I'm lost in admiration of Eddy. I barely achieved a passing grade in algebra myself, and as for chemistry—¡ay de mí!—they very kindly let me take an extra English class instead. Yes, he might have developed into a very clever pro indeed. And he had the orderly mind." For each paper was neatly labeled with the name of its recipient, to be handed over for copying and destroyed later.

"But where does that get us? Damn it, it's going to shock the Blakes. But what does it say?"

"A motive," said Mendoza. He lit a new cigarette and shuffled all those pages, tabulating the names. "Maybe. It's the only thing that might have built up a motive, isn't it? Kids this age are hair-trigger sometimes." He began to separate the papers in little piles, according to the names, and he went on dreamily, "The kids buying Eddy's services would be rather special ones. Kids who are pressured at home to bring in the report card full of A's and B's. Of course, a lot of parents do that sort of thing. A lot of kids do their best and shrug it off if they can't quite make it. But sometimes parents are so misguided as to offer the bribe— bring home A's or your allowance drops, bring home A's and you get a bonus. Yes. I wonder what Eddy's rates were? A dollar for a one-page essay, two bucks for this week's algebra problems. Like that. And isn't this pretty." He contemplated fourteen different piles of papers. Thirteen of them were fairly slim piles, two or three pages to each. The fourteenth contained eight pages. "So now I think we know. Most of these kids were only buying Eddy's services for a couple of classes. Bob Hilton, for instance, doesn't seem to have trouble with anything but English—that's all Eddy did for him this week. Jim Canaletti was buying his algebra problems and nothing else. Frank Hauser also had trouble with English—both English One and English Ten. But there, Arturo, we have the dumb lout Mark Light who was bad at everything. Eddy was doing all his schoolwork for him, from English to history to math. And consequently we can say that the majority of Eddy's extra money was coming from Mark Light. And somehow I don't think Mark liked paying out most of his allowance—probably—to Eddy. I don't know what might have set off the homicide. Killing the goose, and so on. But as I say, kids this age sometimes go off half-cocked. . . . The gun. I think, on the strength of this,'' said Mendoza, ''the next obvious thing to do is go and see Mark Light. With a search warrant. Tomorrow morning. I am now going back to tackle Ursula—''

"Naturalmente," said Hackett. "Our Luis always makes a beeline for the females."

"Don't miscall me. Virtuous and romantic young girls I shy away from as the devil from holy water. No, what interests me is that on the facts she ought to be anxious to have the murderer caught—she ought to have poured out this information at once, realizing that it probably had a bearing on the murder. Why didn't she? The heavily paternal Mr. Marble? I don't think so. . . . You know, risking mayhem from Mr. Marble, I think we'll get a search warrant for that house too."

Which paid off, because tucked away in Ursula's top bureau drawer they found two hundred and thirty dollars. The sports jacket had been a single extravagance; Eddy had been saving his money soberly.

"I don't *care!*" shrieked Ursula. "You were all against us— we loved each other—but he *said*—it was a joke really, then, but he *said* it—if he g-got killed in an accident or something, it was *mine!* I don't care what you say, it *is* mine now and it wasn't up to me to say anything—*tell* on him! Everybody thinking it was such an awful thing to do—what was so bad about it, if he was that smart? I don't *care*—"

"Vaya," said Mendoza to Hackett, "the eternal feminine. And we call them illogical and sentimental. They're born with shrewder minds than Newton or Einstein."

"But it still doesn't say who did kill him."

"Wait till we get that other search warrant."

They got it next morning, and went up to the Lights' house with it. There was, of course, a certain amount of indignant protest and talk about high-handed cops and citizens' rights. Light senior was one of two partners in a well-known local chemical-research lab, a personage of considerable presence. But he was also an honest man, and backed down grumbling before the search warrant.

The boy came in from somewhere as the Headquarters men started the search; he halted at the sight of Mendoza and Hackett with his father in the entrance hall. "What—what's going on?" he asked. And he sounded nervous.

"We're looking," said Mendoza, "for the gun. Do you own any guns, Mr. Light?"

"Why, yes, as it happens target shooting is my one hobby, I have several— But really, Lieutenant, I must protest, Mark was one of the boy's best friends, you can't suppose there was any reason—"

"Look at him," said Mendoza. The boy had gone dead-white; he stood absolutely still as if in shock for one moment, and then turned and bolted.

Hackett plunged after him, but Light senior was quicker. He collared his son firmly and hauled him back into the house. He had gone pale himself. "Mark," he said in a stunned voice, "Mark, you couldn't have—"

And here came Dwyer down the hall, triumphantly bearing a small revolver by a pencil through the trigger guard. "Here we are, Lieutenant. Nice little Browning thirty-two, and a Maxim silencer right next to it. Quite a collection of shooting irons down in the study."

"Very nice," said Mendoza, and turned on Mark, still in his father's grip. He didn't waste any time. He told Mark they knew what Eddy'd been doing, and that Mark was his star customer. He didn't, for this reason and that, have much sympathy for Eddy or Mark or any of these kids, so he didn't pull any punches. "We're requisitioning your gun, Mr. Light, because it's a hundred to one it's the gun killed Eddy. Isn't it, Mark? He needled you some way, or maybe you just got tired paying him—how was it exactly, Mark? You might as well tell us, you know. Ballistics can identify this as the gun that killed him, all scientific. And that puts you right on the spot.''

"I never—"

"Never thought we'd get you for it? You left before he did at the library that night—I can figure how that went. Maybe you waited until you saw him coming, having spotted his car, and asked him for a lift home. Something like that. And shot him as you got in the backseat. Anyway—"

And Mark, the overgrown lout, lost his head. He turned on his father savagely. "All *your* fault! A college boy I had to be, sure! I don't give a damn, see, not one damn—college!—it just wasn't for me, I haven't got that kinda damn fool brain— *Books!* I couldn't care less! But you hadda make a big deal out of it, no allowance unless I get the A's 'n' B's! What the hell, *books*! Every cent of my allowance, almost, gone to that bastard, some weeks I dint even break even—just to get the A's 'n' B's for you, and the money to pay *him*! I couldn't—I hadda go out sometimes, dint I? Have a little fun? I got behind payin' him, and him sayin' he'd tell you how I cheated—he would've too, cold-blooded bastard—I—it's all *your* fault, *I* never wanted to go to any damn college—"

"My God," said Hackett. "Eighteen. A thing like that. And all of 'em from good backgrounds. It makes you wonder."

"I'll tell you, Arturo," said Mendoza, "it makes me wonder what more valuable and important citizen he might have murdered later on, if we hadn't caught him now. The man capable of murder, he'll do it at eighteen or eighty." He laughed. "The privileged classes—we should occasionally spare a charitable thought for them. But I'm sorrier for Mark Light in a way, than for Eddy Blake."

"Not much to choose between," said Hackett.

"*¿Cómo dice, chico?* Brains will always be more important

than stupidity. What it comes down to is—mmh—the individual integrity." And Mendoza added thoughtfully, "That Ursula girl, hanging on to the money . . . However, *en naturaleza,* females quite lawless."

"A waste," said Hackett, a little sad, a little annoyed. "A good brain—"

"My Arturo! I'm a rational agnostic, with common sense—and even if religion does endorse the idea, I believe it—the two forces, good and evil. It depends on which side the good brain belongs. In this case, I think we've saved some trouble for somebody sitting at this desk twenty years from now. That one could have grown into a dangerous pro, *de veras.*"

THE LONG CHANCE

"I've gone along with a lot of your hunches," said Sergeant Arthur Hackett, "but—"

"No hunch," said Lieutenant Mendoza irritably. "Straight evidence."

"*And,*" said Hackett, "I might add that I've seen a lot of your hunches fall flat. My good God above, Luis, the man's confessed!"

Mendoza dusted loose tobacco off his desk, arranged the desk box and letter tray at a precise parallel, straightened the desk blotter. One reason Mendoza had a little reputation on this force—his built-in sense of order. The thing all in a muddle, he couldn't rest until he'd straightened out into sense. "*¿Pues y qué?* The man has also told us that an invisible spiritual guardian warns him about secret enemies. Do you believe that too?"

Hackett regarded him in exasperation. In the last three weeks the L.A.P.D. had been confronted with the dead-by-violence corpses of five middling-to-elderly women—Agnes Hope, Ruth Fleming, Marian Steers, Evelyn Gibbs, and Polly Winters. Four widows and a spinster. Mendoza, his senior sergeant, and a lot of underlings had put in a little overtime looking, and their looking had, six hours ago, resulted in the arrest of one Edgar Edward Fleming, nephew to the late Mrs. Fleming. He had told them about it at once, eager to explain that the women were all powerful secret enemies to him, he had killed them in self-defense; they had been conspiring with Communists—or perhaps with Satan—but fortunately good spiritual forces had managed to warn him in time.

"Five of them?" he was asked. And the names read out to him.

"I don't remember now how many. Yes, five. Six? No, I—I— I don't—you must *understand*, I—"

And the doctor had grunted out the inevitable "Schizophrenia." "Been building up some time, and he blew up all of a sudden. Hell of a thing."

So it was. It was also quite straightforward. All the women had lived alone. Four of them had been killed by a number of head blows, not delivered by any weapon, but as a result of being held in a powerful grasp and slammed down on floor, convenient furniture, and in the case of Mrs. Steers, the kitchen stove. Fleming was a big hulk of a fellow, very strong. The fifth, Miss Winters, had been struck twice on the head with that old friend the blunt instrument. And now Fleming was sitting down there in the county jail, before removal to the psychiatric ward of the General, not only willingly claiming all five as his victims, but talking about an army of invading Martians he'd also destroyed, after his spirit guardians had warned him of their arrival—and about the imminence of the coming of the Anti-Christ.

Which made little better sense, Hackett said, than Mendoza sitting here saying that Fleming hadn't killed Polly Winters.

"Look," he said. "I can reason from A to B too. What you've got in your head is that Winters is the only one of the five he didn't know personally. Hope and Steers were friends of his aunt's, and he'd met them there. Gibbs went to the same church he did. Also you're thinking that all those four lived more or less in the same area, within eight or ten blocks anyway, and Winters lived a lot farther off. O.K., but it's not as if she'd lived the other side of the county—and she wasn't an invalid, didn't have a car and walked everywhere, so we're told. What's to say Fleming didn't pass her on the street, anytime? Who knows what his helpful spiritual advisers whispered to him? There's another enemy, boy—smite hip and thigh! So he follows her—"

"You need not advertise the callousness of the average cop so graphically, Arturo," said Mendoza coldly. "Only another superfluous old maid, good riddance? That I know. I call your attention to the fact that Winters was killed with a weapon, unlike the others. Also to the fact that, by the testimony of her neighbors, she had come home at least four hours before the surgeon says she died. So nobody followed her, came right in after her and killed her."

"What the hell?" said Hackett. "Who knows what one like Fleming would do? They can be damn foxy sometimes. This one you're reaching for, boy."

"It wasn't Fleming who killed Miss Winters," said Mendoza obstinately. "And I know nobody in the D.A.'s office is going to listen to me any more sympathetically than you—some good hard work has to be done on it before they'll listen at all."

"We're busy enough as it is, damn it! My God, go haring off after a wild goose—"

"And find a mare's nest? ¡Zape—no hay tal! Go away and stop criticizing your seniors."

"It's the hot weather," said Hackett. "You've been overworking. You just relax, go and take that redhead of yours out somewhere and have a good time—you'll feel better tomorrow."

"Out!" said Mendoza. "I'm going back to work. I'll tell you what I come up with—if anything—in the morning."

"¡No me tome el palo—don't kid me!" said Hackett, and went away.

The night shift was coming on; it was six o'clock. Mendoza sighed. And he had told his grandmother he'd come to see her tonight. He called her and said something had come up—tomorrow—

"You neglect me shamefully! I do not believe it. It is that you visit another kind of woman, my wicked one!"

"And don't I know, my little pigeon, ten to one you've got another prospective bride picked out for me to inspect!" God forbid it. She'd been trying for years to marry him off to some decent girl who could coax him back to the priests. He calmed her down, said tomorrow for sure. He asked Sergeant Slade to pull the file on the Winters thing, and put it in his breast pocket. He collected the custom-built Facel-Vega from the lot and drove home, to an affectionate welcome from the sleek feline Abyssinian personage who ruled his household, Bast of the green eyes. He fed her first and over his own dinner reread the Winters file.

"*¡Ay de coincidencia!*" he said to himself. But there it was— it had a different smell, somehow. The younger Homicide sergeants were apt to speak with awe of Lieutenant Mendoza's uncanny hunches, but Hackett was quite right: a lot of them fell flat. It was the ones that didn't got remembered.

Miss Winters, aged sixty-eight; retired schoolteacher; lived alone in one side of a small duplex she owned on Kenmore in Hollywood. Didn't go out much; when she did, it was to church, an occasional concert, an occasional play—marketing and so on. Not many friends. She hadn't even that traditional spinster's companion, a cat. She did have a niece, her only relation. Miss Marjorie Gaines, employed at a Bank of America branch in Westwood. Miss Winters had been killed ten days ago, before Mrs. Gibbs and Mrs. Hope, after Mrs. Fleming and Mrs. Steers. She had gone out (the neighbors couldn't say the exact hour) sometime in the afternoon, and she had been seen coming home at about six o'clock. By the evidence in the house, she had had dinner, washed the dishes, and been sitting in her living room reading Rupert Brooke, when she was interrupted. (*¡Caray,* Brooke! These romantic-minded spinsters.) How had she been interrupted?

Mendoza lit a cigarette and went on automatically stroking Bast on his lap. Sure, so the other four Fleming had known; and they'd known him. He came ringing their doorbells; three of them might be surprised to be called on by a very casual acquaintance, but they wouldn't be afraid of him at once, they'd let him in. The aunt, *naturalmente,* wouldn't suspect anything either. But the surgeon said, about Miss Winters, between ten and one A.M. (She'd been found by the tenant of the other side of the duplex, coming to borrow some sugar, at eight the next morning—front door open, screen unhooked, so the tenant suspected something wrong and went in to investigate). Now, an elderly woman living alone, it was on the cards she'd be startled to have her doorbell rung at that hour. *¿Cómo no?* She wouldn't be used to visitors that late. She certainly wouldn't—that could be said definitely—let a stranger into the house at that time of night. Especially a man.

Somebody saying, Western Union—saying, an urgent message from your niece—and getting her to unhook the screen door, and forcing his way in? Yes, but it was a warm summer night, and a good many people nearby—doors and windows open. Sure to God she'd have had time to scream, to struggle?

And why had anybody wanted to murder Miss Winters? Such an inoffensive, unimportant old maid?

Oh, yes? said Mendoza to himself. Had she been? They had asked questions about all these women, because in the average homicide case the deceased had done something, or been something, to produce a motive for the homicide. Of course, now they had Fleming, all that looked rather irrelevant, because Fleming's motive had been irrational. The fact that Mrs. Gibbs had been a bridge fiend, and Mrs. Hope the neighborhood gossip, and Mrs. Steers a rather stupid woman whose only talent lay in cooking, and Mrs. Fleming an extremely devout member of the St. John Lutheran Church, looked unimportant. And of course there were other nuts besides Fleming wandering around, in a place this size. But that seemed to make it sound a little too coincidental, just another nut. And Mendoza, who frequently found it rather difficult to get dealt into a few poker hands because he was such a constant winner, would lay odds that Fleming had never been within a mile of Miss Polly Winters. So what did they have on her?

Not much. She had, as the British put it, kept herself to herself. A rather typical spinster, if there was such a thing: a spare, upright, dignified old lady, very businesslike, a little abrupt. She didn't believe in running bills. She had got the duplex paid for, and invested in a modest amount of sound common stock, all on her salary before she retired. Mendoza the conservative (especially after his grandfather had died and they found all those safe-deposit boxes stuffed with nice gilt-edged five-percent stock certificates) approved. A longheaded, sensible woman. (*¡Ay de mí!* his grandmother, what she called investing, collecting expensive jewelry—the portable value. Nobody could convince her Tel-and-Tel was better. And what did she say? "A fine one you are to talk, with this imported automobile and God knows what spent on your clothes, not to mention your immoral women!" As if that had anything to do . . .)

Miss Polly Winters . . . Mendoza apologized to Bast, stashed the dishes in the dishwasher, after earnest reflection before the mirror changed his tie for a more discreet one, and drove out to Bronson Avenue in Hollywood where Miss Marjorie Gaines occupied a shabby middle-aged apartment.

He hadn't seen Miss Gaines before; that had been Hackett or one of Hackett's men. As something of a connoisseur of females, he was disappointed. Miss Gaines was long, thin, angular, and lacking in poise. At one glance, Mendoza longed to send her to his redhead, Alison Weir, who operated a charm school. Alison would tell her not to wear too much costume jewelry, or that dark lipstick, and not to giggle and gesture so extravagantly. She had an unfortunately aquiline nose, freckles, and a high-pitched voice.

"Well, I really couldn't say," she said. "But it does seem funny, I never thought before. Auntie'd have let me in, of course, or anyone she knew, but I don't think any stranger. Such an awful thing to happen—but with all these juvenile delinquents—"

"Do you mind telling me," asked Mendoza with his most persuasive smile, "what your aunt had to leave? As you were her only relative, I expect you came in for all of it?"

Miss Gaines was neither offended nor puzzled by this personal question; probably she did very little thinking about anything at anytime. "Oh, yes, I do. There was a will at the bank." Her eyes filled with easy tears. "Dear Auntie, I mean, even if she hadn't any other relations, she might *not* have. You know how funny old people get. But she wasn't *that* funny—quite sensible in a lot of ways—and she left it all to me. The duplex, and the man at the bank says it comes to about ten thousand dollars in stock. Quite a lot . . . Well, she hadn't actually *told* me so, but I was pretty sure she was going to, you know."

De veras, thought Mendoza, and so what? It depended where you sat, what kind of money looked important. The duplex, maybe worth sixty thousand. Ten thousand in stock. The hell of a long way from a fortune, these days. But money.

"And just to set the record straight, Miss Gaines—I believe someone asked you before, but—you were out the evening your aunt was murdered?"

She didn't seem to take the implication at all, and readily repeated the story he'd already seen in the records. "Oh, yes, I was at a shower. A wedding shower for Sharon Wilson, she works in the branch I do, some of us got up a surprise shower for her, she's going to be married in November. I took a set of bath towels, awfully cute—I got it on sale— But really, Lieutenant, I mean, why would you want to know? . . . It was at her apartment, 'way out on Western. . . . Heavens, I couldn't say what time I left! Carol drove me out and brought me home, I haven't got a car. I suppose about eleven-thirty."

Very nice. A pretty definite alibi. In any case, he couldn't see this long thin dreep of a female slamming her aunt over the head for the legacy she had to leave.

So, let Hackett say he was woolgathering. *Lo digo y lo sostengo,* he thought, by God there was something here still to be found out.

"Of course I'm terribly grateful," Miss Gaines was saying. "Poor old Aunt Polly. It was awfully good of her, especially when— well, that doesn't matter. I won't say it won't be *useful.* You see, I'm going to be married," and she smiled and blushed at him coyly. "And no matter what Micky says, it'd be silly to pay rent now I own a house, and even if it is sort of old-fashioned furniture, well, it's silly to go into debt for new. . . . But, Lieutenant, have you found out something about who—" The evening papers hadn't had the story on Fleming.

Reflecting that a benevolent nature had so ordered matters that even the most unprepossessing people could find mates somehow, Mendoza gave her a vague answer and came away. He drove out to the General to see Fleming and was told that Fleming had had to have a shot to quiet him down and wasn't available for questioning. So he questioned the psychiatrist who'd seen him instead.

"That's an extraordinary question," said the psychiatrist, staring at him.

"Just an opinion, please," repeated Mendoza patiently. "Would he say he'd killed five women when he'd only killed four?"

"I'm afraid no one could possibly say. We like to think we know quite a bit about schizophrenia, but actually we've only scratched the surface. But are you suggesting that—really, it doesn't seem—that is, from what I've heard of the case—"

"So I'm chasing a wild goose. But I don't think so. If the names were impressed on him again, if he were asked specifically—"

The psychiatrist shrugged and shook his head. "Hopeless, Lieutenant. He's cracked up very thoroughly now. You see, to put it in nontechnical language, he's used up all his nervous energy for a long time in maintaining a normal surface appearance. He realized that his fantasies would seem strange to others, and kept it all inside. When the pressures became too intense, he was driven to these murders, and when he was apprehended, he collapsed suddenly into the worst stage of the disease. Indeed, I might say that—as to your suggestion—it's possible he doesn't really know himself, now, how many people he killed. You probably know that the one most obvious symptom of the disease is an inability to distinguish between fantasy and reality. When he's telling us about these Martians he also killed, and now about a physical encounter with Satan—quite real to him—you aren't likely to get anything useful out of him as to whether he really killed four or five old women."

"Which is very helpful." Mendoza offered him a cigarette. "Why old women, do you suppose?"

The psychiatrist shrugged again. "One can guess. We don't know much about his early history, only the little his aunt had mentioned to friends. That his parents died when he was a child and he was raised by his grandmother. Possibly there were pent-up resentments against the mother-figure, or just against all old women, or widows. Who can say? It's a progressive thing. As I say, he unwittingly aggravated the progress by trying desperately to keep up a normal appearance—you know of course that up to two weeks ago he had earned a fair living as a department-store clerk. Then it got too much for him and he exploded, went all to pieces. That's how you got on to him, I understand, the people at the store talking about his queer behavior and so on, so he was fired. Without much doubt now, he'll spend the rest of his life in an institution for the criminal insane."

"Which is of no help to me," said Mendoza. "But thanks very much."

Too late to do anything more tonight, and what else could he do anyway? No line, no handle at all. The Robertsons, tenants of the other side of Miss Winters' house, had been out until midnight on the evening of her death, so if Miss Winters had screamed, they hadn't been there to hear. But if she had, the neighbors on the other side, the Johnsons, would probably have heard—hot weather, houses all open—and they hadn't heard anything.

So all right, say somebody had rung the bell and said, "Wire for you," or "Special delivery." She seemed to have been an old lady physically active and in possession of all her wits. Surely the moment such a spurious messenger had forced his way into the house, she'd have made some outcry, put up a struggle, or fled to run out the back door, calling for help?

Mendoza went home and read over the file again. It hadn't looked as if there'd been a struggle. She had been found facedown, sprawled in the middle of the living-room floor, and the wounds had been on the back and top of her head. Nothing, so far as the tearful niece could say, was missing from the house. Fourteen-odd dollars in her purse, and that plainly visible on a living-room table. The few objects of value in the house—her modest box of jewelry, silverware, a new portable T.V.— untouched. Which of course had tied it in with the Fleming jobs, because nothing had been taken from those other places either.

But Miss Winters hadn't known Fleming, that they could say for pretty sure. Not by name: nothing to say they hadn't passed each other in the street, as Art said. About Fleming, impossible to say—sure, he might have had a brainwave about one stranger as well as four women known to him. But about Miss Winters, anybody with common sense could say that she wouldn't have admitted a stranger to the house at that hour, and if he'd forced his way in would have screamed. And been heard.

"Eso sí que está bueno," said Mendoza to himself exasperatedly. "What a mess!" He went to bed, telling himself further to have patience—and hope.

As Hackett had reminded him, Homicide was being kept pretty busy (the hot weather, probably: tempers short) and what with this and that it wasn't until after lunch next day that he had time to put his mind on Miss Winters again. His own temper was not improved by Hackett's derisive comments on his abortive evening's work. . . . "Your crystal ball shows you the damndest pictures, Luis!"

"Hell!" said Mendoza. "I'll get some sense out of this if it's the last thing I do!" So the house had been gone over at the time, but he hadn't seen it—and in a business like this he wanted to look at everything himself. After lunch he drove out to Miss Gaines' apartment; it was Saturday and he just might find her home.

He did. Her fiancé was with her. One Mr. Michael Barr. Mendoza marveled again at Providence. Mr. Barr was even less attractive than Miss Gaines, being rather weedy, with no chin and an already receding hairline; but obviously he and his Marjorie adored each other. He called her Kitten. *¡Por vida!* thought Mendoza, and asked if he could borrow the keys of the duplex.

"What for?" asked Mr. Barr curiously. "I mean, I thought

you fellows were finished—since you got this nut. We were just reading about it in the paper—hell of a thing.''

"Yes, isn't it?'' said Mendoza, cutting off Miss Gaines' excited comments. "Just checking evidence. I'd be obliged, Miss Gaines—I'll return them in a couple of hours.''

"Why, certainly, you're welcome, I'm sure. I can still hardly believe it—an awful lunatic like that murdering poor Auntie! It doesn't seem possible, I mean, you read about these things in the papers, but they don't happen to people you *know*—''

"They happen,'' said Mendoza. "Thanks very much.''

He went through the duplex thoroughly. Nothing there at all. Of course, of course. If the convenient clue out of a detective story had been dropped—the cuff link, the handkerchief—the boys would have found it first time round. All he got was a kind of lefthand confirmation.

Because the chalk outline was still on the floor, where the body had lain. A good ten feet from the front door, and she'd fallen facing away from that door. That said she'd let somebody in and turned away from him, leading the way into the room. Didn't it? If she'd answered the doorbell—

Mendoza found the phone, hoping it hadn't been shut off, found it hadn't, and called Miss Gaines to ask whether Miss Winters had habitually kept the screen hooked and the front door locked.

"Oh, yes, she did. Always. A woman living alone, you know—and while it's a respectable neighborhood, the awful things that happen these days—'' He could hear Mr. Barr in the background asking questions, is it that cop again, what does he want? "She always did.''

So what did that say? Not the fake Western Union messenger. A caller, and one she knew. She'd unhooked the screen to let him in, turned away back into the room—turned her back on him. Someone she wasn't afraid of.

But not one single damned thing to say who it had been. Take a look at everybody she had known? At all the neighbors?

He did a little swearing, returned the keys, and went back to his office to brood.

□ □ □

That evening, as promised, he went to see his grandmother, who—since they'd found all those deposit boxes—was enjoying life in a Wilshire Boulevard apartment, telling everyone grand lies about her impeccable Castilian ancestry.

"What, no new candidate for bride to foist on me?" Mendoza asked, kissing her.

"Unfortunately she was engaged for the evening. A very nice genteel pretty girl. You are a wretch! I ask myself what is to become of you!"

"My little pigeon, I do very well as I am—"

"Disrespectful! And most sadly sinful! The good God knows I tried to bring you up respectably! You are not growing any younger, you should be sensibly married long since—"

"And running back and forth to the priests! Don't I know your devious schemes!"

"You are not so foolish and naïve to believe in this notion, true love forever to base a marriage upon—"

"I was never so naïve. God deliver me! We will stop talking of this—"

"Luis, my wicked rake!" she said severely. "Marriage is a serious matter! It is always for the elders to give deep consideration to arrange it suitably, to be sure all is done right— Now what have I said?"

"I'm not sure," said Mendoza, straightening to stare into space. "Something significant? I have the feeling. . . . Oh, the devil, let it go. Have you seen the doctor about the stiffness in your knees, and what did he say, my dove?"

"What would he say except that I am growing old, which I knew already? It is a waste of money."

Sunday was just another day to Mendoza if he was working something. He was in his office by nine o'clock. The trouble was, he didn't know where to go from there.

Yesterday—to Hackett's disapproval, what with the spate of business they had on hand—he'd set a man to looking out what

more there was to know about Miss Winters. And her acquaintances. So here was a report on his desk, which meant exactly
nothing.

Miss Winters had regularly attended the local Episcopalian
church. She marketed mostly at the Country Supermart three
blocks away from her house. She subscribed to a circulating
library nearby. She liked concerts and grand opera. She was a
little stiff and formal with her neighbors, but she liked kids—
didn't mind their being noisy, or using her driveway for roller
skating and so on.

The principal of the school where she'd taught until three years
ago said Miss Winters had always been very well liked. Never
any trouble with other teachers, anything like that. She belonged
to a retired teachers' club, and usually attended its monthly
meetings. Very few people had ever come to see her, except her
niece and two or three women friends of her own age. Names
appended. None of them had seen her for some days before her
death.

"¡Parece mentira!" said Mendoza. He felt frustrated. Because, besides the fact that he wanted to know, there was another
consideration. If Fleming hadn't killed Miss Winters, somebody
else had. And anybody who got away with murder once was a
little readier to be provoked into it the second time. Better to
catch up with him right away.

But where to look?

He let it simmer in his mind all day, and no new ideas occurred
to him. At six o'clock he went home, fed Bast, shaved again and
changed into the new Italian silk, and took his current redhead
out to dinner. He was abstracted throughout the evening, and
Alison complained about it.

A wrong smell, somehow. He'd lay odds it hadn't been
Fleming. . . . On Monday morning, toward noon, for no reason
he drove out to Kenmore Avenue and slid the Facel-Vega into the
curb opposite the duplex. He got out of the car and stood there
smoking a reflective cigarette, looking at the quite ordinary frame

house on an ordinary middle-class street, and brooding over his problem.

About two cigarettes later a black-and-white squad car pulled up behind the Facel-Vega and a uniformed officer got out. "O.K., friend, what you doing here?"

Mendoza was surprised, but produced his credentials without rancor. The uniformed man was voluble, not to say panic-stricken, on apology. "Doesn't matter," said Mendoza. "But how come?"

"Well, Lieutenant, the neighbors—Mrs. Robertson, that is—saw a man come Saturday, go into the house—"

"Also me. Yes?"

"And was kind of curious, you know—and seeing you here again, looking at the house, she called in. And the desk sergeant was kind of curious too, because—well, it was Headquarters business, as soon as you found it was this nut, but you see, on account of the old lady coming in just the day before—"

"*¡Quiá!*" said Mendoza. "She came to the precinct house? What the hell for?"

"I couldn't say, Lieutenant—the sergeant just happened to mention—you know, when the story came out in the papers. Sure, we got the call first at Wilcox Street, but it was turned right over to Headquarters, you know—"

"So I'll see that sergeant, right now!"

The desk sergeant said, "One o' these suspicious old maids is all. You know"—he was looking a little surprised at Mendoza's interest—"we get these people coming in, saying so-and-so's a Communist, a bad woman, a Peeping Tom, and all like that. A lot of old maids . . . Think it had anything to do with her getting murdered? I did not. Why the hell? That was one all of a piece with those other old women, this joker you just picked up. Looked that way from the first, didn't it? Never crossed my mind—I mean, old maids are always coming in with funny stories."

"I know. What funny story did Miss Winters tell you?"

"I tell you how I figure it," said the sergeant. "Psychological, kind of. See, these old maids, they're just naturally jealous of young women getting married. And kind of leery of men—all kinds of men. She came out with some rigmarole, this young fellow her niece was engaged to—said he was a bad young man, she wanted us to look and see if he had a record, so she could convince her niece to break off with him. She didn't have a damned bit of evidence about it, and I told her, all polite, you know, we couldn't—"

"No evidence," said Mendoza, "but some experience of human nature, at sixty-eight. By all we have, an old lady with her head screwed on very damn tight. I wonder. Thanks very much, Sergeant."

A handle was all he'd needed.

Pues sí, the old lady saying. Marriage is a serious matter. . . .

And it might not seem an important enough business for a lieutenant to handle, but Mendoza wanted to wind it up himself. He called Miss Gaines at the bank and asked where Mr. Barr worked. He was a clerk in a big chain drugstore. Mendoza drove out there, found Mr. Barr, handed him a well-polished glossy photograph chosen at random from records, and asked if he recognized it.

"What the hell?" said Barr. "No, I don't. What's all this about?"

"Thank you very much," said Mendoza, drove back downtown and recommended that a car keep an eye on the drugstore until Prints had done its job.

Within forty minutes Prints informed him that Michael Barr indeed had a record. Three juvenile arrests (grand theft auto, and burglary: probation) and a one-to-three count for burglary and assault five years ago.

"Vaya, muy lindo," said Mendoza. "Very nice." It could be nicer. Because he liked the solid evidence and the warrant before he went after a suspect. But as far as it went, nice.

He sought the sergeants' room hopefully, was gratified to find Hackett there, and crooked a finger at him.

"What do you want now? I'm busy on that Davids thing—"

"I want you to come and help scare somebody. You look so much more formidable than me, my Arturo. The pro wrestler, all those muscles. I need your moral support."

"*No hay tal, chico,*" said Hackett, "no flattery. I've been in a couple of roughhouses with you and a nastier infighter I never hope to tangle with, appearances regardless."

"Come along. I'll explain on the way."

On the way, Hackett listened and said he'd been smoking opium. "Insubordinate," said Mendoza. "Wait and see."

They walked into the drugstore and found Barr behind his counter. He went a shade paler when he saw them.

Mendoza leaned on the counter and said conversationally, "It was unfortunate that Miss Gaines' aunt was such a sharp old lady, wasn't it, Barr?"

"I don't know what you mean," said Barr. He looked at Hackett's big bulk nervously.

"You know what I mean. She didn't like you, she tried to persuade Marjorie that you're a wrong one—didn't she? She even went so far as to ask the local precinct to look and see if you had a record—"

Barr went dirty white. "You—she never—"

"No, that you didn't know about. But you were mad—for some strange reason you're crazy about Marjorie, and you were afraid the old lady would get Marjorie to listen to her in the end—you knew you *had* a police record, and if Marjorie should find out, she might—"

"That's a d-damned lie—I never—"

"But you did," said Mendoza, smiling at him. "You went there that night to argue with her, try to persuade her that you're perfectly O.K. and suitable, and you loved Marjorie and meant to make her a good husband. What did she do—contemptuous but not afraid of you, letting you in, turning her back? I don't think you'd come prepared to kill her, but maybe you had. If you had, you had a nice little sap ready in your pocket. But if you hadn't, if you just saw red all at once, there's that handy little bronze reproduction of *The Thinker* on the hall table. You'd clean it afterward, of course—"

"I never—I dunno what you—" But he looked green; he hung on to the counter.

Mendoza looked at him meditatively. "All for this dowdy thin dreep Marjorie! I don't understand it. The homeliest female I've laid eyes on in six months—female is all you can say, nobody but a blind man would—"

And Barr went for him like a tiger, lunging over the counter. "God damn you, don't you talk like that about Marjorie! She's *mine*—she's *beautiful*—you Goddamned bastard, saying—" He put up quite a fight for such a little fellow, and a crowd gathered and a couple of glass cases got smashed before they collared him and got the bracelets on. But he went on talking, incoherent, passionate. "That Goddamned old maid, telling me I was no good—telling Marjorie—trying to get her to break off with me— I *had* to— Damn you! How the hell did you— That fellow you picked up, so O.K., what the hell? Everybody thinking he'd done that one too— Crazy— How the *hell* did you— I couldn't stand it, things she kept saying to Marjorie! She let me in, sure, she didn't figure I'd— But I *had* to! She might've turned Marjorie against me—"

"Straight evidence be damned," said Hackett. "Two hundred years ago you'd have burned at the stake for a sorcerer. Luis and his crystal ball."

"*Qué disparate,*" said Mendoza. "A second look at the evidence, that's all. Don't flatter me."

"That's a laugh. Nothing you like better, don't kid me. I'd hate to think it's because you're so much smarter than the rest of us that you're right so often. But once in a while I can't figure it any other way."

"Never mind, maybe you'll pass the lieutenants' exam next time," said Mendoza.

THE BRONZE CAT

~~~~~~ *I*t is not true that wealthy people are treated
with more leniency by the police—not by a
good police force, and the L.A.P.D. is a very crack force. But
unhappily, human nature being what it is, wealth is apt to get
more attention.

Which explains the fact that on receipt of the news that Mr.
George Cumberland had been found murdered, Mendoza went
out to the scene himself with Hackett and the usual crew of men.
The case had been handed on to Headquarters immediately. The
press would make a little stir about this one; Mr. Cumberland had
been one of the city's wealthiest residents, and had contributed a
lot of money to various civic projects. The philanthropist, in fact:
being unmarried with an older sister as his only relation.

They had lived together in an austere old two-story mansion,
far too large for them, in what had once been an exclusive district
above Sunset. It had not deteriorated, but these days it wasn't as
fashionable as it had been.

The squad-car men first summoned were still there. They led
the Headquarters men back along a dark hall to the study. Or tried
to; Miss Jocelyn Cumberland came pattering after, telling them
their job with fretful insistence.

"It was Martin Gregson, that is quite obvious! I knew that *at
once*! George said last night that he was simply furious at him—
Martin Gregson at George, I mean—because George got that

Arvidian away from him. The minute I came into the study and found him this morning, I saw it *all*! Gregson must have come last night to try to persuade George to sell it to him—very likely he was sorry *then* he hadn't kept on bidding—and they had a quarrel, and Gregson murdered him. A very odd sort of man I always thought him, Gregson I mean, and *not* well-bred. And they never could stand each other, you know, after that Whistler affair. I've never seen George angrier! To question his judgment! He was after all a recognized authority on art, being such a well known collector! If he said it was a Whistler, it was a Whistler—''

"Please, Miss Cumberland, we'll talk to you later on and listen to your suggestions. But now—''

She was a broad, stocky woman of middle height, never pretty, not well-preserved at perhaps sixty. She had a round flat-featured face, very pale blue eyes with sandy lashes, a quantity of sandy-gray hair in a careless bun. She wore an unbecoming flowered silk dress, no makeup, and her nails were black with grime.

"—And even if Gregson is *also* supposed to be an authority, to *question* George's judgment— George never could abide him after that. Of course it is a Whistler, it's hanging in the living room now—and he was quite pleased to have got the Arvidian away from Gregson, yesterday afternoon. George I mean. So you *see*. Besides, he left his hat.''

Mendoza exercised tact and patience and shut her off at last with promises to see her later. He escaped into the study where the crew was already busy. Dr. Bainbridge, kneeling over the body, said that all he could say now was that death was due to a skull fracture and had probably occurred between nine and twelve last night. The squad-car men said the old lady said she'd found him about nine-thirty when she came into the study; they always had breakfast together about then and he hadn't shown up, so she went to see if he was downstairs.

The study was crowded with furniture, solid and heavy, and many *objets d'art*. A dozen paintings large and small, figurines and vases standing about on several small tables. The body of

George Cumberland, a stocky bald man in the mid-fifties, lay facedown beside the desk, as if he'd been knocked out of his chair. Everything in the room was quite neat otherwise— furniture all in place, pictures straight; it didn't seem that there'd been a struggle. Beside the body lay a bronze statuette, a reproduction of the sacred cat of Egypt; it was only about nine inches high, but undoubtedly heavy enough to have been the weapon.

Mendoza looked about the room and said to Hackett, "*Caray,* I have the feeling that I've got into a British detective story. The classic fictional setup."

One of the squad-car men said apologetically, "Not to butt in, Lieutenant, but just looking around while we waited for you, well, it seems like the old lady might have something about this Gregson. See, what I can make out of what she says, this Cumberland collected valuable pictures. And he went to a private auction yesterday afternoon, and bought this picture by this Arvidian who seems like he's a famous artist. This other guy, Gregson, wanted it too, and they ran it up to twelve thousand bucks—so the old lady says—before Cumberland got it knocked down to him. Jesus, twelve grand for a picture! And not a picture *I'd* pay twelve cents for, but there's no accounting for tastes— that's it over there—"

It was a canvas perhaps eighteen by thirty, a study in monotones of an old mill, with black-and-white cattle grazing in a pasture below. At a desultory glance, Mendoza rather liked it; it was restful.

"—And she says Cumberland always sat up late. Her room's at the back, upstairs, and she didn't hear anything. They don't have a servant living in, just a couple of dailies. And it doesn't look like there'd been a fight—just a slanging match, maybe, and this Gregson loses his temper and grabs up this statue and lets Cumberland have it. And he did leave his hat. Maybe he was scared, seeing he'd really done for Cumberland, and just ran off."

Mendoza looked at the proffered hat. It was an ordinary gray

Homburg, very much like his own except that he preferred a
somewhat wider brim and patronized a more expensive hatter.
Inside the sweatband, in gold, was stamped the name of a Sunset
Boulevard firm, and the name of M. L. Gregson.

"Yes, I see," he said. "That bronze cat—any prints? Or can
you say yet?"

"No, clean as a whistle," said Scarne, "except for a little
blood and hair. It's what was used all right."

"This looks like an easy one," said Hackett. "That handy
French door out to the side yard. I can build it up. Gregson
coming a little late, maybe—seeing the light in here, coming
round to tap on the window. If they knew each other fairly well."

"We'll find out. But I have an idea most of these art dealers
and collectors would know each other—on the financial level,
anyway. Alison's told me this and that." His current redhead was
a lesser-known painter herself. "And also, you know, that
kind—sometimes they get very wrought-up over these things."
He strolled over to look at the picture. "Quite a nice picture. The
cows really look like cows. I don't know that I'd pay twelve
thousand bucks for it myself, but Mr. Cumberland obviously felt
differently. So, I'll leave you to supervise the routine and go to
see Mr. Gregson."

Mr. Martin Gregson was a dealer in *objets d'art,* chiefly
pictures. He had a very classy-looking gallery out on La Cienega,
and he exuded quiet prosperity personally. Mendoza, running the
expert eye over his Lovat mixture, accurately placed his tailor (a
craftsman rather more radical than the one Mendoza patronized)
and disapproved his Paris-import silk tie as a trifle less than
discreet; but both had cost money. Mr. Gregson himself, a big
paunchy dark man, blue-chinned, in the fifties, did not look well.
His eyes were bloodshot, his pudgy hands trembled, and he was
in the act of swallowing aspirin when an underling showed
Mendoza into his private office.

"I believe," said Mendoza, "that this is your hat, Mr.
Gregson."

Gregson agreed, happy to see it again. "Very obliging of you, I must say—thanks very much. But where did you—"

So Mendoza told him where, and also that he couldn't have it back; it was evidence. Gregson turned paler, called upon God, and said *what* a hell of an awful thing. "Cumberland! A burglar, was it? My God! He'll be a loss, you know. Fine chap—I knew him well—"

"So I understand," said Mendoza. "Although you had had differences of opinion with him. Yes. We have been hearing something about his getting the best of you yesterday at an auction. A painting by one Arvidian."

"Oh—yes," said Gregson, sounding nervous. "Yes. At old Wantage's gallery. That's so. I wanted that canvas, I—er—had a prospective buyer. . . . Cumberland was willing to go a little higher. . . . Well, yes, I may have been annoyed at missing it, just at the moment, but—really, Lieutenant—I don't see that this has any bearing—"

"Would you mind telling me, Mr. Gregson, where you were last night between nine and midnight?" asked Mendoza gently.

Gregson turned deep puce and burst out, "What the *hell*? D'you think *I*— Why, for God's sake? This is ridiculous! I hadn't any reason— That painting? D-don't be absurd, Lieutenant! Just another b-business deal! Why should I—"

"How did you spend your evening, Mr. Gregson?"

"I—dear God!" said Gregson. He mopped his brow with the silk handkerchief from his breast pocket. "I'll have to tell you, I suppose. I—er—tied one on, Lieutenant. You don't catch me at an auspicious moment—I've got the hell of a hangover. We started out at the Copa, but—"

"We?"

"An—er—party. Mr. Hilary Wantage, and his nephew Bill, and their wives . . . I'm not married, no, sir, it was just the five of us. I think it was about ten-fifteen we went on to the Brass Hat, but—really I couldn't say—"

"You stayed there?"

"Lieutenant," said Gregson simply, "I couldn't say one damn

thing after about eleven. The rest of them went home—young Mrs. Wantage hasn't been feeling well lately. I remember them leaving, but that's all. Liquor takes me that way—I pull a blank. I look and talk O.K., but I don't *remember* next day. Know what I mean?''

Well, it affected some people that way, of course. And an odd sensation it must be. That was one of the few experiences Mendoza had missed, being drunk. Early in his tender youth he had discovered that about three drinks turned him into a belligerent warrior hunting a series of somebodies—preferably somebodies a lot bigger—to fight, and he had consequently curtailed his drinking. His handsome classic profile was too valuable to him in the pursuit of certain other interests, to risk. "I see," he said. "May I have the addresses of these people, please. . . . And how do you explain the fact that your hat was found in proximity with Mr. Cumberland's body?''

"Oh, I can tell you about that," said Gregson with an uneasy, hopeful smile. "My God, it does seem funny, I know, but coincidence— You see, we got our hats mixed up at Wantage's yesterday afternoon. There's no check booth or anything like that—just the foyer with a couple of hatracks—you know. I always wear a Homburg, and so did Cumberland mostly. Either black or gray. And I guess he picked up mine—he left before I did—and so I took his. It wasn't until I got home I found it out. His initials were in it—I always have my name put in mine. So then I saw what we'd done. You see, we're much the same build, wear the same size.''

"Yes. You found you had Mr. Cumberland's hat when?''

"Oh, it'd be about six o'clock.''

"And what did you do with it? You didn't think of returning it at once and claiming your own?''

Gregson looked even more uneasy, produced an ingratiating hollow laugh, and said, "Oh, well—it was latish—and I was going out with the Wantages—and Cumberland would be feeling a bit annoyed, maybe, because I'd shot up the price on that Arvidian—of course by next day he'd have calmed down—just an ordinary business deal, you know! But I—well, the long and short of it is, I thought what the hell, I'll take it back tomorrow, and—as a matter of fact—I wore it when I went out. I—"

"Indeed. And where is it now? May I have it, please?"

Gregson passed his handkerchief across his mouth. "I—well, it's the hell of a confession to make, Lieutenant—but as a matter of fact I—I haven't got it. You know how I told you—the liquor—I must've left it somewhere, just forgotten it—"

"Why haven't you asked for a warrant?" asked Hackett. "I know the motive sounds weak, but the law doesn't require an established motive."

"No. I'd like," said Mendoza, "to pry a little deeper. It looks too easy, somehow, that's all. Maybe I'm unconsciously influenced by the fact that the setup looks like one of those 1930-vintage British detective stories."

"*No hay motivo para preocuparse tanto,*" said Hackett severely. "You're just exercising your tortuous mind. What it looks like is usually what it is."

"You're so right. But you will oblige me to find out whether Cumberland did indeed habitually wear a Homburg. I also want to see some other people who were present at the auction. And I trust you are looking for any traces of Mr. Gregson in the bars adjacent to the Brass Hat."

"Yes, of course we have to think about evidence the D.A. can use. I've got a little already."

No fewer than a dozen witnesses, present at the private auction, testified that Gregson had seemed extremely angry to be driven beyond his price on the Arvidian canvas. No one else there had been much interested in it; after the bidding had passed a thousand, those two had been the only bidders.

Three of the witnesses, all dealers, confirmed that Cumberland and Gregson, never close friends, had on several occasions differed bitterly on the judgment of certain paintings.

Mr. Hilary Wantage, his wife, his nephew, and his nephew's wife, deposed that they had left Mr. Gregson at the Brass Hat at about eleven o'clock. They said he had been high, but not dangerously so. They had gone virtuously home to their respective addresses. Nobody but Mr. William Wantage had noticed what sort of hat Gregson was wearing; he said it was a gray Homburg.

It looked very damned open-and-shut.

And for some unknown reason Mendoza continued to feel uneasy about it.

Hackett said, "For God's sake, what more do you want? Get a warrant."

"No me gusta," said Mendoza. "A weekend won't matter. And I think we'll have a look around to locate Mr. Cumberland's hat, if possible. Was there really an exchange? Did Cumberland possess a similar Homburg? If so, is it where it should be at home? Just because Gregson's story sounds absurd, we can't let it go without looking into it."

That night he took his redhead to dinner. And mentioned the case, knowing she'd be interested.

"Arvidian?" said Alison. "That's an awful lot, but some day he may be worth it. One of the few contemporary painters with real genius. Which one was it? *The Old Mill*—I'd love to see it, I've read descriptions, of course, but I haven't seen much of his original stuff. He's good, you know. Unfashionable at the moment, but good."

"I could see it. He made cows look like cows."

"¡Dios me libre!" Alison laughed. "I know, most unfashionable. I do too, not to claim I'm in his class, so I don't sell any more than he did at first. Of course his suicide aroused some interest. . . . Did I tell you I sold a canvas to Vesperian the other day? Very flattering."

"Well, I'm no critic, *chica,* but personally I liked that thing you did of a suburban street better than this old mill. Nicer colors."

"¡Dios se lo pague!" said Alison, moved. "Sheer ignorance, but nice to hear. I'm one of Arvidian's fans. I'd love to see that canvas."

"Take the afternoon off and come down to Headquarters,"
invited Mendoza absently. "We've impounded it as evidence.
You can examine it to your heart's content."

"Do you really mean it? I'll take you up on that."

A patient check on all the bars around the Brass Hat produced
very little evidence. Gregson had left the Brass Hat immediately
after the rest of his party, and gone into the Tric-Trac a block
down. He had been high, talkative and genial, but still walking
and talking O.K. The barman didn't think he'd stayed more than
ten or fifteen minutes. He had had two double brandies in quick
succession, and then left.

Witnesses present at the auction couldn't say at all what kind
of hat either Cumberland or Gregson had been wearing, but
agreed that both did frequently wear ordinary Homburgs.

Miss Cumberland could not, on the other hand, recall that her
brother had ever had a similar hat. In George Cumberland's
wardrobe at present were a black Homburg, a black derby, a silk
opera hat, and two Panamas. No gray Homburg.

And of course that was no help. If liquor did take Gregson that
way, he might easily have rushed out to Cumberland's house—
brooding over being worsted at the auction—and picked a fight
with him, and snatched up that bronze cat and killed him. And
fled. And subsequently pulled a blank on it. Or had he? So he'd
keep on saying, anyway. None of his prints in the room; he
hadn't been so high that he'd forgotten to wipe off the bronze.
But he was obviously scared green; he had almost fainted when
they asked for his prints. An innocent man might be disturbed
and indignant, but he wouldn't be as terrified as all that, surely?

At that point in Mendoza's meditations, Alison came in. It
was Saturday, and she was free of her charm school. "You *did*
say—"

"Certainly," and Mendoza issued orders. "Sit down, *querida*. Happy to oblige."

"Heavens," said Alison as Sergeant Lake brought in the
canvas, "I hope you're taking reasonable care of it."

"We are indeed. Hypnotized by the figure of twelve thousand

bucks." Mendoza propped it up on his desk and Alison came over to look.

She looked for a long moment of silence, and then she said, "Luis, this isn't an Arvidian. I don't *think*. I knew him very slightly, you know—and being a fan of his, I've seen all his stuff I can. This isn't like him, a rural subject and the way it's handled too—" She gestured. "Oh, it's a bad copy of his style, not Arvidian himself. Of course I'm no expert, but— Take it to Vesperian, or Wantage, and have it vetted."

"It's a forgery? I'll be damned! But—" Mendoza stared at it, trying to fit this into the plot. "Yes, I'd better have an expert opinion. Who did you say?"

"Vesperian. Out on Santa Monica. He'll know for sure."

So Mendoza asked Vesperian. Who looked at the canvas and made tut-tutting noises. "Of course *Wantage*—" he said, and shrugged. "But all the same . . . Well, of course one cannot consider that Wantage is always—er—scrupulous. . . . An original? Dear me, no. No. I knew Arvidian. This is none of his work. A copy of his style, yes, that I grant. But not an Arvidian. I wonder, now, who Wantage got to paint it for him? Young Fairbrother, possibly? Or do I wrong him?"

"Wait a minute, let me get this clear, Mr. Vesperian. In your opinion, Mr. Wantage was aware that this is not a genuine Arvidian, when he sold it as such?"

Vesperian smiled, stroking his fine white sidewhiskers. "No one will ever prove it, Lieutenant, because he will say no, and even eminent art critics make mistakes. But there is small chance that he did. He was Arvidian's agent, you know, up to his death last year. If you ask my opinion, it is quite possible that Wantage privately commissioned this forgery, and with George Cumberland in mind as—what is the term?—the sucker."

"Why do you say that?"

"Dear sir, Mr. Cumberland—" Vesperian threw out his hands in expressive gesture. "A very fine, pleasant, charitable gentleman, but *no* eye whatsoever! Every dealer who had any transactions with him soon knew that. And he believed himself an expert judge. It was a little comic, you understand. He went to sales and bought old obscure canvases, swearing this was an undiscovered Dufy and that a lost Renoir. Well! Of course he was laughed at, and that only made him more obstinate."

"Can you tell me anything," said Mendoza, "about a quarrel he had with Mr. Martin Gregson over a painting of Whistler's?"

"My dear Lieutenant! It was *not* a Whistler. And this quarrel, if you choose to call it so, was not with Mr. Gregson only but every dealer in the city. He offered it to me also—he did not collect Whistler. He had picked it up at some little estate sale, a thing rather in Whistler's manner but no more a genuine Whistler than— Well!" Vesperian hunched his shoulders in a massive shrug. "He went to Gregson first, expecting that Gregson would buy it at a nice round figure. Even a millionaire is not averse to making a little profit, why not? And after Gregson laughed at him, he came to the rest of us one by one. I assure you he was quite infuriated at myself also, and at Mr. Wantage, and others. It is quite true that he seemed to have taken particular exception to something Mr. Gregson said—I believe he used to go to that gallery fairly often to look and buy, but not recently, after that affair."

"I see," said Mendoza. And suddenly light dawned on him, and he began to laugh. "I do indeed. Thank you very much . . ." He stowed the spurious Arvidian in the back of the Facel-Vega, debated on what tactics to use, decided on a straightforward attack, and drove out to Gregson's gallery.

Gregson turned pale and started to shake when he saw him come in. "Lieutenant, my God, you've got to believe me—I didn't—I hadn't any *reason*—" Then he saw what Mendoza was carrying, and turned a delicate green and fell silent.

"Nobody's accused you of anything—yet," said Mendoza. "Let's go into your office, shall we?" There, he laid the canvas on the desk and surveying Gregson laughed. "You'll never make a successful criminal, Mr. Gregson—you have too nervous a conscience. Now I know why it's been troubling you, and you've been so upset at our attentions. Not because you committed a murder, but because you conspired with Mr. Wantage to put over a little fraud on Cumberland. That's it, isn't it? I can see that Cumberland must have been heaven's own gift to dealers, and you'd been missing his patronage lately, I think. Maybe so had Wantage. However it came about, Wantage acquired this fake Arvidian—somehow, we needn't go into that—and wanted to put it over on Cumberland for a nice profit. But he couldn't hope that any other dealers or private bidders would go very high on it, so he roped you in to shove up the bidding. Which made Cumberland all the more determined to get it. I don't think either of you liked or disliked Cumberland particularly—it was just a business deal, as you said.''

"Oh, hell,'' said Gregson unhappily. "It was a dirty little trick, I know—how in hell did you find out about it? Wantage— well, my God, you can understand it was always a temptation, with Cumberland! Yes—I've got to say that's how it was—and dear God, if it has to come out in the papers—ruin both of us! But there was Cumberland, trotting around writing five-figure checks without thinking twice—a gold mine—funny, the old lady, his sister, is miserly as hell, always yapping at him about wasting money, but Cumberland would get rid of ten thousand in one afternoon and never turn a hair. And—''

"Oh, is that so?'' said Mendoza. *"¡Qué interesante!* Well, Mr. Gregson, I don't think this business is relevant to the murder at all, and probably it needn't come out—''

"I hope to God!'' Gregson mopped his brow, beginning to regain some color.

"Its only relevance is that you were at the same place as Cumberland that day, and inadvertently exchanged hats. . . . Yes, I do think I see daylight in this affair. I wish you could say where you went that night after you left the Tric-Trac.''

"Lieutenant, I don't even remember the Tric-Trac.''

"Any favorite places you might have gone? Not in that neighborhood, because we've asked in all the bars within six blocks.''

"My God, it might've been anywhere, I don't know. If you could find the cab driver—''

"Yes, we're looking for him. Nothing on that yet."

Gregson mopped his brow again. "I used to hit a place called Farano's, out on Santa Monica, a lot. But I don't know. My God, it's a sort of relief to get this off my chest, but what a hell of a thing—getting myself suspected of murder—"

"Well, you're not now," said Mendoza.

"And what makes you say Gregson is innocent just because he pulled a fast deal on Cumberland? That doesn't say anything about the murder," said Hackett.

"I think it says quite a lot. We know now that Gregson had no reason to feel resentment against Cumberland. That was just an act, to shove up the bidding, help out Wantage. More. Gregson had every reason to want Cumberland alive, not dead—the nice pigeon, as he said, trotting around writing five-figure checks. True, none of Cumberland's money had come his way lately, but I'll lay you long odds he'd have worked up a little deal, maybe with Wantage's reciprocal help, to lure the bird into the net again. Yes. Well, the pigeon being plucked, they went out celebrating that night. And then what?" Mendoza leaned back in his desk chair and swiveled around to stare out the window. "Do we say that about the same time Gregson pulls a blank—unfortunate the rest of them went home so early—a burglar is getting into the Cumberland house, being discovered by Cumberland and snatching up the bronze cat to bang him over the head and get away?"

"*Pues no*. It was too early for a burglar, and besides, anybody intending to break in would have seen the light still on in the study—the curtains weren't pulled, anybody would have seen Cumberland there, up and awake."

"*De veras*. Not a burglar. And that leaves us just one answer, doesn't it? *Por lo general,* women don't have logical minds, of course—but didn't she stop to think that Gregson might have an alibi, and certainly still had her brother's hat? Only unfortunately for him, he didn't. And of course if Gregson did have an alibi, she could always say, a burglar."

"But why, for God's sake?"

"We may get to hear. But I heard a suggestive little thing this afternoon. It may be she couldn't bear watching George throw away money any longer. . . . She heard about the exchange of hats when he came home, of course. We may never know whether the murder was premeditated or not—if she thought of it then or if it was a later impulse. I think they were arguing, and there may even have been a little struggle. They were alone in the house, of course—nobody to hear. She got Gregson's hat from the closet and left it there, hoping to incriminate him. I wonder why she didn't call the police then, say she'd heard a struggle and run down to find George? Instead, maybe thinking to make it all look even more natural, she goes up to bed and waits for morning to discover the body. *Caray,* I wonder if she slept?"

"But there's no evidence, Luis."

"I'm afraid there won't be, no. But we'll have a damn good hunt anyway."

Before the search warrant came through, Dwyer came in with a statement from the bartender at Farano's, and Cumberland's hat. Gregson had been at Farano's from about eleven-thirty to one A.M., and had forgotten his hat when he left. The bartender hadn't known his name, so all he could do was keep the hat in case he came back for it.

Which cleared that up. Gregson wouldn't have had time between leaving the Tric-Trac to go and kill Cumberland and still be in Farano's at eleven-thirty.

But Hackett was having doubts. "Look, this is wild. There are a lot of people who knew Cumberland and might have had a reason to kill him besides Gregson and Miss Cumberland. Why should you say—"

"Ah, but it's a very long chance that anybody else knew about Gregson's hat being there. Cumberland would have put it tidily away in the closet, you know, not left it out where it was found. Whoever put that hat there, to incriminate Gregson, knew about it. And it was a woman's trick. . . . I wonder if we'll get her."

They went out and confronted Miss Jocelyn Cumberland. She heard Mendoza through stony-faced, and denied everything; she gave no signs of breaking now or later. A very tough old lady. And no concrete evidence against her at all.

Until they found a green silk dress with quite a lot of blood on it, hanging in her closet. The blood was type A, the same as Cumberland's, and Miss Cumberland's blood was type O, the lab reported. So she could hardly claim it as her own blood. And she hadn't been wearing that dress the morning the body was officially found, so she hadn't got the blood on it then—indeed, couldn't have, for the blood had then been dry for some hours.

They brought her in and charged her, and showed her the dress. She eyed it impassively and said, "I daresay I should have explained before—it was very foolish of me, perhaps, but women are sometimes foolish—I did find George that night—yes—I'm not sure of the time, but—I was still dressed, I came downstairs for a book—I found him, and that's when I got the blood—I was quite terrified—"

"So why didn't you call the police then, Miss Cumberland?"

Her mouth moved uneasily. "I—why, I was so frightened—I thought the criminal might be still *lurking*—I ran upstairs, and there's no phone there—"

"That's not very plausible," said Mendoza. . . . When she'd been taken away, he said to Hackett, "I wonder if she'll get away with it. She would have got away with it entirely—no legal evidence at all—if she hadn't been a miser. She couldn't bear to throw anything away. Any sensible woman would have got rid of that dress at once, anticipating police in the house and possibly a search. But she was too miserly. . . . Me, I'm all for thrift," said Mendoza, fingering his twelve-dollar foulard tie, "but like anything else it can be carried too far."

NOVELTIES

*T*hat once renowned man-about-town Lieutenant Luis Mendoza was getting a little tired of sly jokes about his newly married state from his colleagues. Consequently he was pleased when, meeting his senior sergeant Art Hackett at lunch, for the first time that day, he found Hackett looking gloomy and aggrieved. Was it possible, he wondered hopefully, that Art had at last had a fight with his Angel and could be baited a little also? He slid into the booth opposite Hackett and made innocent enquiry.

"What?" said Hackett. "Oh, Angel's fine, sure." Mendoza sighed. It was too much to have hoped for, of course; unlike himself and his redheaded Alison, Art and his Angel were a nice quiet domestic couple. "No, it's this damned Schwartz thing."

Mendoza cast his mind over the current homicides and said, "Old woman died alone in her apartment—run-down old place on Flower. Just routine, wasn't it? I thought Palliser was filling in all the forms. What about it?"

"For once," said Hackett, "I'll lay a bet with you, Luis. It was murder. But nobody's ever going to prove it, and I can't see how it was done."

"*¿Qué tal?* I just glanced at the report—what's all this? Old woman lived alone, died of a heart attack. It only came through Homicide because it was a sudden death and she hadn't had a regular doctor."

"Yes," said Hackett. "I know. But you know Palliser—the eager beaver, and he's a good boy. He looked at it twice and asked me what I thought. Sure, so she lived alone. Greta Schwartz, seventy-eight, an old hellion by all accounts. Widowed about fifteen years. Tight as the proverbial bark on a tree. She was worth in the neighborhood of a hundred thousand—securities mostly, a little real estate—but she lived close to the bone, in that—well, call it almost a tenement. She wasn't neighborly. Hardly ever let any of the other tenants in—suspicious, you know, if they tried to be friendly. She was scared to death of burglars—had extra locks on all the doors. A regular old maid, lived by strict routine, you know the kind. Supper at five o'clock and if something delayed it five minutes, she'd be in a tizzy—out to market at two-seventeen, and if she found her clock was slow and it was two-twenty, upset the rest of the day. She—"

"All right, I see her. Who wanted her dead and how did he, she, or it induce a heart attack? Was there an autopsy?"

"Yes, and damn it, it *was* a heart attack. Her heart was bad—she'd been told so. We found a doctor who saw her about two years ago. Said any sudden shock might put her out. She hadn't been to him since, wouldn't take the stuff he prescribed—too expensive. As for who had the motive, there's only one answer on that. Her nephew—one Rudolf Klopfer. Only relative, and he comes in for everything. And the doctor had told him her condition, as her only relative. He's a salesman for a wholesale outfit, and I don't like him. Neither does Palliser."

"Which does not say he's committed murder," said Mendoza.

"Well, damn it, he did," said Hackett. "Go on and laugh—can't anybody but you have a hunch? I swear I knew it as soon as I looked at him." He regarded his Dieters' Special Plate unhappily; to the detriment of his last physical, Art's Angel was a dedicated cook. "I don't see how, but he did. The way he looked, the way he talked— You know how you sense these things?"

Mendoza did. Probably a lot of it was just experience—sometimes specialized knowledge. But there was something else too—just a feeling. "Nothing to say so to the D.A.? So he came up behind her and yelled boo, or slammed a door, and she had the attack?"

"No," said Hackett, "that's just the hell of it. And one of the reasons— Well, I don't know, Luis. I tell you, if it had been like that, if he'd been there and yelled for an ambulance, poor Auntie's had an attack, I might have believed it. But—the autopsy says she died between nine and midnight on Wednesday, and Rudolf was way out in Long Beach playing pinochle with three respectable friends, from eight until one A.M. And I do mean respectable—and not such close friends that they'd set up an alibi for him."

"Awkward," said Mendoza. "Offhand, I don't think much of your hunch. Any other interesting facts?"

"Greta's one weekly outing, usually, was to church. Lutheran. She had a couple of fairly close friends who also went there. A Mrs. Prince, one of 'em, says that Greta disapproved of her nephew's social life and had been talking about changing her will and leaving everything to the church."

"She thought pinochle was sinful maybe?"

"I gather she'd found out he has a girlfriend who's been divorced. One Ruth Yorke, dumb blonde."

"*¡Qué atrocidad!* But because he had a motive doesn't say— You're really serious on this?"

"He killed her," said Hackett stubbornly. "And it's a waste of time talking about it, because nobody could ever prove how, let alone that it *was* murder. She might have died any minute, naturally. But he wasn't taking any chances that she'd change her will first. I mean, it happened just too convenient for him."

Mendoza was interested; it was a funny little business to use imagination on. If Hacket was right—and he not only had a lot of experience as a Homicide cop, but he'd majored in psychology up at Berkeley, of course. "Any more details?"

Hackett spread his hands. "Nothing to point anywhere. She was found by a Mrs. Breck, another friend from church, coming to call on her next morning. When Greta didn't answer, Mrs.

Breck surmised something was wrong—everybody knew she had heart trouble—and called the nearest traffic cop. They had to break down the door, those extra locks. And then they notified Rudolf as the nearest relative. And Palliser looked at him and didn't like him, and neither did I. I swear he made it happen. But don't ask me how.''

"Mmh,'' said Mendoza. "A sudden shock of some kind— Did she have a phone?''

"You think that wasn't my first thought? No, and these pals of his say he didn't phone anybody all evening anyway. Neither did Ruth Yorke—I asked there too. She was at a girlfriend's apartment that evening, at a party. Everybody vouched for her.''

Mendoza finished his coffee. "It looks to me, Arturo, as if your little hunch is like just a few of mine—a dud. *Nada de eso.*''

"I swear to God Rudolf managed it somehow,'' said Hackett. "But it looks as if he'll get away with it all right.''

Mendoza was just sufficiently curious (and hopeful of finding something to point a lead and prove his superiority) that he made the fifteen-block journey to the late Mrs. Schwartz's apartment. It had been looked over, of course—no faint indication of anything but natural death, except Hackett's absurd hunch. It would now be up for rent again, the nephew having had Mrs. Schwartz's few belongings removed. The superintendent let Mendoza go up alone.

It was just a bare, shabby three-room apartment. Rather unusually for its vintage, it had two doors; there was a back door off a tiny service porch, leading down rickety wooden steps to the squalid rear yard and a line of refuse cans. The extra locks had been left on the doors: all Yale locks.

Any papers she had had were gone, of course. Nothing to be seen in three bare rooms empty of furniture.

But the fact that the stolid, shrewd Hackett had had a hunch at all was interesting.

Mendoza went back downstairs and called his office on the

phone he'd had installed in the new Ferrari. "Where does Rudolf Klopfer work?" he asked Hackett.

"Kleinfeldt Manufacturing Novelty Company," said Hackett. "But it's just one of those things—never get any evidence. And something's broken on this Carey business, that chef's decided to tell all—you'd better come and listen to him."

"*¡Segura mente que sí!* I will indeed," said Mendoza, losing interest in the late Mrs. Schwartz.

It was six-forty when he got home, to find Alison full-length on the couch lazily studying a catalogue. Three of the cats huddled together alongside her, and El Señor was sitting on the record cabinet brooding darkly on one of his deep plots, by his expression.

"*¿Qué es esto?*" demanded Mendoza, dispersing cats. "Didn't anybody ever tell you that when a sober, hardworking husband comes home after the day's labor, a respectable wife should be in the kitchen preparing a—"

"I thought the Cuernavaca," said Alison, kissing him back abstractedly. "I made reservations for eight o'clock. You'll have to shave again. I've been Christmas shopping. . . . Yes, very beforehand, I know. And when I came in, all these awful catalogues—"

"God deliver me from a managing wife!"

"Yes, *amante*," said Alison. "I don't, do I? I should think the post office would put a stop to it, you know, it must quadruple the work—and where on earth they get the names I can't imagine."

"What are you talking about?"

"These catalogues," said Alison, sitting up. "Your moustache needs trimming, *querido*."

"Leave my moustache alone. Go and put on that amber thing and I may condescend to take you to the Cuernavaca."

"*¡Vaya con el mozo!*" said Alison, handed him the brochure she'd been looking at and started for the bedroom. Mendoza wandered after her, looking at the thing.

He found himself looking at a photograph of two trousered legs, one ending normally in a decent oxford and the other in an outsize naked human foot. The small print underneath said: "A million laffs! Fool your friends! Realistic plastic feet fit over shoes! Only $1.98!"

"What the hell is this?"

"What? Oh—I told you. Of course, some catalogues have quite nice things," said Alison, diving back into the closet again after brief emergence. "But some like that—you can't imagine what awful little nastinesses— Talk about elementary humor. Fascinating in a way, to see *how* awful they can get, you know. Like exploding cigars, only worse."

"I believe you," said Mendoza. He sat down on the bed, stripping off his tie with one hand. The next thing to meet his eye was an illustration of "Fun-filled toilet paper—a laff a second!" And at the bottom of the page, there was a photograph of a grinning gentleman with about seven feet of snake wound around him: "Realistic plastic Python turns you into a snake charmer! Flexible, inflatable, real-life colors! Scare your lady friends? Wow the party—only $2.98!"

"*Por vida,* people really buy these things?"

"They must, I suppose," said Alison. "People who like practical jokes, you know." She vanished into the bathroom; and Mendoza, turning a page, sat very still and stared at it.

And after a moment he said very softly to himself, "*¡Quiá!* I wonder. I do wonder. It's a little idea, anyway. But how in hell to prove it?"

It was Saturday night, and anything remotely incriminating in Rudolf Klopfer's possession would have been got rid of since Wednesday.

But he haled Hackett into his office next morning and showed him the catalogue, open to the right page. "Suppose, *hermano,* you're an old lady with a weak heart, and you come into the kitchen, or your bedroom, say, and see that? You're an old lady scared to death of burglars, remember."

Hackett looked and swore. "I'll be damned! But—" What he was looking at was four fingers of a hand bent around the edge of a door; two smaller cuts showed it dangling from a lavatory basin, from the door of a refrigerator. The print below said happily, "Shock your friends! Realistic colored plastic, easily attached anywhere with tape! A million laffs, only $1.98!"

"Say on a half-open closet door, or the door to the service porch," said Mendoza pleasedly. "I notice these—things—are called Novelties. I wonder if Mr. Klopfer's firm manufactures them?"

"My God," said Hackett, "it'd have been a way to do it all right. A gamble, but— But look, it'd have still been there when they found her, they wouldn't have missed—"

"Not necessarily. Where was she found?"

Hackett was still staring at the photograph. "My God, what minus IQs go for this kind of—! Where? In the kitchen. She always had a glass of hot milk before she went to bed, Mrs. Breck said, and—"

"Yes. But she hadn't started to get it before she had her heart attack, had she? No. Came in, switched on the light, saw this— or something like it, that snake would have done the trick too, I'd guess, coiled realistically on the floor—and *terminar*."

"But when—and how—"

"Nothing very difficult about it. A rudimentary sort of plot, which—if Mr. Klopfer has the kind of mind to sell these, mmh, novelties successfully—we might have expected. She was an unsociable sort, I don't suppose the other tenants kept tabs on her callers. He'd know her habits, which were—you said—rigid. He'd come to see her just after she'd finished supper and got the kitchen cleaned up, so she wouldn't be going in there again until she went to get her hot milk. He'd make an excuse, wanting a drink of water, and set his little booby trap, switching off the light behind him. Some time previously, he'd have got an impression of the back-door key—the one to the Yale lock, the regular one wouldn't be any trouble to pick—and had a copy made. You said up to recently she'd been on good terms with him. Yes. Well, so off he goes for a happy evening of pinochle, and when he knows his alibi's well established—if the gamble's come off O.K.—he comes back, up that back stair, quietly lets himself into the kitchen, sees the gamble *has* come off, and removes the evidence. . . . It's a way it could have been done, *de veras*. I wonder if he did."

"But—"

"I think I'll go and verify your hunch, Arturo. After all, I'm the expert there."

"But we'll never prove it—"

"Wait and see," said Mendoza.

He found the Kleinfeldt Novelty Company—which did indeed manufacture, among other things, the practical-joke novelties— and found Mr. Klopfer in his cubbyhole of an office. He eyed Mr. Klopfer with interest, while he outlined his theory of Mrs. Schwartz's fatal heart attack.

"In your place, I think I'd have chosen the snake," he said, smiling. "But you knew her better—possibly the burglar's hand round the door would have been more effective. Or was there some other diabolical little prop? At any rate—"

Hackett was quite right. Klopfer was a paunchy bald fellow in the fifties, and he was sweating and panting incoherent protests. " 'S a lie—I never thought of—perfeckly natural death, poor ole lady—what the hell, a damn cop comin' try to lay it on me— You can't prove— Goddamn dumb cop—"

"Well, as to proof, at the moment, no," said Mendoza. "But we'll be looking around, Mr. Klopfer. We'll be looking." He bent a benign smile on Klopfer.

"You," said Alison, "are looking disgustedly pleased with yourself." She regarded him with misgiving. "And the way you keep chortling over that idiotic catalogue— Are you going to disillusion me and turn out to have that kind of sense of humor?"

"*¡No hay tal, gatita!* I've been visited by inspiration," said Mendoza. "A very melodramatic inspiration . . . It must be marriage, I've never been tempted to anything so unorthodox before. But it might just work, you know—he's in a very nervous state, and he's got some old-fashioned ideas about cops. . . ."

□ □ □

"Give him a nice plausible-sounding name," he said to Hackett next morning. "Like, say, Mr. Philip J. Paulson. Living in the Flower Street neighborhood. Knowing Greta Schwartz casually. Coming home late that night, about one-fifteen, and seeing a light-blue Ford sedan just like Mr. Klopfer's parked outside there. Leave the details vague. And a man looking like Mr. Klopfer heading for the rear of that building. You know the sort of thing—just so he gets the idea. Hint at blackmail."

"Well, but—" As Mendoza went on talking, Hackett began to grin.

"—And leave the rest to your uncle Luis. I hope." When Hackett had left, Mendoza called Sergeant Palliser in: his newest sergeant and a promising young man. "I have scruples about these things," he explained. "Art's one of my best friends, I could hardly murder him with much enthusiasm. Besides, there ought to be two of us there. Do you mind being a murderer in a good cause, John? It'll look more artistic in the back, and he can't do that himself."

Palliser laughed and said he'd try to reconcile himself.

Mr. Rudolf Klopfer plodded up the stairs to his shabby apartment, getting out his keys and telling himself for the hundredth time that he hadn't a thing to worry about, they could never prove anything on him. This crazy story that bastard Paulson tried to put over— What the hell if he did tell the cops? No proof—there'd never be any proof—Paulson wasn't going to get anything out of him, anyway.

But how the hell had that slick cop come to suspect?

He opened the door, stepped in, and pawed for the light switch. Light came, showing him the familiar, untidy, dusty living room—and the body of a big sandy man sprawled prone on the floor in the middle of the room. A black-handled knife thrust up from the sports-jacketed back, surrounded by a red welter of gore. That Paulson guy—

Mr. Klopfer let out an involuntary screech and stepped smartly backward, into the grip of a tall dark young man who'd followed him in, and who now growled, "Caught in the act, by God! See, Lieutenant?"

"Very convenient," said Mendoza, coming around Palliser to confront Klopfer. "Disposing of the witness who could identify him. This is Mr. Paulson, isn't it, Sergeant?"

"Sure is," said Palliser.

"Very dead," said Mendoza. "How did you entice Mr. Paulson here, Mr. Klopfer?"

Klopfer found his voice. "I never— It's a frame! Damn cops trying to frame— Goddamn lie, he or nobody couldn't have seen me then, it was three A.M., not one-fif— *Oh, my God!*"

"Was it indeed?" said Mendoza, pleased. "You might as well finish the sentence now— When you came back to remove the evidence. Go on, please."

But Mr. Klopfer slumped to the floor in a dead faint as the corpse stood up.

"So I guessed right," said Mendoza, "it was the burglar's hand. Damn realistic indeed," and he bent the painted plastic hand back and forth thoughtfully. "Of course he's not very big-time—easy to scare, but it's always gratifying to get a full confession like this. And what you might call—"

"Poetic justice," said Hackett. "Sure." He looked at the knife hilt in its red plastic bed of blood ("Startle your friends! Easily attached with adhesive— Realistic! Only $1.59!") and laughed. "We'd never have proved anything on him, of course. It was funny how I just *felt*, somehow—"

"Mmh, yes," said Mendoza. "And I wonder if it *is* marriage. You starting to have hunches, and me being tempted into melodrama as per all the fiction—"

"My God," said Hackett, "that reminds me, I never called Angel to say I'd be late. I'd better run— You, of course, have got yours trained, the autocrat you are—" He snatched up his hat.

Mendoza sighed to himself. Just inviting insubordination to tell Art how wrong he was. . . .

PART II

HAPPY RELEASE

Mr. Deasey sat on the side porch of the Sunnyrest Home and thought about the late Mrs. Pope and other things. *Sunnyrest,* he thought disgustedly for the hundredth time: just the kind of damn fool name a woman like Mrs. Beauchamp would pick. And just the kind of damn place all of them were, like he'd expected. Never mind, he wasn't in for life like the rest of these poor bastards.

"Yessirree," quavered old Mr. White beside him, "that was in nineteen twenty, I think—remember clear as yesterday—"

Mr. Deasey looked at Mr. White with irritation. It beat all how some people let themselves stagnate: that was the word. Hell, White was a year younger than he was at seventy-one, and here he was a drooling piece of senility, couldn't talk about a damn thing nearer than about 1925. Mr. Deasey wished he'd shut up; he wanted to think seriously about the late Mrs. Pope.

Nice enough woman, she'd been. . . . This Sunnyrest place was an old house, kind of a house that was called a mansion when it was first built about 1890, and besides all the big upstairs rooms and servants' rooms, there'd been the back and front parlors downstairs, the sewing room and conservatory; so Mrs. Beauchamp—who pronounced her name the Southern way—had had plenty of space to squeeze people in. She'd taken the back parlor and breakfast room for herself, and upstairs let the wide hall divide what she called, in her Goddamned silly way, the

Girls' rooms from the Boys'. And packed three beds to a room. Making a damn nice thing out of it, if they were all paying what he was, three hundred and fifty a month. Private rest home for old folks, not one of these big places where the charge was the hell of a lot steeper.

Mr. Deasey, his mind temporarily sliding away from Mrs. Pope, looked at his surroundings with hatred: at the ancient wicker chairs, the quiet lawn and flower beds, the quiet street. Six damn blocks from a bus and a good two miles from the nearest bar. He looked at the surrounding company, and thought of the presently invisible rest of it, with equal dislike. Him, Dan Deasey, cooped up with a pack of senile characters like this! Old White. That Armitage who went on telling the same old stories about when he was a sergeant-major about fifty years ago. The Lacy woman who sat over a ouija board in the parlor every night, old fool. The Potter couple, by damn, only in the sixties and it was perfectly O.K. with them, pay for separate rooms in (my God) the Girls' and Boys' sections. Ex-Captain McCarthy. That Goddamned silly Pepper woman with her cheap perfume, making eyes at him over her knitting. That—

Pack of senile idiots. It was damn depressing. Mr. Deasey sighed, remembering back wistfully to six weeks ago and his snug little room in the Crescent Hotel on Santa Monica Boulevard. He'd knocked around a lot in his day, and his third wife had died nine years back; he was used to doing for himself, and he kept everything neat and shipshape. Not that he'd been in it much. There was a bunch of them usually congregated down at the Black and White Bar about noon—Bill and Fred and Joe and Harry—all different ages, all good fellows—and later on he and Fred'd usually wander on up to Rosie's Grill, and meet some other guys there, and hit a couple of places for the evening, maybe run into old Jim or Duke or Pete—

That damn doctor, thought Mr. Deasey. He hadn't had a drink in two months. Hell of a thing. But he was feeling just like himself again now, he'd get out tomorrow and pick up a bottle, see him through the week he still had to stay at this damned place.

The Sunnyrest Home had been an almighty affront to Mr. Deasey. So he was seventy-two, and just getting over a bad bout of flu. "And no family," Dr. Katzman had pointed out, "to take care of—"

"What the hell d'you mean, no family?" Mr. Deasey had said, bristling. "That I know about, six boys I got—the first three by Jenny, and then the redheaded one, that's Mike, by—"

"Sure, sure—but not around," young Dr. Katzman had said. So, not around. Bill in the army, and Denny on construction somewhere in Mexico, and Mike on an oil tanker— "You need a good rest with somebody waiting on you for a while, old boy," Dr. Katzman had said. "Say six weeks. I know better than to try to stick you in an old folks' home permanently—but six weeks will make all the difference."

Mr. Deasey, up to this morning, had been bitterly agreeing with Dr. Katzman that it sure as hell made all the difference— he'd got to feeling twenty years older, listening to all these senile old crocks. Having to sit next to old White at the communal table—old White wouldn't wear his false teeth, and of all the repulsive sights— But this morning, Mr. Deasey had suddenly acquired an object in life (besides the major one of getting out of this damned graveyard and back to the congenial company at the bars along Santa Monica).

The late Mrs. Pope. And the late Mr. Jensen. And the late Mr. Swann, whom he'd never laid eyes on, just heard talk about.

And, of course, Mrs. Beauchamp.

Mr. Deasey had disliked Mrs. Beauchamp the minute he met her. She was a large, round, pink woman with a perpetual smile pasted on her rosebud mouth. She dressed in nurse's uniform, much starched, and was fond of the nurse's editorial We. Like most proprietors of old people's rest homes she treated her charges as children to be guided with playful jocularity. ("Time for our nice supper, now! Everybody washed up? *That's* right! . . . Time for beddy-bye!") The desiccated mummies in this place didn't seem to mind, but Mr. Deasey—in, thank you, full possession of his adult faculties and intending to stay that way—loathed the fool woman. Not that he liked White or

Armitage or McCarthy or the rest of them so damn much, but he resented on their behalf (maybe just because they didn't seem to) the implication that because they'd lived a certain length of time they must have got into second childhood.

And up to this morning that was about all he'd felt in re Sunnyrest—a dumb hatred of it and of Mrs. Beauchamp. He'd had the impulse to start a calendar the way convicts did, mark off the days until (his six weeks of rest done) he could escape to his old familiar haunts. Damn flu hadn't set him back at all; he felt fine now.

Then this morning—or rather last night—Mrs. Pope had died. Undertakers called for her about ten; he'd seen the car come up. Mrs. Beauchamp had found her dead—woman had been poorly the last few days, bad cold turning into incipient pneumonia, and Mrs. Beauchamp had brought her down to the little spare room across the hall from her own— "So we can keep an eye on you, dearie, in case you want anything during the night, you know." Just the way old Jensen had been.

Well, people did slip off like that—ones with no stamina. She'd only been sixty-six. Turned into pneumonia, the doctor'd said so: all open and aboveboard, she'd been due to go to the hospital today.

On the other hand—

"And then in nineteen twenty-one," burbled old White, "I remember I bought my first auto. 'Twas an E.M.F., and we had a little joke—"

Well, in his day (which wasn't over by a long shot) Mr. Deasey had knocked around. Never had so much schooling, but he'd picked up this and that—done a stint as a hotel dick, he had, and gone to sea awhile, and straw-bossed construction gangs from Tucson down to Vera Cruz—and he might be seventy-two, but that didn't say he'd all of a sudden stopped being that same Dan Deasey. Hell, he still had an eye for a pretty girl and he could outdrink most men he knew—*and* he wasn't senile any other way, damn it.

He said impatiently to old White, "Yeah, I know, I heard it—

Every-Morning-Fixit. Listen, you knew this Swann that died here last month, you said.''

''Oh—Mr. Swann. Yes,'' said White vaguely. He was a fat old man, bald, with a pendulous chin; Mr. Deasey, who was lean and spare and had kept all his teeth and most of his hair, found him a repulsive sight with or without his false teeth. ''A happy release, poor fellow,'' said White. ''No family, you know, he was quite alone, never had visitors, and his heart was shaky—very shaky. The doctor had warned him—'' he sighed. ''It's a terrible thing, Mr. Deasey, to grow old all alone like that.''

And that he'd picked up from Mrs. Beauchamp. Hadn't the damned woman sat here in that very chair, this morning, after they'd taken Mrs. Pope away, and said the same thing? ''Quite alone in the world, poor soul—a happy release, we must all feel. No one to visit her, and so little money, no real family—''

Well, hell, thought Mr. Deasey (sliding to irrelevancy again) he'd just as soon *have* nobody to visit him than the kind some of the rest of 'em had! That hard-faced skirt in the mink coat came to see the Potters—their only daughter—and her fat husband: ''How are we today, darlings?'' Scared to death, you could see, the Beauchamp woman'd say, prices going up. Didn't give a tinker's damn for the old folks, you could see that. And that young lout came to see Armitage—grandson. Shoe on the other foot there, Armitage had a little money and the young lout wanting some of it. By damn, if any of *his* boys'd ever got themselves rigged up in a damn womanish outfit like that plaid jacket— *Or* gone to blandishing at him about money for art lessons— Art lessons, for God's sake . . . But of course his boys, thank God, were O.K. Knew all his money, and not so damn little money either, had gone into a nice fat annuity, and what the hell? They were doing all right. Still his boys, and him still their dad. *They* knew he wasn't going senile yet.

No visitors, said the Beauchamp woman, and looked at him pityingly too. Mr. Deasey had wanted to say to her, No, by God, ma'am, all my boys are off doing their own job of work someplace. They know I can take care of myself. They got round to writing, of course; and at that, they didn't—he figured—write just the sort of way Mrs. Beauchamp might approve of. . . . He pulled Mike's latest letter half out of his shirt pocket (it started out, *Hello, you old bastard, what's the price of rye gone to now?*) and then shoved it back. He was thinking about Swann. And Jensen. And Mrs. Pope.

There was a word for it—cliché. Sure. Things people said without thinking. A happy release. The Beauchamp woman had said that about Jensen too.

Jensen had been sixty-nine. Dry stick of a fellow—retired pharmacist. (Swann, retired bank clerk.) Always coughing: a weak chest. He'd got a cold—that was the week before Mr. Deasey got here—and just hadn't got better.

"A *happy* release," the Beauchamp woman had said. In the parlor after dinner (if you could call it that, thought Mr. Deasey, whose standing order at Rosie's Grill was a New York steak medium-well and a double order of French fries). She'd sat on the couch between Mr. Deasey and Mrs. Potter, and said earnestly, "We must all feel, a happy release for the poor lonely old man. No family, no friends to visit him—cheer him up. I do feel so, for such lonely souls. You know, it's the main reason I started Sunnyrest, to be a haven for these poor elderly folk—so few people appreciate the sadness of old age, the way old people feel— I try to understand, and do what I can."

"Oh, indeed you do," the Potter woman had bleated. "Dear Mrs. Beauchamp! I suppose we must feel that the poor soul is better off—"

Nobody, thought Mr. Deasey, is better off dead, damn it!

And today, Mrs. Pope. Nice enough woman, a bit too fat, a widow, and talkative. Been a pretty woman once. And she'd had a daughter, but the daughter'd never come to see her—that was a whispered piece of scandal around the place: like a damn girls' school, any little gossip grabbed at to tell around.

The Beauchamp woman, on the porch this morning— "Poor lonely old soul! I really feel she's happier to be gone, you know, Mr. Deasey. Only an ungrateful, selfish daughter who never came to visit her—and she was failing rapidly, you know. I could see that. We must all feel, now she is happy in the arms of Our Lord.''

Well, doctors, he thought. Sure. Dr. Katzman. Dr. Sayers. One or the other of them coming to see patients here. Dr. Katzman who'd stuck him here. Good enough doctor, seemed like, but— What the hell did it say? You take a lot of people, the namby-pamby ones, in the late sixties, early seventies, they'd let any little thing carry them off. And it wouldn't be like anybody twenty-five or thirty slipping away—the doctors wouldn't be too surprised. *Or* concerned. He had a weak heart, she had pneumonia pretty serious, the flu's been bad this year.

Never suspecting—

Mr. Deasey had begun to suspect (or was a better word wonder) only because he had sharp eyes and a lot of time to ruminate lately, and he wasn't half-senile like everybody else in this place. Mrs. Beauchamp's little eager black eyes on him— that other time and this morning— ''I really feel for elderly people, you know, Mr. Deasey. How terrible it is for them—so many of them—alone and friendless and poor. Really, if we have any religious faith at all, we must know that they are so much happier to die and win *permanent peace* and bliss in the heaven we are promised. Don't you think so?''

Mr. Deasey had never thought peace a very desirable state, or being dead either, so he hadn't said anything; but there was a funny look in her eye he hadn't liked. The Beauchamp woman was too damn religious, come to connect it up—always praying at you before and after meals, and so on. And could that be the reason?

It was the hell of a crazy idea, but he just wondered. . . . Even in a place like Sunnyrest, where everybody was sitting around just waiting to die, wasn't three deaths in six weeks a little bit too damn much?

Well, young Katzman was coming to see him tonight. . . .

''Surprised?'' said Dr. Katzman. ''What d'you mean? Pneumonia, it carries off a lot of old people—ones not as tough as you,'' and he grinned. ''I hoped we'd bring her through, but I wasn't surprised she didn't make it. Why? . . . Now what the hell have you got in your head about this? Certainly Mrs. Beauchamp's a competent practical nurse. There wasn't the slightest—''

"O.K., O.K.,'' said Mr. Deasey. "So I'm going senile with the rest of the inmates. Thank God I'll be out next week.''

"And back on a pint of rye a day. Well, I can't stop you. And I'll be damned,'' said the doctor, putting away his stethoscope, "if your heart isn't sound as mine—God knows why.''

"Seeing I haven't had one damn drink in two months, I'm surprised it isn't kicking up like hell,'' said Mr. Deasey. But of course that told him the doctors wouldn't listen to a word. Good-enough doctors, but what the hell, an old woman in a rest home dying of pneumonia, an old man with a shaky heart popping off sudden (maybe his medicine kept back?—maybe, with the old woman and the other man, a window left open and no blankets on the bed?). Some old folks, damn easy to put them out, make it look natural—and who to take notice, no money to speak of, nobody much interested in them?

"A *happy* release,'' the Beauchamp woman had said. And for a second she had looked really happy. "To think of this dear soul entering into eternal bliss with Our Lord— Much the better way than continued loneliness and suffering here on earth!''

And the rest of these senile mummies nodding solemnly and agreeing with her.

It was a crazy thing all right, but Mr. Deasey had seen a lot of crazy things in seventy-two years, and he figured he wasn't cracking up yet to see craziness where it wasn't. Not yet, at only seventy-two.

"That,'' said old White,'' was in nineteen thirty—''

"Yeah, sure,'' said Mr. Deasey absently. No good to tell the doctor. Young people, that hadn't lived long enough (or knocked around enough) to know that with human people you just shouldn't be surprised at anything—well, you just couldn't reach them. But, hell, this old idiot here, and the Lacy woman, and McCarthy—rest of them—senile or not, he figured they wouldn't want to be hustled into heaven ahead of time. And he could swear—

□ □ □

"No, ma'am," he said pathetically, "my boys don't come to see me. Haven't got much time for an old fellow like me." (Hell they haven't. Mostly wrote pretty faithful, and asking advice too—dames and poker, mostly.)

"That's terrible," said Mrs. Beauchamp, her eyes filling with easy tears. "I feel so for you poor old people, this younger generation just heartless, so they are! I nursed both my old parents faithful, I flatter myself, Mr. Deasey—every sacrifice made, right up to the end. It was the reason I started my Sunnyrest home—I have a kind of affinity for old people, you know, I understand them. It must be a dreadful, dreadful feeling—that you're all alone, no one caring for you at all, and death so near."

Mr. Deasey coughed, trying to sound more pathetic. "Well, I guess it is, ma'am. And I told you my heart's awful bad too—the doctor gave me some pills to take." He produced a little bottle. Actually the pills in the bottle were vitamins. Little white tablets. Some fool idea of Katzman's.

"Oh, dear, how sad," said Mrs. Beauchamp.

"I got to take three every day," he said, "or no telling—"

"I'm so sorry," said Mrs. Beauchamp sympathetically.

"Oh, well," said Mr. Deasey (he'd done a stint in summer stock back in '42, but hadn't liked show business much), "I guess we just got to make do as we can, up to the bitter end, ma'am."

"You must have *faith*, Mr. Deasey," said Mrs. Beauchamp.

Mr. Deasey left the little bottle of vitamin pills on the cheap pine bureau in the room he shared (a martyr to Sunnyrest's regime) with Mr. White and ex-Sergeant-Major Armitage, when he went down to dinner that evening. (Dinner, my God—one thin slice of chicken and a boiled potato! He thought wistfully of Rosie's Grill. Well, only another few days.)

When he went upstairs again at nine o'clock, the bottle was still there right where he'd left it. He twisted off the cap and shot the contents into his palm.

Aspirin.

"Umm," said Mr. Deasey to himself. So he had been right. Hell of a thing.

Crazy religious fanatic. Happy release.

"I'll be damned," he said aloud.

And then a sort of righteous indignation took possession of him. Just suppose he *had* had a bad heart, needed those pills?

Nobody—but nobody—thought Mr. Deasey, blind, deaf, or dumb, seven or seventy, was better off dead!

And nobody here would believe him. Their nice kind Mrs. Beauchamp. My God. And a damn lot of use, tell the doctors. Damn it to hell, you got to be seventy, everybody treated you like you're a kid, can't think anymore, don't see straight anymore, don't feel anymore. Just a back number, not working on all cylinders. And didn't he know, no use to tell the cops either. Even if a lot of them were the hell of a lot smarter than they used to be, now. On an offbeat thing like this— The Beauchamp woman'd just deny the whole thing, say he was going senile and didn't know what he was talking about. And Katzman would speak up and say he'd never prescribed any heart medicine. And he hadn't known Dan Deasey long, just since the flu. He might not want to think Dan Deasey was going soft in the head, but he couldn't be sure—a wild story like this. If the Beauchamp woman denied the whole thing— Damn it, you got to be seventy-two, people treated you like— And what proof was there? Damn all. Even if they dug up the bodies, no damn proof at all! And of course they'd never believe him that far. Likely try to tuck him away somewhere as a lunatic.

What the hell could he do?

"The Goddamned impudence of the bitch," said Mr. Deasey. "I will be damned."

The next morning he told Mrs. Beauchamp he'd walk down to the drugstore to get some cough drops.

"Oh, you're sure you're able, Mr. Deasey?"

"I'm able," said Mr. Deasey.

He was feeling fine now, damn the doctor, and he walked down and got the number seven bus up to Fairfax Avenue. He got off, lighting a cigarette (hell of a ruction at Sunnyrest if you so much as struck a match—tobacco so *bad* for the heart), and made a beeline for the nearest bar. After a couple of drinks, he felt a lot better still.

He found a liquor store and bought a pint of rye and a bottle of cheap burgundy. He went on feeling better and better as he waited for the bus back. . . . Had trouble sleeping, he had, when the damn doctor took him off the rye—too weak to go out and get himself a bottle then, and those damn hospital nurses, anyway— So, the little bottle of tablets. Still six or seven left—and the doctor'd said it was common, easy to buy, anywhere. . . .

"Oh, but Mr. Deasey, you shouldn't have *alcohol,* should you?"

"It's not that kind of heart disease, ma'am," he said. "The doctor said I ought to take a little stimulant— And I feel kind of self-conscious drinking it alone, Mrs. Beauchamp, I just thought if you'd join me in a little glass— Before bedtime'd be best, he said, like now—"

"Well, it's very thoughtful of you," she said, beaming at him. "But you mustn't forget to take your pill, Mr. Deasey."

"Hell, no," said Mr. Deasey absently. "Well, happy days." He nearly gagged on the burgundy—damn Dago stuff.

"Look who's here, for God's sake—welcome back, Danny boy!" "What the hell, couldn't kill you with an ax, Dan, old boy, old boy!" "Set 'em up, Barney, the old boy's back with us—"

It sure as hell sounded good, all the old bunch, and the bar smelled good and familiar too, and it felt very damn good, get back with his own kind of people. Damn doctor. Those desiccated mummies. Sunnyrest, my God—for Dan Deasey. He set them up for the boys, and agreed they sure as hell couldn't kill him off so easy, and he was feeling fine—just fine.

"—Something in the paper, Dan boy, about the dame that

ran that rest home place you were at—dying kind of sudden—''

"Oh, that," he said, swallowing rye. "Yeah, they decided she'd made a mistake, took too many sleeping pills. Like people do, you know. They found the bottle in the trash." Of course, minus any label—just in case the number could be traced. He'd had to say he'd heard her mention taking the stuff sometimes, and by God if old White hadn't backed him up—power of suggestion like the saying went. Funny all the same. "Only about fifty-five too. Kind of a shame . . . Same again, Barney."

It was kind of a shame. If the doctors would have listened— But you couldn't have a crazy female running around loose like that. Hell no. And by the time you got to be seventy-two, any kind of a man, you weren't afraid of taking responsibility.

Those poor bastards up there at Sunnyrest. Get transferred somewhere else now, he guessed.

"Hey, Dan, you got anything for Hollywood Park this afternoon?"

"Think about it later, Charlie," said Mr. Deasey. "I'll look. Right now I got a letter from my boy Pat to read—he likely wants some advice about a dame, he usually does. Then I'll look over the field and pick a couple for us."

RANNYSORE

"I didn't mean to do it!" sobbed Brenda Reade. "Only we were playing tag-you're-it and Betty tagged me so hard she sort of shoved me and—and I just stepped *one foot* into Mr. Shipley's yard—only he said it was on some new seeds or something and he was mad—he—"

"Oh, dear," said Jane Reade. "Again, darling? I know you don't mean to, but you must be more careful—all of you!"

"Damn it," said Bob Reade, "why can't you kids play somewhere else besides around Shipley's? We've had—"

"But it's the only place *to* play, Daddy—"

"—Nothing else ever since the man moved in but complaints about kids doing damage to his damn garden!"

"Oh, well, Bob, he is rather a crank. That corner lot's always been more or less the neighborhood playground, and now he's bought it and made a garden, the kids naturally play in the street there, and I must say it's a good place, because of its being a dead-end street. You can't expect children this age—and he doesn't like children anyway—"

"Of course he's a crank, Jane, but kids have got to learn about private property too. Why doesn't he put up a fence?"

"Maybe he can't afford it," said Jane vaguely. "I wish to goodness he'd never moved here!" Just as Bob said, ever since the man Shipley had bought the house next to the end lot on Primrose Lane, and that lot, neighborhood peace had vanished.

This was a fairly new suburban area, of upper-middle-class homes; the twelve children on this block were not slum-bred hooligans—but children would be children, after all. As Jane said, the younger ones were used to playing in that lot, and had transferred their activities to the street-end, perilously near Mr. Shipley's carefully cultivated new garden. There had been a fuss when Stevie Brent ran through it flying his kite; there had been a bigger fuss when little Bruce Brent, who was only three and couldn't be expected to understand, pulled up some new seedlings along the sidewalk. There had been complaints when Brenda trespassed after her ball, and when Betty Pollack's spaniel puppy dug up a bush, and when— There had been several complaints to the Reades about Brenda. Brenda was something of a tomboy, a leggy active seven-year-old; she promised faithfully to *remember* and *be careful,* but somehow further incidents occurred.

"He was so mean, Mother! He looked at me something awful—he—"

"Well, just please try to be extra careful," said Jane. You'd think they would, she thought, because none of the kids liked Mr. Shipley; they were even a little afraid of him. Bob would laugh, but she thought she could be a little afraid of Mr. Shipley herself. It wasn't exactly anything he did or said—she knew just what Brenda meant by saying he *looked* at her—it was something about his eyes. He was a tall, lean man, very dark, with thinnish dark hair; his age no one could guess. And you wouldn't think dark eyes could look cold, but his did. On the few occasions Jane had met him, she had felt vaguely repelled.

He lived alone with a manservant as unsocial as himself; in the six months he'd lived on Primrose Lane, nobody had found out what Shipley did. He seemed to have no regular job; he came and went at odd hours, and twice had been away for a week or so.

"I wish," she repeated to Bob, "he'd never come here."

"He ought to put up a fence," said Bob irritably.

"Yes, well, if he calls you can tell him so. I'm going over to see Edna Brent. I do hope Brucie's better." As she walked down the block, she hugged to herself the reassuring sight of Brenda, restored to her usual volatile self, absorbed in a game of jacks with Betty Pollack on the Pollacks' front steps. Poor Edna . . . and poor Brucie. Not as if Edna was careless about watching him, but a three-year-old could be out of sight in thirty seconds— these awful things happened however careful you tried to be. Edna said she hadn't had her eyes off him ten seconds—down there on Broadway yesterday—when it happened. Brucie running out into the street after an escaped toy, and that big bus—

Edna looked haggard. She said Jim was at the hospital, had made her come home. "They don't know for sure yet. They just say, maybe. He's—he's still in a sort of coma."

Jane said all the right things, feeling obscurely guilty because she still had her Brenda. And she tried to cheer Edna up, knowing how she'd hate that herself, but it was (wasn't it?) the social convention—tried to take her mind off it a little, with casual talk. She told her about Brenda's latest brush with Shipley. "It's a pity he ever moved here."

Edna said with a little effort, "Oh, well, Jane, I don't think he's as—as funny and cantankerous as he seems sometimes. You know how these fanatical gardeners are. I think he just loses his temper for a minute and is sorry afterward."

"Well—" said Jane doubtfully. The times Shipley had complained to her about Brenda, he hadn't been in a temper; coldly sarcastic and bitter was more like it, quite under control.

"Because after he'd been so angry at Brucie, he came and apologized, and brought him a present."

"He did? How funny."

"Quite an expensive present too, one of those battery-operated trucks—they were eleven dollars at Keenes'—Brucie's just crazy about it. I was surprised, but he was really quite nice about apologizing, and—oh, dear," said Edna, groping for her handkerchief, "I shouldn't have let Brucie have it, it was that truck he ran out in the street after—"

Jane said all the appropriate things over again.

It was that evening that Shipley came with the thing. When she found him on the doorstep, Jane was afraid he'd come to offer more criticism of modern parents who couldn't control their children, but he was astonishingly amiable. She still didn't like him, but she saw he was making an effort to be friendly. He apologized a little stiffly to Brenda for being cross with her—"I know you didn't mean any harm, child"—and as a peace offering presented her with an enormous parcel. "I do hope you will like it, my dear."

Jane gasped faintly when she saw the contents. It was a stuffed animal of some sort, quite three feet high, and she knew the prices of such toys. For a moment she was ready to protest, and then—remembering what Edna had said—she thought, Well, if the man is really making that sincere an effort to be friendly, we can't rebuff him. He's just a little crotchety, not knowing much about kids. And not working at a regular job, maybe he has quite a lot of money.

There was no doubt that his gift had captivated Brenda. Like most little girls her age, she loved stuffed animals, and she'd never seen such a magnificent big one as this. She clasped it ecstatically, said *"Thank you!"* without prompting, and spent the rest of Shipley's brief visit silently adoring it.

"Well!" said Bob when their good neighbor had taken himself off. "I'll be damned. He's not such a bad guy after all—seems to realize he's made an ogre of himself to the kids."

"That's what Edna said," said Jane. "He brought a present to Brucie too. But look at it, Bob!—it's awful, really, we shouldn't have—why, it must have cost fifteen or twenty dollars!"

"Let's see it, sweetheart. Now, I can *hold* it a minute, can't I?—I'll give it right back! What on earth is it, anyway?"

"A—a—a kangaroo," said Brenda.

Bob laughed. "Well, no, honey, I don't think so. I'll tell you what it's meant for," he said after a moment's study, "that prehistoric thing—a dinosaur, what's the name? *Tyrannosaurus rex,* that's it. The one that walked on its hind legs."

"Is it?" said Jane doubtfully. "Maybe so. They make so many different kinds of stuffed animals now." The thing was covered with good thick plush, and colored slate-gray all over except for a scarlet open mouth and a white underbody.

"Rannysore," said Brenda instantly. "That's his name." She snatched it back, cuddling it.

Jane had quite an argument with her on Monday morning about taking Rannysore to school. All weekend Brenda had been inseparable from the thing. Finally she went off, sulkily late, extracting a promise that Jane wouldn't touch it.

Jane had no desire to touch it. She looked at it where Brenda had left it, carefully propped up at the head of her bed, and she didn't like it. She had the quite absurd notion that the thing was watching her slyly with its shiny black-bead eyes as she dusted and straightened up Brenda's bureau top.

Brenda sometimes dawdled on the way home from school, but today she was home punctually at two-forty, making a beeline for her bedroom. She emerged with the thing cradled in her arms and announced, "Rannysore and me are going to play in the backyard."

"All right, darling," said Jane. "You'd better put a sweater on. Is Betty coming over?"

"Uh-uh. Rather play alone with Rannysore."

She did, the rest of the afternoon—off among the old oak trees at the rear of their lot, out of sight. Which wasn't like tomboy Brenda; but kids went through these phases. Nevertheless at dinner Jane asked, "What kind of games do you play with—with Rannysore, darling?"

Brenda shot her a swift secretive glance. "Our *own* games. Just *games*. Rannysore talks to me and—and everything, when we're alone together. Just when we're alone, because he doesn't like other people to know he *can*."

"Yes, I see, darling." Jane exchanged a little smile with Bob. As modern, educated parents they knew that all children had these fantasies, quite real to them.

But Brenda's fascination with the ugly thing continued to puzzle her. Every morning when she came in to dust, straighten up, there it was looking at her—*watching* her, she thought—and absurd as it was, she found herself feeling uneasy to turn her back on it. Which was ridiculous: a stuffed toy, even if it was so big!

On Wednesday Brucie Brent died. Everyone on the block went to call, express sympathy, offer to run errands. The silly meaningless little things one did and said at such times—the cake, the flowers.

Jane came back from her condolence call feeling exhausted, and found Brenda home from school, and ran to hug her (feeling guilty, *I still have mine*). Brenda didn't want to be hugged. "You *promised* you wouldn't touch him, Mother! He doesn't like to be touched by anybody 'cept me! He—"

"Who, darling?"

"You *moved* him!" Brenda pointed accusingly. Certainly the last time Jane had been in Brenda's room, that Thing (as she was calling it to herself) had been propped up at the head of the bed. Now it was lying across the foot.

"I didn't, really I didn't, Brenda." And she hadn't. For a moment Jane had a very queer feeling: how had it got moved? "I promise you I didn't."

"Oh—well, then, maybe Rannysore just moved himself, maybe he wanted to lie down awhile. But you mustn't touch him, Mother, because he might bite, you know. Anybody 'cept me."

How had the thing been moved? Of course it had just fallen over, Jane told herself robustly. She was being perfectly idiotic about it—a silly stuffed animal, of all things—but she felt she'd almost rather pick up a snake than Brenda's Rannysore.

"Bob," she said hesitantly as they were going to bed. "That—thing. She's obsessed with it. Do you think it's—well, healthy?"

"Oh, kids get these crazes, honey."

"But she never seems to play with Betty or Dorothy anymore—just by herself, with that thing. You'll think I'm crazy, but I just hate that—that creature! There's something *not right* about it, Bob."

"What d'you mean?"

"I don't know," said Jane miserably. "I—all right, I'm crazy, but I feel it's *watching* me!"

"Hey, now!" he said, and came to kiss her. "You need a headshrinker? What's this all about?"

"Every single minute of her own time, she's off alone with it. I *hate* it, Bob. It's—it's—uncanny."

"You've got a complex or something. Maybe your unconscious mind connects it with something you were afraid of as a kid. You know."

"Oh, sure," said Jane, trying for the light tone. "Just another little old neurosis."

"Look, honey," he said gently, "I guess we're all worrying a little more about our kids, on account of Brucie. You know? Don't fuss, Janie. Brenda's O.K., you'll see, in a little while this craze'll be over and she'll find another one."

"I hope so!" said Jane.

But the next morning, looking at Rannysore leaning against the headboard eyeing her, she had the momentary hysterical feeling that its expression was no longer sly, but insolent. *It's got Brenda,* thought Jane, panicky, it needn't be sly anymore. And pulled herself together. This was absolute nonsense—she must be coming down with something, or maybe she really did need a psychiatrist.

She turned her back, dusting the bureau. When she straightened and turned again, the thing had fallen over on its side and its black-bead eyes were staring at her sideways. Her heart gave a little extra thud. Of course it had just fallen over. But she couldn't bring herself to go and set it upright.

She felt that it really *might* bite.

"—And I'm going to take Rannysore, Mother—"

"You can't take—it—to school, dear."

"But I've just been *telling* you! It's a special day, a sort of party, Pets' Day it is, and kids who haven't got any pets are supposed to bring Favorite Toys, and so I'm—"

"Oh, dear," said Jane. "All right." She hoped Mrs. Woods wouldn't think it very funny; but of course this nonsensical feeling she had about the thing was all her own little neurosis—probably any other adult would see only a big stuffed toy. "But, darling, please don't—don't tell people how it talks to you and plays with you. We know that's just playing—just make-believe—but some people—"

"It's *not*!" said Brenda. "He does *so*! And he's not an—an it, he's Rannysore!"

"Oh, all right," said Jane, defeated. She stood at the door to see Brenda off—only six blocks to school, and a guard at the one main crossing—in her new red car coat, with the thing held in her arms. She turned at the corner and waved, and Jane waved back.

Not twenty minutes later Anne Pollack dropped in. "I know it's too early, but I couldn't wait to spread the news. Tom told me when he got in last night, of course, and then it was too late. You'll never guess, my dear—we've found out at last what Mr. Shipley does, and of all the things you can imagine—! Tom had to stay late in the office for a client yesterday"—Tom Pollack was junior partner in a city law-firm—"so he had dinner in town, and somebody had left this brochure thing on the table, so he looked at it casually, you know. And you'll never guess! It was an announcement about a lecture—on alchemical research—and it was Anthony Lewis Shipley lecturing! Our Mr. Shipley!"

"Alchemical research—" said Jane.

"The most absurd thing! Tom was so intrigued he went there—and it was one of those shabby little public halls on a side street—and it turned out to be a meeting of one of those queer sects, you know— Yogi or Zen or something, only not as respectable as those—they call themselves the Association of Modern Alchemists. Tom said he had to come out in the middle of the lecture or he'd have laughed in the man's face. My dear, he—Shipley, I mean—was lecturing on *sorcery*—or something like that anyway—quite seriously! He talked some rigmarole, Tom said, about what he called Sending—he said he'd mastered the art of sending a spirit to possess inanimate objects! Did you ever hear anything like it? I should think he must have a private income, shouldn't you? Well, I mean, we all knew he's a little peculiar, but I never suspected he was as peculiar as all that!''

"Yes—no,'' said Jane. "How very odd.'' And she was not at all superstitious or credulous, of course—a modern sensible woman—but as she went on talking to Anne, she thought to herself, I won't have that thing in the house another day. Not another day. I don't care what fuss Brenda makes, out it goes! And let everybody say I'm a silly hysterical female all they please. As soon as she comes home from school—

But she didn't come home from school. She didn't come home at all. By four o'clock Jane had called Bob, and called the police—and they both arrived at the same time.

"Mrs. Reade, we're very sorry to have to break this news to you—'' The young uniformed policeman looked as if he hated his job, right then, and probably did. She leaned against Bob, hearing his words numbly, disconnected phrases—the railway crossing at Fifth and Greenstone—red car coat—name tag in the coat—freight train—

"No,'' Bob kept saying. "No. Not Brenda. No.''

"I'm afraid—no doubt, Mr. Reade . . . very sorry. We—''

"She never came home that way, along Greenstone instead of Maple! She wouldn't be at that crossing— No—no—''

"I'm afraid—'' said the young policeman wretchedly.

"Why? In God's name, *why*—''

And Jane said suddenly, loudly, "I know why! Ask Rannysore! Rannysore told her to go that way! It was Rannysore—'' And she began to giggle weakly.

They looked at her as if she was mad. Perhaps she was mad. She put her hand to her mouth, stopped the giggling. "Please,'' she said to the policeman, "please. Tell me. Was there a—a big stuffed animal—there—with her? A big gray stuffed animal?''

"No, ma'am, nothing like that at all.''

"Honey—'' said Bob.

"Of course not," said Jane. "Of course not. He wouldn't be found—at the scene of the crime."

"I don't get what you mean," said the policeman uncertainly.

"She's hysterical," said Bob. "Janie—"

She leaned against Bob, letting their voices go over her, unhearing. Quite rational explanations there would be—but she *knew*.

THEY WILL CALL IT INSANE

She sipped after-dinner coffee and made inane talk with Beatrice Foster beside her and thought about killing her husband.

It was quite ridiculous really because in stories people had important reasons for killing people. Wills. Deathless love. Blackmail.

What with all this emphasis on realism in fiction these days, she wondered that writers didn't consult the newspapers, to see that so many people were killed because of, really, nothing at all.

A man shot his wife because she insisted on putting on that red dress he didn't like.

A woman shot her husband because he teased her, not telling her where he'd gone last night. (Actually an innocent sales meeting.)

That kind of thing.

"Don't you think I was right?" asked Beatrice. "I mean, she'd been really insinuating that there was something funny about the election for secretary."

"Oh, I do," she said. "Of course." A nice quiet dinner party they were having, for people they knew well. The Fosters. The Andersons.

She wondered if Beatrice ever got very tired of the way Andrew Foster said "Tell you what I mean" twice in every sentence.

People all had mannerisms, of course. Tiresome and otherwise. You learned to put up with each other, or you were very depraved (or very brave, which she'd never been) and got a divorce.

"Tell you what I *mean*," said Andrew Foster, "it's un-American. That's what I say."

"Well, I guess that's obvious," said Bob Anderson.

"*I* figure," said George, "damn nonsense to worry about it. You know. Be afraid of 'em. Bunch of damn peasants, you might say in the feudal age up to thirty, forty years back— a threat to *us*? Don't make me laugh!"

"Well, the missile program, what we get to hear of it—" said Bob Anderson.

"Oh, dear, they've got on to politics," said Judy Anderson.

Please, George, she thought. Not the funny story about the Russian private in Berlin after the war and the water faucets torn out to send home. I've heard you tell it so often. Please.

No, the funny thing was, they never—the people who wrote that kind of thing—could imagine any sort of motive but an important one. They never wrote stories about a man murdered because every single solitary morning he came to breakfast and said cheerfully, "Well, another day, another dollar." Or because he always told you about things three times. I'm going to have the oil changed on the car, he'd say. And, I left the car to have the oil changed. And, I picked up the car after the oil change. Nothing to do with you, as if it was relevant information, when you didn't drive. Or because, when he told a story about something that had happened to them (the old Indian in New Mexico, the funny hotel in Maine) he always started out, Was it Monday or Tuesday . . .

"The cutest line," said Judy. "Plain, you know, but smart. Dressmaker suits and what they call cocktail dresses. Expensive—eighty-nine fifty and up—but worth it."

"Where'd you say?" asked Beatrice.

"Websters'. A new line—Antoine's, they call it."

George always started the story about the Russian private, "See, we just don't realize how far behind us they are." It was one of his favorite stories, like the one about the cow and the one about the Pentagon clerk. The kind of story you could tell in mixed company.

Not that George had ever been much given to the other kind. "Taupe?" said Judy. "It's a difficult color to wear."

"All the thing this season, they say. But it's not a shade I like much either. Too neutral. And these sheaths, my dear, fatal except for the perfect figure. But I—"

The odd thing was that George had never been given to the kind of thing which eventually built up motives for murder. The extracurricular blonde. The embezzlement from the firm. Dear me, no.

He was a responsible, honest man. Good George. Honest, honorable George. Straightforward George.

He had sometimes (she thought) been a little hard on the children, but probably for their own good. Children were never hurt by sensible discipline, were they? In any event, it was over and done now, for good or bad: John married and living across the country, Marian in a good job in Cleveland, Betty married to nice kind Jim and quite happy in Florida with her two sweet children. All *right,* all of them? They seemed so.

In effect, the job wound up.

"These rockets—" said Bob Anderson across the room.

"Tell you what I *mean*—"

"Lot of nonsense, all newspaper hysteria, *propaganda*—"

You really couldn't imagine George being cruel. A good husband and father. Only he would go on facetiously calling her *the old lady* to the children, and thinking it funny. The rest of the time he called her *Mother.* Quite an unpleasant habit, implying that she was *nothing else,* and she had spoken to him about it, but he never remembered. *Mother,* he said.

He was getting quite bald, and a little too fat too.

Dear George, really, she ought to feel. A responsible husband and father.

Insensitive, of course. A great many men—a great many *people*—were. Never getting the nuances. But he meant so well.

She'd been a good, accommodating, hardworking wife to him for thirty years.

She wondered how many times she'd finished laying the breakfast table to hear him come thumping downstairs and say heartily, "Well, another day, another dollar!"

Accommodating. If she was quite honest with herself, she must admit that for a number of years now George had bored her terribly. With his Let's see now was it Friday or Saturday, with his endless repetition of irrelevant information, with his Heard a good story about that (the point inevitably a ten-year-old-mentality one).

Good well-meaning George, she thought desperately, please don't tell the story about the Russian private.

Because if you do I think I'll kill you.

"—An upswept hairdo," said Beatrice. "You know. They say it makes you look younger. I keep thinking, though, suppose I had it shingled and didn't like it? It'd take ages for it to grow out."

"I know what you mean," said Judy earnestly.

It just occurred to her, did perhaps to every woman fifty-one years old feel and think these things? Very possibly. It wasn't, heaven knew, that she wanted her youth over again. By her limited experience, lovers (George) and husbands (George) would all be much the same, insensitive and well-meaning. It was just, it seemed a pity there wasn't something *more*. When one was led to expect it.

He would come out of the bathroom and grin at her apologetically and say, "Well, old lady, what about it?" As if that was conducive. In his pink-striped pajamas, and still working that three-tooth bridge back into place. Not that it'd been often the last ten or fifteen years. No. He was a man who *settled down*.

Every single morning, Another day, another dollar.

He earned a decent living for them. He was a good responsible well-meaning husband, so he was. He'd been a good father.

The only thing was, quite literally she felt she simply couldn't bear to hear the story about the Russian private again.

She didn't know much about Russians, she didn't know if it

was a *likely* story or not. She just knew she couldn't stand hearing it all over again.

And anyway, the articles on etiquette said you should make the conversation general.

"George darling," she said, "not that story." In desperation.

There were newspaper stories. Read between the lines. If there hadn't been a gun *available*— She'd never thought it a valid argument. If you were going to kill someone, you'd do it anyway, gun or no. But she rather saw it now, because there was a gun in George's desk—a license, all legal, of course.

"George," she said, "I'll kill you if you tell that story." Because she couldn't bear it again. All the well-worn phrases, the broad tag line. Not possibly could she stand it.

"We just don't *realize*," said George, "how far behind us— Hmm, what'd you say, old lady?"

"You've got to have an absolutely perfect figure," said Judy Anderson. "I said to the clerk—"

They didn't know about people, the ones who wrote about murders. But it was conceivable that they knew a little about crime, because it was quite true, that argument about If there hadn't been a weapon available.

The revolver he kept in his desk, because of sometimes having money belonging to the firm overnight. She thought it was loaded.

"Excuse me," she said politely to Judy and Beatrice. She went into his study and got it from the desk drawer.

Every single solitary day he came down to breakfast and said, Well, another day, another dollar.

"George," she said from the door, "George, if you tell that story again I'll kill you. I really will, George."

He didn't see the revolver. "You're a card, old lady," he said, and went on to the other men, "See, we just don't *realize* how far behind. . . . There was this story I heard, see, seems there was this Russian private—"

She kept her finger on the trigger a long time after he'd stopped twisting and jerking. After somebody had gone to the phone.

She thought, I warned him. God knows I warned him.

CONUNDRUM

ow, Robert Patrick Doyle is about the brightest of the up-and-coming younger officers of plainclothes detectives in the Dublin city police. His mother was English, which gives him some of the perseverance a detective sometimes needs; but there is a saying that all things have the defects of their advantages, and there's no denying at all that the English blood in him deprives Doyle of that extra bit of imagination which is also frequently useful to a detective.

I am his superior officer; I know. I tell you, when I heard this story from him—for this is Doyle's story—I could not bring myself to speak to the man for a week. Called for strong waters I did and just turned my back on him. For all that he'd brought in Tom Devesey *and* the evidence.

Later on when I felt a bit stronger I saw Detective Slade and asked how he felt about it. Not the world's disciplinarian I am, which Slade knows; and he said, "Sir, I coulda killed him, justabout, when he told me. I read a story once, by an American fellow, about a lady—"

"And a tiger," I said. "Yes, my boy. So have I."

"Not," said Slade, "that I'm *superstitious*, sir."

And God knows I hope I'm a rational man, as a superintendent of police has to be, and I'm not superstitious either, a reasonable agnostic with a university education. All I will say, we don't know all about everything yet, queer things happen, and you'll know the classic quote from Shakespeare. More things in heaven and earth.

But this is Doyle's story, and as my old grandfather used to say, may the black curse of Mora fall on— Well, no, now I won't say it, for he's one of my best men indeed. And I will just set it down as it happened.

It was not the first time Bryant and Reed's had been burglarized. Nor I daresay will it be the last: a fashionable jewelers' shop has a natural affinity for burglars. Since their last burglary they'd put on a night watchman (being too penurious to install a modern alarm system)—a poor old fellow not much use at anything but staying awake reading the *Irish Mail* all night. Certainly not much use against Tom Devesey. I will say (and Doyle agreed with me) I don't believe Devesey meant to kill him—just put him out of action. But he struck a little too hard.

We knew it was Devesey about two hours after Bryant's discovered the outrage next morning, for the fool had obligingly left a few prints on the office safe. Well, it's a delicate operation, and gloves are clumsy things. It was only the second time Devesey had tried a safe. Devesey was what the official jargon calls a recidivist. The other name is nuisance—to the public and police. He'd started out with petty theft, graduated to burglary, and to that date had served two sentences for that and one count of assault; he was a man turned violent in drink.

Doyle was put on it, and he took his immediate junior, Slade, and they went hunting. A very good man Doyle is at routine hunting. But sometimes the luck runs contrary. Especially (human nature being the frail thing it is) around the waterfront east in our fair city. The unfortunate fact is, when for several hundred years in this nation the law was foreign, biased, and unjust, a few Irishmen got it firm in their heads that all law is so, and a bare sixty-five years of the opposite hasn't unfixed the notion. There are those who don't like the proximity of constabulary, uniformed or otherwise.

Which is to say that Doyle and his men, cautiously poking

around a couple of waterfront pubs known to be haunts of Devesey's, put up the game early. Devesey they found—one man actually had his hands on him—but Devesey being a big tough young fellow, he got away, leaving behind a plainclothes man with a broken jaw. He got away with the aid of several people of the type aforementioned. That was early the next morning after the burglary. The routine I'll not bore you with; suffice it that Doyle discovered Devesey had got a car—an old Morris it was—and had driven out of Dublin in the general direction of Kildare.

Once Doyle gets a scent he'll never leave it—that's the English in him. He sent out wires to various stations, to be on the watch for the car and the man; but he'd prefer to catch up to Devesey in person, so he took a car—one of our new lot, a big Riley—and Slade, and started off that way himself.

They found the Morris in a ditch at Newbridge, and a local garage owner jumping up and down in a black wrath swearing about car thieves.

"What was stolen?" asked Doyle.

"If ever I get my hands—"

"What car did he take, man? Did you see him?"

"Did I— Mary and Jesus, if I'd seen him d'you think he'd've got off? The Colonel's Jaguar it was, just in for an oil change—"

They went on, casting right and left—slow work—and picked up traces of him in Mullingar, of all places. Of course Doyle had wired all stations of the change in cars from Newbridge. "What in hell's name is he making north for?" said Doyle to Slade.

"The border," said Slade. "Belfast maybe."

"He's going the long way round for that," says Doyle. "But it might be." Once over the border in the Six Counties, he'd be on foreign soil; and it must be admitted it's easy as buying a drink out of hours to get over the border between guard stations. Even with a Jaguar. All those side roads— So Doyle wired up to the Ulster police and to Belfast, and (having his teeth in it by then) drove on.

Meanwhile, of course, messages from here and there came in to Dublin, and anything suggestive was relayed on in Doyle's general direction, in duplicate and triplicate to catch him somewhere. He was caught at Cavan (he'd made north for the border) with the news that the Jaguar had been abandoned at Carrick-on-Shannon, and he sat down and swore. Doyle is a mighty swearer on occasion and Slade listened with respect.

"Now what in the name of all devils in hell is he making northwest for?"

"Confusing his trail," said Slade brightly. "He knows we know who he is and are after him. Maybe he'll double back, sir."

Doyle wired frantic queries to Carrick. Carrick took its own time to answer, but finally wired back that an old Ford station wagon belonging to the local parish school was missing, and had been seen proceeding northwest toward Drumshambo, but not stopped as the observer did not then know it had been stolen.

"Hell's hot fires!" said Doyle, and got the Riley filled up and set out due west. A perseverant man he is. He had left Dublin at ten in the morning, and it was now four in the afternoon and he ninety miles north and west. He was to be farther. He had sent off wires from Cavan, but we all know the northwest counties are provincial, not to say bucolic, and when he got to Carrick they had no news for him. He was hungry by then, and a right he had, so he and Slade had a scratch meal and drove on to Drumshambo, where the local constable said he'd seen the Holy Family School car pass. Roundabout four o'clock it'd've been. He hadn't taken much notice; the father sometimes drove up this way visiting friends.

Doyle swore some more and went on to Drumkeerin. Now, you understand—if you've never been up that way I'll tell you— every mile he was going backward, you could say. That's the loneliest and emptiest part of the country, northwest. No big towns at all this side the border, once you pass Sligo. It's barren open country—little villages, and little farms, and hills, and that's every last damn thing. Good fishing in the lakes, but not many decent hotels; and people living just about the way their great-great-grandkin did—and thinking the same thoughts, by damn. There are police, and telephone wires—in places—but they're not frequent, nor much regarded.

Well, Doyle went on, getting a hint of the Ford in Sligo (from a petrol-station attendant); on up into Leitrim he went to cross the Donegal border by Pettigoe. The Riley was going sweet and kind. Not so Doyle's thoughts. Why was Devesey running up into the barren wilds like this? It made no sense at all. He voiced his doubts to Slade, who said, "Oh, well, sir, these fisherfolk along the coast—you know the reputation they've got for smuggling—he might be figuring to get away by sea, maybe across the border to Derry and take ship for England."

"By God, that's so," said Doyle, struck. "You've got it, and I'm a fool—he'll have the loot on him, sure, jewelry doesn't take up much space. And he'd find a fence in London easy enough. . . . By God, I *am* a fool!" For he'd just remembered something from Records in Dublin. "Devesey's a Donegal man—came from some little place here. He might have a relative or two—or friends—still here."

"Is that so, sir? Then that'll be the reason, all right."

They got to Donegal town about seven o'clock (I said the Riley was going well). Doyle heard that the Donegal police had nothing for him, and sent a wire to Dublin demanding from Records the name of Tom Devesey's native village. He stood Slade a drink while they waited. Back comes the answer, Dunbarra. Very efficient we are in Dublin, all modern methods.

"Hell and damnation!" said Doyle over a map. "Another forty miles north, good! But I'll lay ten English pounds on it, *avic*—it's there he's making for, to some old friend or relation who'll get him over the border to the night mail at Derry for England—and maybe tonight! We'll press on."

They did. Doyle at the wheel, be sure they did! Observe them running downhill at half-past nine, out of the Derryveagh hills, into the village of Dunbarra—a little coastal scattering of fishermen's cottages and one inn. The Green Man, it was called.

At this point I sympathize with Doyle. Indeed I do. The

townsman he is, with a quick sharp city mind, used to all the modern conveniences. He says to Slade, "Be sure he's here somewhere—hidden up, and the stolen Ford too—all we need is local reinforcement to locate him." In they go to the pub and introduce themselves to the landlord.

"A tellyphone?" says the landlord. "Now that's a pity, sir, there's none here at all, you'll have to drive on to Burtonport to find such a thing. The wireless, sir?—what you'll be callin' the tellygraph? Oh, indeed, nothin' o' the sort here at all, at all. The *garda,* you are? Indeed . . ."

I don't blame Doyle at all. A hard and frustrating day he'd had, as you can see, and little food or drink. He said this and that about backward villages that didn't know what century it was; but he was hungry and tired. So he said to Slade, "Look, boy, we'll have a drink and something to eat before we start asking questions." To which Slade was agreeable.

See them then in the one public room, over cold beef sandwiches and whiskey that never paid any tax. Among the thickheaded bucolics, the half of them talking somewhat antique Irish. Which is a habit they have up there; and one damn good thing (in this case) that the damn-fool government insists on teaching it in school down here, as a relic of our glorious past— for Doyle understood it.

"Cahill was all of a shake," so an old granfer by the fire was saying. "It is indeed bad luck to see The O'Derrigan. Took to his heels and ran he did."

"And so would I," said another man, "with no shame."

"But it was not The O'Derrigan's regular hour to ride," says a third man. "Never that early he rides out, but at midnight. I do not believe it was The O'Derrigan at all, but some man on nefarious business."

They sat over their beer and whiskey, young and middle-aged and elderly fishermen, and ruminated, and drank.

The second speaker says, after a while, "Reagan's mare was found running loose. The fence is sound enough."

"Ah!" says another man. "That there motorcar. But who knows what The O'Derrigan might be up to, Mick?"

Now, this conversation roused interest in Doyle, and he went up to them to ask questions. They accepted him very reservedly—the bucolics don't like police much either—but they told him that indeed a motorcar had been found, all alone, just outside the village—run off the road into the sea, only it were low tide and the widow Connell's son had seen it, about dusk. Constable? Oh, aye, Will Brady were constable here, likely he'd been told—or would be sometime.

"And who," asked Doyle (hot on the scent of some friend or relative of Devesey) "is O'Derrigan?"

I ask you to imagine the contempt they turned on him, the incredulity. One by one they said, "You never heard of The O'Derrigan?" and spat on the floor or gave him pitying looks. In the end one venerable patriarch pronounced sentence: "One o' they southron folk as had t' learn the Tongue all new." They are dismally insular, these northerners. "See you, outlander, I tell you. The O'Derrigan, a great chieftain he was about here, a thousand year and more back. When it came his time to die, die he did not—for cause of his greatness. No, not never. Sleeping he is, see you—waiting he is. So the tale does say it—waiting for the time of Ireland's greatest trial and trouble. With his hundred bold brave young champions, he sleeps underground—somewhere about Sliebh Laught—and their tall white war-chargers and silver armor and silver lances and swords all to hand. In a dream like they lie there, until the hour is struck. Between the seawall and Dunvegan Castle, somewhere there—no man can be sure just where—they sleep underground, until the hour they're needed. Then the horn will be blown and the spell wound up—and they will wake and come out, to make Ireland a whole and free nation. So it does tell."

Another man emerged from his beer and added to that, "It do go on to say, The O'Derrigan to be High King of all Ireland—and I won't say I'd not be agreeable, this electing idea it do seem just put all the wrong fellows in to run things."

"Never mind all that," said Doyle impatiently, "that's nonsense! Did you say someone saw a stranger—something about a horse—"

"Every full moon," says the patriarch, nodding slowly.
"Every full moon, at the hour of midnight, so is the charge laid
on The O'Derrigan—a very great and noble chief he is—to
rouse him from his sleep, and come out, and mount his tall
war-horse An Dubh—the Dark One—and ride about his land, to
see how it fares with his people. We do not venture out to see—
it is ill luck—we bide in and let him come, and pass, and see,
alone. His own appointed time he shall know. And no man
knows where the entrance is to that underground cavern—save
by ill luck—for there is no entrance at all, save on the one night
at the one hour. Stories there are of men who have stumbled on
it, yes, my woe! There is a cleft in rocks where no cleft is by
day, and the unlucky one who stumbles and falls there sees of a
sudden a marvelous light—and then that vast vaulted chamber
inside the hill. And all about are the noble warriors, each at the
side of his great white war-charger all clothed in gold armor and
harness—all in a dream trance. And at the head of the hall is
The O'Derrigan, the tall fair war-leader, with his black war-
charger An Dubh—waiting in trance his appointed hour. The
cavern is all lit within by a strange pearly light. It is a place
made for the repose of champions. The chargers are shod with
silver, and silver and gold are the armor and weapons of the
champions, the knights of righteousness. Yes, yes, secret is the
entrance there—but once each full moon it cracks open, and The
O'Derrigan alone, that great chief, comes out to view the world,
to see if his hour is come. It is said that in that vault is a hunting
horn of silver, and when the hour is struck, he will blow upon
it, and all the warriors will waken and come out to win the last
battle for truth and righteousness."

"Oh, for God's *sake*!" cried Doyle impatiently (you may
imagine how he received all this—he had had two years at Dublin
University). "What I'm asking you, man, you said a stranger had
been seen—when and where?"

There was a long pregnant silence. Somebody said, "The
gentleman disbelieves in The O'Derrigan. A townsman, like
some we see now and then. Calling us fools they are. But it is

so—it is so, for all their foolish scorn on it. Haven't there been men saw with their own eyes? There have. Stories there are—my own granfer knew one of them, old Jamesy Barrett. Out hunting a loose foal he was, by dark, and stumbled into that secret cleft—aye, right smack down. My granfer heard him tell it many's the time. And there they were before his eyes, aye so, in that great hall—the hundred sleeping champions each with his war-charger aside him—silver armor and weapons to each—and at the head of the hall there was tall O'Derrigan, bolt upright in a tall carved chair. And the silver horn hanging at his side. All of which did Jamesy Barrett see with his own eyes.''

''Ah! I've heard it. And how, the brave foolish fellow he were, he goes up closer to look, and stumbles accidental over some gear lying at the nearest champion's hand, so the warrior stirs and mutters, *Is it the time yet, is it the hour?* By Jesus, weren't old Jamesy struck with terror! He can only justabout get words past his teeth—No, 'tis not the time, he says—and runs, through miles of wet dark caverns, so he used tell it—until he comes to a place he can climb out to solid earth, and finds himself five miles north up about Sliebh Darra.''

''So I've heard,'' nodded another man. They all looked silent scorn at Doyle and Slade, and then the last speaker drank, coughed, and said, ''Indeed. But of course it is true that it was not midnight when Cahill saw him, riding about the lee side o' the cliff.''

''When?'' demanded Doyle.

''Why, this very dusk, in the mist as the dusk came down. Very shaken up Cahill was, no wonder.''

Doyle dragged Slade off from these paganly superstitious villagers. ''Now mark,'' he said. ''There was something said also about a stolen horse. All right. Devesey's calling damn canny, he knows we're on his trail. He's got in touch with someone here—or is hoping to get in touch—who'll help him away. He got rid of the Ford, or thought he did, and borrowed this horse for a little way, but he's lying up somewhere now. And where easier than some place local superstition makes the natives shy of? It's God's gift to him. And him being from about here, he'd know.''

"So he would,'' agreed Slade.

"So, look. You take the Riley and get on to the nearest telephone and telegraph. Call up reinforcements—he's about here somewhere, I swear, we've only got to hunt. He wouldn't risk a cottage, even with everyone in it friendly—they're too easy searched—he'll be lying up out of the village. We'll need a dozen men to search thoroughly—you go and fetch them up. Meanwhile I'll do some reconnoitering with the local constable.''

And that was a sensible plan, of course. Off Slade went, and Doyle found the constable, Brady. Very reluctant the constable was to have anything to do with him. But he showed Doyle the abandoned car, and it was the stolen Ford, which made Doyle all the keener to get on. I can imagine the scene—Doyle firing questions at that beefy slow-minded yokel, more impatient by the minute. . . .

Well, no, Brady couldn't call to mind any Deveseys about. Might've been some whiles back, he couldn't just say certain sure. Couldn't call to mind any mention of the name roundabout. A burglar was it, and him killing a man too? Oh, God save us, none in Dunbarra'd be knowing one like that, all honest folk they were here—

"Yes, well, never mind that now,'' said Doyle. They could find out later what man was maybe helping Devesey. The main thing now was to get Devesey; it might be his benefactor was planning to help him away on tonight's tide. There was no time to be lost. He impressed this on the constable. "You know the country—are there any caves or places like that he might be hiding?''

"Oh, ah,'' said Brady, "plenty o' caves in the cliffs. Clefts there be all along. And up in the hills too. And the ruins o' the castle— But whyfor should this burglar from Dublin—''

"I've *told* you—never mind! This place where that ghost or whatever it is is supposed to be—where is it? I think that might be the likeliest spot.'' For indeed Devesey knew they were close behind him, and even for six hours or so would choose the safest possible hiding place.

"Oh, you don't want to be going up there, sir," said Brady, horrified.

"Damn it, I do, that's what I'm telling you! How do I get there?"

" 'Tis the first night o' full moon," said Brady. "Very ill luck it is to see The O'Derrigan. You don't want to be doing that."

"Oh, the hell with your O'Derrigan! You and I are going up there after Devesey, for I'll swear it's somewhere about there he's hid. Where—"

"Oh, indeed, no, sir!" said the constable, backing away. "I'll not be doing no such thing—"

"Hell and devils take you!" says Doyle. "Call yourself a policeman—damn' superstitious idiot! Wouldn't the bastard come to a place like this! I need you to guide me, damn it— I can take Devesey alone once I find him, damn lot of use you'd be— and you're coming if I have to hold a gun on you!"

"Oh, now, indeed, sir—" Brady was looking ready to cry. But Doyle, as indicated, is a very determined man, and though it nearly came to gunpoint, in the end he dragged Brady along with him. He charged the landlord with a message for Slade, when he got back from Burtonport with more constabulary, to let him know where he was so they could follow; and he set out with Brady pointing the way, and making sounds of distress every step. Some of these villages, no denying they're backward in their ways.

They went on foot, though Brady said there was a bicycle track partway up. A nice fool he'd look, thought Doyle, chasing Devesey on a bicycle. He put his gun in the outside pocket of his trench coat, nice and convenient, and urged speed. Now he thought, it seemed unlikely that Devesey hoped to get away tonight, if all these ignorant peasants were so terrified to venture out at full moon; or maybe one of them wasn't? But his blood was up then and the sooner he laid hands on Devesey the happier he'd be.

The moon wasn't up yet, and it was bitter cold but clear; the sea wind bit through his tweeds and trench coat. They climbed up through thin trees, north from the village, and came out on a bare open cliff. The constable began moaning that just along here was where The O'Derrigan came riding. "Shut up!" said Doyle. "Did you not say midnight? It's not eleven yet." This seemed to cheer Brady up a bit, and he came on with better will.

They rounded a rocky headland and Doyle saw, about half a mile ahead, ruins of some kind towering up against the sky. "That'll be the castle," said Brady. Doyle reckoned they were a couple of miles out of the village.

"Very good," he says. "Now, what convenient hiding places are there around here, where a man might lie up a day or two?"

"Oh, indeed I couldn't say," said Brady. Doyle could have brained him. "Acourse there's liddle caves like in the cliff—"

"Ah, that sounds promising—"

"But they do all be covered at high tide, and he'd surely be drowned," said Brady brightly. Doyle exercised patience and went on asking. "Well, there's the low ground behint the castle. Like a liddle deep gorge it is, and there's liddle holes either side in the rock, but it wouldn't be just so comfortable a place—"

"He'll not be thinking about that. Lead on, we'll try there first."

Behind the stone ruins, the cliff divided sharply and made a narrow little cleft, with steep sides about twenty feet deep. Doyle sent Brady to the opposite side while he took this; they both had torches. Brady objected. He said it must be past eleven now indeed, they'd not be finding a man all in the dark, and better to stay together— "For the love of God!" said Doyle. "Do what you're told, man! The moon's coming up."

Brady said in faith he had noticed it. It didn't seem to make him any happier. But he followed Doyle, puffing, down into the little gorge. The moon was a great help: a bright white light sliding over the terrain.

Well, to cut a long story short, Devesey wasn't in any of the small caves in that gorge, and next Doyle thought of the ruins of the castle above—several walls still standing, and piles of stones all about, a good place to lie hidden. He dragged an increasingly reluctant and uneasy Brady up there. And flushed his quarry almost at once, flashing his torch around— Devesey it was, just sliding round a corner of the wall. Doyle called on him to stand, tugging at his gun. Devesey ignored that and ran like a hare, with Doyle after him. Out on the open headland Devesey fled, and Doyle fired once over his head and then at his legs, but missed him. Devesey swerved left to rougher country, running toward a belt of trees higher up where he might lose himself—but Doyle was hard after him. He was in better condition than Devesey, and began to gain on him. Everything was clear almost as day now, under the full moon, only without color—black rising hills and rocks, sparse moor growth underfoot, empty land all about, black trees ahead up the hill. Doyle pounded on, gaining, after the black fleeing figure ahead with the bag jouncing on its shoulder.

Have I said that he had been a notable football man at college? It was his old tackle he made on Devesey at the last, and the two of them came down sudden and hard on hard ground, and rolled. Down a sudden sheer drop they rolled, and Doyle found himself on top of Devesey at the bottom of what felt like a narrowish hole in the ground. He shook his head, sat up, and discovered that Devesey was clean out. But for all that, he knotted his belt round Devesey's wrists and went over him for a gun—which he pocketed.

And he'd misjudged Brady, for here he came pounding up valiantly and calling. "It's O.K.," called Doyle, "I've got him, but we'll need help to get him out of this crevasse or whatever it is. A rope or something. He's dead out." The little chasm was only about fifteen feet deep, but Devesey was a big man. "You chase on back and get help—he's safe enough here. But hurry!"

Brady didn't like it, but they couldn't get Devesey up any other way. He went off, and Doyle sat down beside Devesey and lit a cigarette, feeling very pleased with himself. He hoped Brady would have the nerve to come back—whether any others did or not—to rescue him. These damned backward superstitious yokels.

But what the hell, he had Devesey. He flashed his torch around the little cleft idly; it was like a mine shaft, and at one side was a dark vertical crack in the rock wall.

He had finished that cigarette and two more before sounds approached him. Slade and reinforcements, by the voices. Good. They lowered a rope and hauled up Devesey, still out, and his bag of loot.

"Just a minute, sir, we'll have you up."

"Right," said Doyle. And just at that moment—so he told me—he heard a very curious sound to hear in his situation. He heard an iron-shod hoof stamp once on stone, and it came from that little cleft in the rock. Very clear he heard it. He turned quickly, to face that cleft, and it was not dark anymore. It was emitting a strange, pearly, misty light that seemed to wax and wane. Or that was the effect. And he heard, quite loud, a jingling that was like to the sound of horse-harness shaking as the horse moved its head, and he heard something that was very distinctly the stamp of a booted foot on rock, from inside that cleft.

"Here's the rope, sir," called Slade.

So Doyle felt for it and got his arm through the sling and called up, "Carry on," and was hauled out. Moonlight, he said to himself, plays queer tricks, and natural noises echo in small spaces.

And so we'll never know—that's the pure crying pity of it—we'll never know for certain. Not, you understand, that I'm at all a superstitious man. No, indeed. But—thanks, yes, I'll have another drink indeed—but just out of curiosity, you know— Yes.

But then Doyle, as I said, is half English. Which puts too much reason in him. One of my best men—a rising man in his job—but it's a handicap to him, so it is.

NEED-FIRE

——When Marriott came into the hut Wesley gave him a look and a nod, said, "The boys are creating about the Sunday work again—want to reconsider it?"

"No," answered Marriott shortly. "They're getting paid, aren't they?"

"Well," said Wesley. And after a moment, "You're not looking up to par, Adam. What's all the rush over this job? If there's anything under your mound it'll still be there next month."

"It's there," said Marriott. He sat down at his table, stared at the fragment of bronze on the blotter: the one fragment they'd dug out in three weeks. "I want to see it. You've got to take advantage of the weather, you know that as well as I do. This damned English weather—the finest spring since the war, and it might be the wettest summer."

"All right," said Wesley. "We're getting paid. After a fashion. You needn't kill yourself at it, that's all." He gave Marriott another look, his mouth tight. "And if you don't mind my saying it, you'd do better not to mix your love life with business. Half what's the matter with you. Dividing energy." Wesley was something of a Puritan.

"And you'd do better to mind your own damned business," said Marriott without heat. He turned the bronze over in his fingers. Part of a spearhead, it looked like. The oldness of it was

· 175

warmth in his hand. He thought Wes was a damned prig, though they had been friends: proximity. Wesley had nothing to do with Sheila. Wanted something to do with her maybe? Or just disapproval on general principles. He wrenched his mind away from Wesley and Sheila and put it firmly on the dig.

All these damned people, a whole country, sitting smug on top of an archaeologist's buried treasure. There were places in the world you could dig and find without disturbing a dog. The waste places. Not here. God, what there probably was under England, under France, under Europe, and never to be found. This little England: government took a dim view of digging up arable land on the chance of finding some old pottery and a few spearheads. You couldn't take up a high street or make a hole in the mayor's back garden. Towns every mile. Sitting smug and snug on history. He swore in a whisper at the bronze, and laughed shortly. Why couldn't he specialize in some field where the material was available? Never mind: the problem came with the job.

Well, he'd persuaded the Institute into this dig, and they'd had really less trouble than he expected in getting permission. Nonarable, of course, marshy land; and Nugent would make enough out of letting them dig to have it reclaimed next year. It was one of the hundred spots on Marriott's map of the British Isles: one of the places knowledge, hope, and hunch marked: *try here*. He had prowled round this place several months, planning the dig. Now he was anxious to get on with it, find something or nothing and have it done. And get away: from Sheila? Yes; no. Damn it, why did she have to stay with him, leechlike? Not important; only another woman. It was not his fault if— Remnants of damned silly Victorian notions instilled in the growing boy.

He got up abruptly and went out, away from Wesley's eyes, down to the dig. Sheila was her own problem: let her solve it. She was distracting him from this dig, Wes was too damned right about that, he conceded. Shouldn't have got mixed up with her at all. A bit different from the Glorias and Dianas, the stupid careless ones, the easy give-and-take ones. But it was her own affair. And his. Wes needn't be so damned righteous.

The men were spading up damp soil leisurely, efficient; Bagshot nodded at his greeting. Bagshot and his crew were resentful all right, mild but stubborn, over the way he was shoving at them to finish the job. Weather still holding—he scanned the sky—and the way things looked they were getting down to the important level. He stood silent at Bagshot's side, watching the black wet earth as it came up.

It was a burial dun, he knew: he felt. The barrow of earth and stones originally raised would have sunk in the passing of centuries, in this marshy ground. Only suggestion of outline remaining. They had found the bronze fragment yesterday; today, tomorrow, other fragments—if they were lucky. Maybe the man, or part of him, the priest or warrior buried here: more valuable, the weapons and amulets buried with him, the trappings of his time and place—Britain of the Druids.

He had a damnable headache. If only he could get a good night's sleep. Two nights, three, and no sleep. He was not overworking; that was nonsense. Old Foster: "That's your biggest fault, my boy. Rush at these things. You can't do it. Take it a bit easier." And: "It's your dig, in a manner of speaking, but if you aren't feeling quite the thing Wesley can handle it alone, you know. You're looking a bit run-down."

He heard his annoyed, defensive reply: "I'm quite all right, sir. The last couple of summers in Arabia got at me, rather, but this isn't anything like a hard job—in England." It wasn't. Lovely spring it was; he'd had some doubts himself about starting as early as the first of April, but the weather had held. If only he could get a night's unbroken sleep. Damned fool to get involved with a woman now.

Never mind: that stuff he'd got from the chemist in the village would help. Take some tonight.

Funny how indifferent they were in the village. He remembered old Mackenzie telling—grand old boy Mackenzie—in his time, it hadn't been unusual for country people to resent digging. The feeling persisted, vague but obstinate, over centuries of time, about the sacred places: sanctity become superstition. Up to this century, places where village folk kept up rituals tracing back to the Druids—if they only knew it. Immemorial custom: they didn't know why or whence. They wouldn't believe when they rolled a wheel downhill on Midsummer Day, lit the fires, named the last sheaf gathered, chose a mock king-fool—tradition, excuse for a little innocent merrymaking and a day off from work—that they were paying lip service to the oldest gods, the sun god and the gods of the wood: and once there had been blood spilled at these festivals. You didn't see that much now. A few isolated places, perhaps. The young people got away, there were magazines, films, more education. They weren't interested.

The landlord at the pub about expressed it. "What you chaps doing up by Nugent's old hill field?" And when Marriott explained, "Oh, aye—Druids and that. I heard of them." A bit amused that a grown man should spend his time digging after Druids. "There was some folk last year over other side of the county looking after Romans."

"This was a long time before the Romans," said Marriott. He wondered, fancifully, if the old gods were angry at neglect. While people went through their rituals, however ignorant of the ritual significance, they had some service paid, some lingering respect. Now no one feared them or propitiated them at all anymore, were they restive and jealous? Now that the need-fires were not made, the blood not shed? Now that the fearsome Pookah was turned to harmless Puck of mere mischief, and Pan was no link with panic, and Lugh's name dead on the tongues of men?

"There you are," said Bagshot. In spite of their small resentment at Marriott the men sounded pleased; it was always nice to know you weren't digging just for the exercise. Wesley heard the shouts and came down from the hut.

"For God's sake be careful," said Marriott. They poked

around in the last few spadefuls brought up before the circlet of bronze. "We'll put everything through the sieve from now on. You never know." It was an amulet—decoration? Talisman? That broken edge might have been a hole for a neck chain. Circle: symbol of the sun, and remnants of a rude design maybe when it was cleaned up. So probably the grave of a priest and not a warrior. He put it away in a little canvas bag; they set to work with their hands, the sieves. In the next three hours they found another spearhead, a squat worked-stone fragment that was part of a figure, and a whole breast amulet that might have designs graved on the surface, but it would need much cleaning to uncover them, and delicate handling.

Marriott felt fine about it when they knocked off. He was even liking Wesley again as they drove back to the village together. Wes suggested darts after dinner—they were both staying at the pub; Marriott said, "Sorry, I've got a date."

"Taking the car?" asked Wesley. And at the affirmative his mouth tightened and he said softly, "I know it's none of my business, Adam, but you're seven kinds of a damned fool."

"Because I don't know a nice girl when I meet one? Be your age, man." He heard the defensive note in his own voice; he took the turn into the village too sharp and fast. "The original species is extinct."

Wesley said nothing to that, but his expression spoke for him; might as well have said it, and maybe added, It's the Institute's car. Well, all right, he could admit to himself it was a mistake— Sheila. Only you took what was offered: or what was nearest. After Fran you knew a lot too much to want it legal again: you'd been in that trap. But there was just enough sentimentality left that you couldn't get away from a little guilt about Sheila, which was after all nonsense because it was her own choice and responsibility. Only—she wasn't a Gloria or Diana from behind the bar or the cinema ticket window.

For one thing she liked to talk, intelligent talk, which felt odd with a woman now. She asked about the dig, what they'd found;

she was interested. He felt her intelligence a presence, an eye on him in the intimate dark—obscurely embarrassed by it—he cared nothing for her mind or character, only her warm mouth and arms and the rest of Sheila as female, only a warmth to keep the cold out but—impersonal. And was embarrassed at his embarrassment; he lit cigarettes for them, talked, answered her questions.

"It's really the one thing you love, isn't it, Adam?" she said. "The one thing that stays, with you."

"Love, lovely? I wouldn't say—"

"Oh, don't be clever," she said. "Don't, what's the American phrase, give me a line. We've never done that. At least you've been honest with me." She was staying with an aunt, on a three months' rest after a bad bout of flu; she'd been a secretary in town, but wasn't sure they'd hold her job; she did no complaining about that, it was how things were. They had met a couple of months ago when he came down to plan the dig. "You never pretended to be serious, I can't say you deceived me."

"No." Better finish with Sheila. You didn't have to explain, have these analytical postmortems, with the other kind. "I knew we'd come to this," he said. "It always does with—"

"With my sort. Say it. Nice girls."

"All right," he said irritably. "You want it both ways—enjoy the freedom and push the responsibility off on the man. Always the same story."

She moved sharply and sighed. "You can't put us all into a couple of classifications, like filing letters. . . . You know there was never anyone else, for me, before."

"I know that. Your own business. Nobody forced you."

"No. It's all right, Adam. It's not me, but you. You're— thinking all wrong about—things. I know your wife made you feel bitter—but—we're not all like that."

"Does it matter to you how I feel?"

"No—I suppose not. I'm just sorry," she said quietly. "And I'm not expecting anything. . . . Maybe you'd better take me back now."

For once he was glad to be away from her. The headache was

a steady hammer behind his eyes. In his bedroom at the inn he stood at the window to take his sedative tablet, grimaced at the tepid water; he could see across the fields the dim outline of his mound against the night sky.

They always made their rituals on hills and rises, and lit their fires in those places, and buried their important dead. Nearer the sun, the giver of life.

The chemist had not wanted to fill the prescription. "Have this recent, sir?" Marriott lied and said yes. He'd had it nearly two years; he'd got it from the surgeon in New York when he had that infected molar out. Never had it made up because he'd left in a hurry next day and the pain hadn't been as bad as he'd expected. It was just a sedative, stronger than anything you could buy off the shelf, that was all.

"You want to be careful with it, sir," the chemist said. "It's a newish combination to me, and pretty strong. You don't want to use much."

"Yes, that's all right, thanks." All he wanted was a little something to help him sleep. Everything went to circling round his mind, tight and concentric, and if he did manage to sleep a bit it did him no good, he woke feeling like death. It was a small bottle the chemist gave him—a dozen tablets, and he'd printed plainly on the label: *one only to be taken.*

Have a good night's sleep tonight, better tomorrow—put in a good day's work—Sheila again Wednesday night, and better make that the last. A clean break. She was too interested. If he wanted to admit it, so was he. Not ever again the trap.

He went to sleep at once, but woke in the night with the quick-vanished memory of bad dreams, and lay with gradually slowing heart; groped presently for his watch. It was half-past three. He did not sleep again. That chemist couldn't have known what he was talking about; the stuff wouldn't give him a whole night's rest. When you were overtired, they said, sedatives sometimes took little effect. It wasn't so much overwork, though there'd been work enough in Arabia the last three seasons. Whole miserable squalid business with Fran, the debts—mostly hers—money; going round and round the bottom of his mind while he tried to put the top part on work. Not all like that, she said. Maybe not; he wasn't taking a chance on it. Why the hell couldn't he stop thinking of that? All over now. And he still had his headache.

They worked all Tuesday without finding anything. Marriott went up to his room after dinner, undressed, took two of the tablets and went to bed. He slept easily, instantly, and slept the night through; but he did not feel rested in the morning; he had dreamed, vividly, perhaps frighteningly, but could not remember his dreams: only a vague uneasiness held him.

That day they found the man.

Not much of him: enough to tell he'd been there. Bones, another breastplate, a piece of a bronze armband.

It was not an important dig; nothing spectacular was going to come out of it, nothing they hadn't known before. But Marriott always knew more excitement for a dig in his homeplace, the smallest fragment taken from this soil. There was so little, comparatively, they had out of England. It was his field. Logical or illogical, he felt a kind of kinship with those bones. Three, four thousand years?—three at least—lying there, the priest who had made the sacrifices and chanted the spells and in his turn been sacrificed . . . King of the Wood.

He was keyed up, he wanted to talk about it. Almost he forgot he was talking to Sheila; and she listened, interested. "King of the Wood?"

"The priest. It was a primitive society, you know—he had to defend himself against rivals. One day he'd be killed and there was a new priest."

"They were sunworshipers—I remember."

"All primitive people are. But there were many other gods too—all your old gods are the same, only they had different names over Europe, Asia . . . their three important festivals were all based on the sun calendar. Midsummer Day—the summer solstice. The Church never invented a real excuse to take that over— Christmas is the winter solstice, of course. Easier for them to make the transition with festivals at the same time." He laughed suddenly. "That's an omen—we're only three days off Beltane . . . the spring festival, the one the Church substituted Easter for."

"They made sacrifices," she said. She sounded a little tired and troubled; he did not hear it.

"Oh, yes. You used to see remnants of the ceremony, late as the last century. They put out all their fire the night before—so the fire they made, the bone-fires on Beltane, were really need-fires— *tein-eigin*. There was a maiden sacrificed, or a man, to Bel. Names," he said. "That's the great god Baal of the Old Testament, turned into Beelzebub in Christianity," and remembered he had not yet kissed her. She moved away from him. He was annoyed at her and at himself. "Sorry to bore you," he said sharply.

"You haven't. Only—it's no good, Adam. There's no sense getting in any deeper—me, I mean. I thought—it doesn't matter what I thought. I'm going back to London next week, and—we'd better just forget the whole thing."

"That suits me," said Marriott. "Just fine." Familiar, strangely new, the odd impulse to apologize to her. She was silent awhile at his side as he drove, and then spoke in a thin voice.

"You've made quite a study of—all that. You know something, Adam?—you've got back to those people. Somehow. It's a queer way to think of it, but— Primitive society, you said. They never knew any of the civilized feelings—tenderness and sympathy. Love. What's called empathy. Did they? And you've deliberately turned your back to forget those things."

"Now you're going feminine on me all right," he said amusedly.

"That's what you've done. I thought maybe I could help. If you ever think—I still can—I would try." And when he let her out at the house she put a hand on his arm and said gently, "We're not all like her, you know. Really."

"Luck, Sheila," he said, brittle, and didn't hesitate to see her in. Better have it dead and done. Once a fool always a fool. If he'd said what he wanted to say—but you couldn't know. They all seemed like that—until you knew. Then it was too late, you were in the trap.

He hadn't been rid of the headache for a week, dull, persistent. He took two tablets that night. But he did not sleep; he lay wide awake, and vivid flashes lit the darkness behind his eyes, poundings of the hammer in his head—Thor's hammer—that turned to red visions' half-dream though he did not sleep. He saw the man whose bones they had uncovered; the man was tall and lean and his eyes were mad. He danced by a fire and drew the knife across the black cock's throat and the blood jutted crimson. He saw the lightning on the hill, the gods angered for it was but a little cock—the knife at the throat of the bull, and the stallion, and then the naked maiden with flowers in her hair, and the lake of crimson blood.

They didn't go any deeper that day. They went on sieving the earth they had dug up, carefully, for more bones, other fragments. They found bones, but not human. "Hare or something," diagnosed Wesley. "Probably later period. Shift of rock worked it down." Marriott was not, for some reason, conscious of any tiredness now; he felt keyed to alertness still. He sat in the hut working on the biggest bronze fragment; in six hours he got most of the top crust of age from it, started to polish carefully. There was what looked like a faint pattern, the conventional circle and rays, showing.

"Are you feeling all right, Adam?" asked Wesley over dinner.

"Fine, just fine."

"Well, you don't look it," said the other man bluntly. "You look fagged to death."

"I'll turn in early. I'm all right." But he beat Wes at two games of darts first, for two rounds of drinks. Belatedly cautious, he hesitated over the tablets. Perhaps one would be enough to give him sleep now, after this long time without. He took one, and lay awake. At two in the morning he got up and took another, and slept until dawn, fitfully.

That day the weather broke and it poured. It didn't matter; everything was under cover in the hut, and they'd put up a rude canvas canopy over the mound. Wesley took the day off and went up to town to see Foster. Marriott sat in the hut working on the bronze. It was an extraordinarily nice piece, or would be when he'd got it cleaned up properly. He thought the headache was not from insomnia at all, but the other way round: it was his eyes. Close work: maybe he should see somebody about it when he was back in town. Maybe he shouldn't take chances, go up now, soon. Eyestrain could play tricks.

Sheila was going to London in a few days. He was finished with Sheila.

Was already playing tricks. The circle design on the bronze amulet widened slowly as he bent to it, and surely there'd been no color on it before—no crimson dye . . . they had no dye for crimson, that was Phoenician. No. He blinked, shook his head: the bronze was just as it had been. Eyes, certainly. He stopped work, lit a cigarette.

"We'll want a crate for that?" Bagshot jerked his head at the canvas bag beside the table.

"Better—they're brittle. The medicos will want a look at him before he's put in a glass case." Marriott flipped back the canvas, touched the half shell of brown-veined bone. "Maybe we should have sent him back to town with Wes. . . ." He laughed and Bagshot looked at him sharply. "Don't want him getting up to tricks tomorrow night, do we? It's Beltane. Very important day to this old chap, Bert." Bagshot laid down his bit of rag and bronze. "Maybe we shouldn't have dug him out until after Beltane," said Marriott in a half-whisper to himself. "Did you ever stop to think, those old gods must be feeling neglected these days. This fellow—they were important to him, you know. He'd want to do what he thought—should be done—for them."

"Yes?" said Bagshot. "I reckon he's past it now, Mr.

Marriott. You been working like a slave the last couple weeks, why don't you knock off and get some rest like?''

"I think I will." Marriott yawned. He recognized his own symptoms, from certain days of the war: this abnormal alertness false, from starvation for rest; yes. A mental weariness now. But it came to the same thing, sedatives or not: when you'd gone just so long, you would sleep. Change of routine sometimes helped. He walked to the village through the rain, hardly feeling it, forcing himself to walk briskly. He had no hunger at all, but got down a small portion of what he was offered, had a large hot whiskey and went up to bed before nine. The headache was only a dull memory above his eyes.

He never knew if he slept or not, but it was a bad night. Very bad. He took two tablets, but he did not think he slept. He went through it all again, with Fran, every moment of it from the day they met. He went back to all the Glorias and Dianas, too. Every now and then Sheila came and whispered in his ear, Not all like that, not all.

She said, You turned your back. You tried to forget all the tender part, the real warmth there is. You said it is only fox fire. Like your little cold flames of desire for women since. She said, Like those old ones who were cruel children in an old world, un-understanding of love—only bodies. You need a better fire than that, Adam, to warm your soul.

The false alertness had worn away that morning and he was deathly tired, his mind slow; it was an effort to shave, dress. It was the first of May, it was Beltane. This night was that called Walpurgis across the Channel in Europe. The rain had stopped, but the sky was gray and low. He knew he would be good for little at any work, but he could not sleep either, or stay here alone any longer.

Wesley took one look at him and said, "You're not well and you know it. You'd better pack up and go home, see a doctor. Sleeping?"

"Not much. I ought to sleep tonight." He must sleep tonight.

He was irritated at Wesley's concern; Wes thinking of last year in the desert when he'd had a go of this before. Cured itself that time—go without sleep long enough, you'd sleep eventually. Tonight.

"Taking anything?"

"Yes . . . none of your damned business."

"All right," said Wes mildly. "Look here, Adam. You're not fit, you need a rest. Foster wants to see this stuff, suppose you drive up with it tomorrow—see a doctor and stay home for a bit. I can carry on here."

"All right," said Marriott. "I'll do that then. . . . Where's home?" He pressed his eyes; the headache had come back full force. Home, he thought: I have none. Easy tears starting of weakness, hot, and he wanted her warm arms and softness that was home *and the trap and the trap.*

"You'd better go back to bed," said Wes.

"No. I'm all right for today. Tonight I'll sleep." Tonight he must sleep.

He was afraid not to sleep. Now there was the lightheadedness, the sensation of being not quite here or there, a disorientation in time. He analyzed his own state with deliberate effort, pleased that his upper mind still functioned clear. Like being, he thought, just a little tight—the need to be careful with sudden movement, the need for attention to details and details with importance just a little larger than life. But he would be all right if only he could sleep. Only a little.

He explained that to Wesley, carefully, and Wes nodded in agreement. Wes said something in return that did not penetrate, and then he was standing at the bureau in the dim inn bedroom, and he had undressed though he'd no memory of that, and the little bottle was in his hand. He was afraid not to sleep, not another night like the last. You want to be careful with it, sir, said the chemist; that was what Wes said, something about being careful. But the chemist had been wrong; but he ought to take care all the same. Two hadn't been enough, and he must be sure of sleep.

He took three, carefully, put the bottle back on the bureau recapped, opened the window and got into bed. Gray light came in the window once the sudden dark dissolved, not moon for the night was lowering but the light promising summer-long twilights to come. Lying in the bed he could just see the outline of bureau, chair, table, and the humped shape of box inside canvas bag where he'd put it ready to start in the morning. All bedded down in wrappings of cotton and odd what care they took with what had lain careless deep in black earth three thousand years. Tomorrow. All right to drive? If he could sleep. Take it easy. It's the Institute's car, said Wes. Yes, I know, all right.

The light was growing stronger, perhaps the moon had come through. It concentrated circling on the outline of box in bag.

It was not, of course, the moon. It was the fires. Full dark, and they were kindling the fires on every hill. They were making the rituals for the sacrifice, and lighting the way for the gods to see. He thought, I should get up and go out and watch, but the keen academic interest was yet not strong enough to raise his body, set it in movement, and he lay supine. In just a moment, he thought, I will make the effort, I will get up and look. It is Beltane, they are lighting the Beltane fires and I should watch, make note of the ritual. He made a tremendous effort to sit up, his body heavy as lead, as iron, as bronze.

Come, said the man. It is time, we must go. He looked, turning his head with slow difficulty, and the man had risen out of the wrappings and the box, and stood beside the bed, a tall man, lean and dark, and his eyes glowed mad. Come. It is time, you must see the ritual.

Help me, said Marriott, yes, I must see.

Come then. It is easy, come, try.

He rose from the bed and was light and joyous and saw the fires from the window, burning disciplined on every eminence of ground into the distance. He went out free and strong again to them, the man at his side. There were trees where he remembered road, and the grass was tall underfoot and wet against his bare legs.

They will not care that I watch? he said, and the man laughed high. The ritual is for you, without you is no dance, no fire, no spell. Come.

He felt that he was naked and should return for his clothes, the air chill on flesh, the grass wet on his ankles, but the thought passed vague across his mind and was gone. He ran, he skimmed the ground light and swift, and the man ran at his side laughing, tall naked man flashing white in the dark up to the fires.

They had begun the dancing about the fires, all white, so white and loud and leaping with the flames to heaven, and singing. The fires were singing with them and the flowers in the girls' hair and the oak sang loudest from the heart of the fires, a thousand thousand fires on every hill. He danced and sang with them and it was a joyous thing.

O look, cried the man, see, they are coming, they are here, them we do honor this night! Look, pay homage! And all the people cried, Do homage, they are come, they give goodwill unto us that we worship them!

O Lugh, he shouted, great Lugh the light-giver, giver of life! All your images, all your names, show us favor of your countenance O Lugh O Baal O Ra the mighty! Mithras god of the morning, see and smile that we do you honor and Dharmè of far Bengal and Indra and Huitzilapochtli of the fierce mountains and Ollthair and Horus and Seb, come, come near and watch! The old ones are remembered again, you old and mighty ones jealous and lonely.

He had never been weary to the bone, his mind and heart never stronger, and he sang with the fire and shouted for joy.

O come you all, sang the man, and they came and gathered hungry and tall as the sky. O Lugh of the Celts come, the eternal light-giver, and Ra and Baal and Tammuz of the Persias and Vishnu come Moloch of the greedy bloody hands thou Thoth come thou Ghansyam Dea of the Gond, Baldur come, see, thou Prussian Waizganthos the bloody come! They come and gather, see and worship. Ammon grant us Anubis have mercy upon us Quetzalcoatl take the sacrifice and be glad, thou Shamach of

Babylon. Tiw, come hence, Wodan, Samain of the women look on us Donar rejoice now Astaroth hear O Grannus be glad we remember! Take thou the sacrifice and be glad O Siva O Typhon O Odin O Mars Silvanus! Eat and drink of the sacrifice O Seb O Perun O Gouri O Apollo O Zytniamatka O Keremet!

The sacrifice the sacrifice, he shouted with the rest, and the gods surged hungry about hands hard on his body and the knife flashed in the hand of the priest *But you are the sacrifice you.* Fear hammering hot not the knife not the knife and the mad eyes too close the Beltane sacrifice not with the knife no the fires the bone-fires blazing on the hills, O Baal see and hear and take and be glad.

Fear forgot and he leaped beside the fire and through the fire crying on the god and it was not fire. It was cold and death, cold and unburning and would not consume him. The god would be angry without sacrifice and it would not burn. The oak cried in a cold voice yet he was whole white leaping in the fire that blazed and consumed not and the god thundered in anger and all were crying his name in rage that he did not burn Marriott Marriott Adam Marriott thou fool this night is thy soul and the fire was cold and he wept aloud for the sacrifice could not be made Marriott O Marriott come but the fire was too cold to burn heart of oak of oak and no use no good no worth no truth at all. Eyes mad too large very close must use the knife then mad eyes too large and gleaming and.

"That's the boy," said the voice behind the round gold-bows of spectacles, "that's the boy. Come on, now, come up." Sounded pleased.

Marriott said clear, "Sacrifice must be made."

"And you very nearly made it," said the spectacles cordially. "If you hadn't a heart like an ox . . . right, he'll do now. Another ten ccs in half an hour."

"But too cold," he said.

"Good, he felt that."

□   □   □

It was all very white and bright. Foul taste. Too cold. Too hot. Burning in arms and legs. And his name.

He turned his head, an immense effort, and saw Wesley at an odd angle. Above, looking down. "Well," said Wesley with a tight grin. "Taking notice at last, are you? It's about time. You damned fool, Adam."

He thought all Wes had done lately was call him a damned fool. He said, "You go to hell."

"Thought I'd never hear you say that again. Or anything. You've given us a lively time with your little bottle. I hope you didn't mean to."

"Go to hell," he said again in a whisper, and, "Sheila."

"All right," said Wesley.

He woke, and slept, and woke, and she was there. "Adam . . . you're awake? Mr. Wesley said—you asked—"

Not properly awake. Chemist must have been right after all. It was great effort to get a hand from under the blankets but then hers was there to meet it warm. "Sheila," he said contentedly.

"Yes—if there's anything—?" Hesitant; stiff. But he could not say it all now, he was simply too tired, and she would go away and never know. There was so much to explain and he could not. Desperate, he tried to tighten his grasp on her hand. She was leaning closer.

"Fox fire," he managed it, hearing it mumbled, impatient with his tired mind. "Sorry—they say—better tomorrow. Then—tell you. Sheila. Please."

"Yes, Adam."

He said more strongly, "I was through the fire and it was cold. You were right. Don't leave me."

"No," she said gently. "I won't leave you. I'm right here."

But not yet quite sure, he could not let go of the warm hand reaching down to him through the spaces of dark.

THE PRACTICAL JOKE

I will admit it was a silly thing to do. But you know the atmosphere in a group of friends enjoying themselves, when everybody's had several drinks. I don't mean any of us was tight. Just relaxed and easy. In the ordinary way, too, everybody there was a rational sort and not given to practical joking, that most obnoxious of minor cruelties. Bob and Ruth are a writing team—juveniles—and Ruth does their charming illustrations; Kenny is a commercial artist, his wife, Pat, is intelligent, Neville is a well-known photographer, and if I am a crime-novelist it's a purely commercial venture. All responsible people, you see, and all moderately successful—so it isn't a question of our envying Griffiths.

But we all knew him; and liked him. Yes, I can say that. There was no malicious intent. Griffiths never had any sense of humor; that's the worst anyone can say of him. He and Bob and Kenny and I had been at the same school, and Griffiths was always like that. When you get a Welshman without a sense of humor he can be grim: so damned earnest. But Jevon Griffiths is intelligent, kind, clean, honest and a good talker, and most people like him well enough. He has a private income, enough to let him amuse himself writing the kind of thing he wants to. This was just after he had published *Nemesis of Nonsense,* and everyone was a bit surprised it was having such a good sale. Perhaps it was a sign of the times—more people appreciating pure cynicism. I expect you remember the book. He had covered all the superstitions, as he called them—from witchcraft to wolf-children to ghosts and poltergeists and apparitions—and methodically, dispassionately dissected and destroyed them—to his satisfaction anyway. As a lot of them deserve; don't mistake me, broken mirrors and black cats hold no terror for me. He'd made a good job of the book; its cool analytical style was effective, and even the chapter on religions was not as offensive as it might have been. He was an agnostic, of course—a practising sincere agnostic; and reason was his whole rule of thumb.

Well, there we were that evening in Kenny's flat and, as I say, everyone was feeling nicely thank you but quite under control. I don't remember how we began to talk about Griffiths. I had met him somewhere the day before and he'd said he was looking for a country place to rent for the summer; he'd begun a novel and wanted some peace and quiet to finish it. I mentioned that, and we speculated what kind of fiction he might turn out. It was Ruth who took such violent objection to *Nemesis*. She said of course she wasn't superstitious, but Griffiths' book showed him as a complete materialist; and she thought he was unnecessarily dogmatic when he said so definitely that everything of the so-called Supernormal was impossible and nonexistent. Quite a few serious scientists, she pointed out, were researching in that field. Somebody mentioned Rhine and Bob wanted to bring in Dunne's theory of time but Pat interrupted.

"Maybe some day Jevon'll be sorry he said ghosts don't exist," I think she said. "Wouldn't it be marvellous if he actually met one?"

"He wouldn't believe it," I said.

"He'd never see one," said Ruth, "*because* he doesn't believe in them. You only meet ghaisties and ghoulies if you believe they're there."

"Well, damn it," said Bob, "if I was a ghost that's exactly the kind of man I'd appear to. Griffiths is a man any ghost might be proud to haunt."

"*I'm* not dogmatic about it," said Pat dreamily. "I just say queer things happen you can't account for. I don't believe we're just several gallons of water and eight-and-sixpence worth of chemicals or whatever it is. I agree with Bob. It'd be a kind of judgment on Jevon if he did meet a ghost.''

Kenny said yes but there weren't any; and Pat asked how he knew. Neville said, ''It's a noble thought anyway. An unsuperstitious Welshman is an impossibility if you ask me. I'll bet if Griffiths went up to bed one night and found something horrible gibbering at him from the top of the bureau, he'd break the mile record.''

''No, he wouldn't—he wouldn't see it,'' insisted Ruth. ''He's too materialistic.''

''I wouldn't say Griffiths is materialistic in that sense,'' I said. ''Actually, he's very sensitive and imaginative—look how crazy about animals he is.''

Pat and Kenny were arguing about ghosts and Bob told them to shut up. We were in that mood, rude and gay: adolescent, you know? ''There's no point arguing that. What I say is that, underneath, Griffiths is just as superstitious as the average man. The primitive isn't far below the surface in any of us. We may ridicule ninety-nine silly superstitions and believe the hundredth ourselves. I think Neville's right; if Jevon ever did see a ghost or something he thought was a ghost, he'd be terrified. He couldn't help it. He may claim to be a materialist, and consciously he is, but there's just as much Neanderthal in him as in the rest of us.''

''I'd love,'' said Ruth wistfully, ''to see something like that happen to him.''

And Pat objected, ''But it's no good just saying it, there'd be no way to prove whether he—'' And then they both had the idea at the same time and squealed delightedly.

Bob was keen on it from the first; Kenny and I tried feebly to raise objections, but . . . well, it was an entertaining idea, you know. Or seemed that way at the time. Griffiths was always so sure of himself. I don't think I really believed we'd do it; it was amusing to discuss, that was all.

"But it's got to be good," Bob kept saying. "He'd never be taken in by a sheet and groans—it's got to be subtle."

"We'll make it subtle, darling. We'll show him a ghost he's got to believe, and I bet we scare him stiff! Oh, and look—what Alex just said!—he's going to take a cottage in the country. We'll haunt it for him. Work out the details later—produce a ghost to go with the house, and see how Jevon reacts."

Well, we made some definite plans, and I daresay if we hadn't that's as far as the thing would have gone. Because it looked a bit different next day; and I, at least, never found amateur theatricals amusing. I'm not sure now what made us—six reasonably normal adults—go through with such a thing. Partly it was Griffiths' own fault; he was always so *damned* sure of himself. The basis of practical joking is egotism: to bolster up one's own ego by making someone else look ridiculous; we all have impulses to it. Is there any right-minded person who doesn't get an unholy thrill out of seeing some pompous dignitary step on an orange skin and take a toss? I don't fool myself; it was a childish thing and we'd no business to do it. Damn it, we all liked the man well enough. I said at the time, it wasn't so much a practical joke as a scientific experiment, to test whether Griffiths had the courage of his convictions.

And I must take the blame for most of the plot, such as it was. After all, plots are my job. I'll tell you what we did and I refuse to apologize anymore for what we've admitted was a schoolboy trick. The point is, we did go on with it.

Griffiths' flat in London was not far from mine, we all knew many of the same people, and it wasn't unusual for us to meet fairly often. But as a matter of fact it was Kenny who got the go-ahead signal. We had to wait, you see, until Griffiths had actually got his country cottage. He told Kenny about it one night a week or so later, and the evening after that we all got together and polished up our plan.

The cottage Griffiths had taken was in Somerset, up toward the Mendips, outside a small village. He had told Kenny he was going to settle in in about a week. I drove down there the next day to see the agent and have a look at the place. Of course it all depended on the agent; if he wouldn't play, it'd make it a lot more difficult. But he did. He was a youngish, pleasant fellow named Barlow, and he was tickled at the whole idea. He had read Griffiths' book, and having met him he thought Griffiths wouldn't turn a hair at the most convincing ghost who ever walked, but he was quite willing to test it. In fact he offered to lay me a quid on it. He *was* a practical joker by nature.

He called it a Sporting Proposition. "I'm going to enjoy this," he said. "Most sporting proposition I've run across since I came down from Cambridge. Just tell me the story you've fixed up."

We'd had quite an argument over that. Bob kept insisting that we had to be subtle, and I saw the point; most kinds of hauntings have been tediously overdone, as it were, both in fact and fiction. But the more subtle we were the more difficult it would be to produce a plausible apparition; besides, Griffiths wouldn't consciously find one sort of ghost essentially more believable than another. In the end we'd borrowed the standard model, you might call it: the tale we wanted Barlow to pitch to Griffiths was the one about the murdered young wife and the husband hanged for his horrid deed—"And dress it up, you know," I said to Barlow. He nodded enthusiastically.

"I can do that on my head. I know what you want. Pass it on as amusing local history, laugh ha-ha at the superstitious villagers. I'll do you better than that. I've a couple of pals around who'd be happy to oblige—get 'em to back me up, all very casual—"

"For heaven's sake don't spread it over the whole county," I begged. "He'll suspect something at once if you shove it down his throat."

"Soul of discretion," said Barlow. "Trust me, I'll put it over all right. Are you on for the bet?" I said I wasn't; if he stood to win anything if Griffiths unmasked us he'd be too apt to let us down putting the tale over. He grinned and said he was a better sport than that, and I'd better have a look at the place to see the possibilities for ghost production. We were very much pals together. I suppose along with the Neanderthal there's a good deal of adolescent in all of us.

So he took me out to look at Griffiths' cottage. (I should have explained that we knew Griffiths was tied up in town that day and wouldn't be dropping by.) . . . You know that country? I don't care for it myself. It is such terrifically calm country: those rolling sweeps, open to the sky and unearthly still, and then little patches of wood that are quieter than woods should be. The cottage was only a couple of miles from a decent-sized village, at the end of a short lane off the main road, and it was a nice little place, not really isolated, only quiet. It had been built about ten years ago, Barlow said, and looked solid and comfortable, two-storied, all modern conveniences, and a wild little garden. Actually it was for sale, but Griffiths had said he wouldn't buy it until he was sure he liked living in it. In spite of its general pleasantness it wasn't a place I'd have liked to live; but I'm a townsman. We went round it, and I saw there was a closed porch built on at the back, with a sloping roof and no windows. But I was mainly interested in seeing how the ghost could appear. We decided the husband had drowned the wife in the quite sufficiently deep stream that ran down behind the fence at the rear of the house, and the ghost came up from there trying to get in.

"There's plenty of cover in the garden," Barlow pointed out, "and it can come and gibber at the study window." He laughed. "My God, if it doesn't scare Griffiths it's likely to keep him without a daily help!"

I said we weren't planning to make a full-time job of haunting. He said regretfully he supposed not, and how did we propose to go about it? We'd argued about that too, and thought Griffiths might recognize either Ruth or Pat—even under adverse conditions as it were—so Pat had got a friend of hers to play ghost, and delighted to be let in on it. Blond girl named Jean—her husband was overseas. Oh, we were being clever about this, I tell you. When grown-up people indulge in pranks they do the thing seriously.

I told Barlow the gist of the idea. And I started to make a

sketch of the house and garden for our ghost. About then Barlow swore and said, "I suppose if the trick works he'll decide not to buy the place after all. Doing myself out of a commission. Oh, well, I didn't really expect to sell it."

"No? Well, it's not everyone'd care to live in such a spot."

"There's nothing the matter with the *house*," said Barlow. "We never have trouble renting it in the summer—weekenders and so on. But sell it?—no."

"Don't tell me it really is haunted."

He laughed. "No, though it has rather a queer history. The fellow who built it was bats—old chap called Graves, and a damned appropriate name too. No, he didn't murder anyone exactly. He gave out that he was a scientist, never said what sort—and he stuck on that porch thing at the back as a laboratory."

"Mmh?" I was making a sketch of the grounds then.

Barlow jingled coins in his pocket. "Well, people up here live and let live, you know, and though the daily help—old Mother Hatwell and her daughter Rosie—talked about the awful noises in that laboratory, nobody thought much about it until one day old Graves wandered into the village in his birthday suit and held an animated conversation with somebody he said was Satan under the war memorial."

"Good Lord," I said politely.

"So they took him off to the asylum, and there he is yet as far as I know. But when they came to go through the house—" Barlow broke off and hunched his shoulders, grimacing. "They found about a hundred dogs and cats and mice and guinea pigs in that lab, in cages, and the bones of hundreds more in the boiler and buried in the garden. The live ones were in an awful state. He was a sadist, you see—I suppose he was too timid to use people, so he worked on animals instead. Some of the things he'd done to them . . . Well, they all had to be destroyed and, as I say, the old chap was tucked away where at least he hasn't any live playthings."

It was a queer, rather horrible story, but I paid little attention to it. I was putting the finishing touches on the other story.

Another thing we had decided was that only one of us could keep an eye on Griffiths. We could hardly descend on him in a body, and Kenny and Neville couldn't get away from town anyway. A couple of broad hints had got me an invitation to spend a weekend with him early the next month; and a couple of weeks before that Bob and the three girls went down to stay in a rather primitive rented cottage the other side of Bristol, an easy drive to Griffiths' place. We'd give it two weeks, producing the ghost a dozen times.

You will think it all absurdly elaborate, and so it was. We were all a trifle younger and sillier then.

I arrived at the cottage, ostensibly for the first time, late one Friday afternoon. I was to stay over Monday. Griffiths came out to welcome me and I had a look at him for any evidences of agitation. He had been living there a bit over a month and he'd had ten days of the ghost. I could imagine Barlow putting the tale across him all right, in that ingenuous manner; and Griffiths' testy answer, too. At first glance he looked just the same as usual, and I thought, well, that's that; he hasn't even begun to fall for it. Then . . .

Griffiths is a little chap like a lot of Welshmen, tough and dark and peppery. But he wasn't looking so cocky now. It wasn't that he seemed apprehensive; after an hour or so, while we said all the usual things and he made drinks, I identified it—he looked *anxious*. Like a man in a house of illness, waiting for the doctor. He said his work was coming on slowly.

"I should think you'd get peace and quiet here," I said. Mind you, I was feeling foolish about this thing by then, but it had gone too far for me to back out. "Don't tell me you've been bothered by the ghost."

"The ghost?" he repeated absently. "Oh, no. How did you come to hear of that?"

"Stopped in the village to ask direction," I said mendaciously, "and heard they did hope as how Mr. Griffiths wasn't troubled with the poor sperrit. Who is the ghost and why does he, she, or it haunt?"

"Oh, the ghost," he said, and after a moment laughed. "It's some local story—the house agent told me—a woman, I really forget the tale. He seemed to think I might want to get out of the agreement, apologized for not telling me before." Yes, clever of Barlow to put it like that. "Curious," said Griffiths, "how these things hang on. Of course it's a practical joke of some sort. Somebody has even thought it worthwhile to dress up and flit round the garden, hoping to frighten me, I expect."

"That's extraordinary," I said. "Surely nobody'd go to that bother."

"Oh, someone might. Someone who'd read my book. It's queer, you know, how angry people are when you attack some set idea. They look on it as a personal insult." He spoke like a scientist discussing the behavior of guinea pigs, talking of people. That was one way he was irritating. He didn't mean it like that, of course. He's a lonely, solitary chap, and though he is liked he is never intimate with anyone; perhaps that troubles him. It started in shyness, I suppose, so he's abrupt when he wants to be quite otherwise. I believe that's why he's so fond of animals, because you can be natural with a dog or cat. He had his two dogs with him, a very old and dignified spaniel and a Scottish 'errier.

"Yes, but it seems an extraordinary length to go to," I said, watching him. "Are you sure it *is* somebody dressed up?"

"Am I sure? What d'you mean? Of course I'm sure. I could hardly think it was a real ghost." He looked at me and laughed. "By God, Alex, I think you'd be pleased if you thought I'd been taken in by a thing like that. It'd suit your peculiar sense of humor."

I told him not to be a fool, filling my pipe.

"I expect that's what it is—someone who's read the book— trying to make me admit I'm frightened after all." And that was surely an odd way to put it. *Make me admit*—not just *frighten*. He was not quite as usual; there was something on his mind. I thought he was reacting very much in character; he was startled by the ghost, and the primitive in him was frightened, but Griffiths the conscious man would never admit that, and all his intellect was setting up a defense.

"How long has this been going on?"

"Oh, most of the time I've been here. You'll probably see it yourself. The twilight hour," he said with an angry little laugh, "is the favorite. It comes through the back garden and taps on the window to get my attention. It wants to be very sure I notice it, you see."

Well, I did. I saw that he was annoyed, but he wasn't giving anything away; possibly the first time he had been frightened, but after that his reason insisted that it was a lie. All the same, I'd watch him this evening when the ghost appeared. There was something besides annoyance in his voice and eyes.

There were two good-sized bedrooms upstairs and a modern bathroom. I had a wash and unpacked, and when I came down we had an early dinner. As it turned out there was no question of scaring off Griffiths' daily; a woman from the village came out every morning, washed up dishes for him and so on, and went off at noon. He'd been catering for himself; he seemed to like pottering around a kitchen. He had laid out a scratch meal on the table in the study, which was just behind the little parlor and substituted for a dining room. The dogs came in and lay down beside his chair. He had arranged it so both of us had a view of the one large window.

"It'll be along presently, you'll see," he promised. I knew that; I was more concerned with watching him. In the stronger light he looked even more strained. Being so dark, he was naturally sallow and blue-chinned, but now he looked almost haggard. He did not again mention the ghost, but kept up a flow of desultory talk. But I thought he was listening and watching with another part of him. And I thought, it's got to him after all. His trouble is a contest between the primitive and civilized pulls in him; he has found his reason of no use to him for once. And I'm afraid that as a writer I was clinically interested.

For all that I was expecting it, the ghost gave me the hell of a start; it was effective. It was nearly dark outside, the uncurtained window a blackish square. Suddenly a pale shape outlined itself there, and made a faint tapping on the glass, and thrust a staring white vague face to flatten on the pane with two white starfish of hands. I started and exclaimed, "Good God," or something, and the dogs went wild, rearing up to the window and barking.

Griffiths did not start at all. "There it is, you see," he said softly. I tell you, I was having to remind myself it was that friend of Pat's—amateur theatricals. They'd made a good production of it. "That's flesh and blood," said Griffiths; he had not moved. "The dogs know. If it was anything else—if it could be anything else—they wouldn't take any notice."

The thing disappeared from the window and I got up to look. "It's only wandering around the garden," said Griffiths calmly.

"I always understood animals could detect the presence of a spirit before humans," I said at random.

"According to superstition. Actually there could be no sensory perception whatever, and an animal has only physical senses to perceive with. Any hallucination convincing a human being he sees—something like that"—he nodded at the window—"is a product of the unconscious mind, which animals don't possess. That's the second reason I know it's a practical joke."

"The first being?"

"Why, that the 'supernormal' doesn't exist." He was infuriatingly undisturbed. I was unreasonably angry with him, and with myself, for—even one moment—finding the ghost startling. But one thing was clear, the experiment had failed. The anxiety in his eyes and his nervousness was all for his work; perhaps it was going badly. Not for the first time I felt ashamed of all this elaborate and juvenile hocus-pocus. I should have to stay the weekend, though I'd found out what we wanted to know, but after that I'd see we called off the joke and left the man in peace.

In fact I stayed only until Sunday. I didn't have to invent a reason for leaving then; I said frankly to Griffiths I didn't know how he stood it. And I like dogs too; but it wasn't only the dogs. When we went upstairs that first night he was again looking slightly uneasy. He said, "I hope you'll sleep all right. I don't think this place is very well built, you know—and there's a more or less steady wind—all the open country. The house is rather noisy at night.'' I said I wouldn't mind that, I was a sound sleeper. I usually am; but I never put in a night like that before. We had gone up about midnight, and I had not got to bed when the dogs started to whine. They slept in Griffiths' room across the hall, and he had shut the door; I heard him speak to them and they quieted down. I switched off the light and went to bed, and then the house started in. It looked solid enough, but perhaps (I thought), it had been green lumber. You notice small sounds at night you'd never hear in the daytime, of course. The change in temperature contracts the boards. Anyway, there was a succession of creaks and cracks and rustlings, interspersed with silences, and just as I was drifting off more cracks and groans— exactly like a restless, fussy sleeper settling down for the night. Then the mice. There must have been a whole colony of them in the walls—of course you get them in the country, and no cat would share a house with two dogs. They pattered and rustled, and noises are deceptive in the dark; it sounded as if they were running about the passage and on the stairs, and perhaps they were bold enough to come out like that at night. Big mice—or even rats, they sounded like. Hundreds of them.

Presently the dogs started whimpering, and I heard Griffiths' muffled mutter at them. After a while his door opened and shut quietly. Dogs wanted out, I decided; and turned over for the dozenth time. There were stealthy noises as he crept downstairs, and I heard the front door open. An interval of silence except for the mice, and then it seemed he had not let the dogs out after all, for they began whining excitedly from his bedroom and scrab- bling at the door. This went on for some time—to my exasperated ears it sounded like a dozen dogs—and the floorboards and walls creaked and groaned steadily (a strong wind had got up about the house) and I was just about to get up and let the damned dogs out when I heard Griffiths coming up the stairs again. I must have fallen asleep then, for a very short time. What woke me was an appalling howl from one of the dogs. Of course once I woke it was for good, though the dog stopped. The boards were still creaking and the wind muttered round the corners of the house and the mice (or rats) seemed to be holding a dancing party on the stairs. I lay awake cursing; the last time I looked at my watch it was past three. I was just beginning to drift off again when I was brought wide awake by the thud of the closing front door downstairs. The dogs were whining and scratching at the door across the passage. Well, perhaps I had slept; for now the house was wrapped in deep heavy silence, so that Griffiths' step on the stair was loud out of proportion. I couldn't make out why the man was prowling about the house all night. It was just faintly getting light; of course some people are early risers. He came up the stair very slowly, and I heard his door open and shut and his voice speaking to the dogs. I did not sleep again, and was down before him; he appeared after the daily woman had come, about half-past eight. He looked tired and preoccupied, and I said I wondered how he could sleep at all, what with the dogs and the house and the mice.

"Yes, it's rather a nuisance," he agreed. "I certainly shan't buy the place."

I could have suggested he leave the dogs out at night, or put down traps for the mice; instead I said I supposed it might be the position of the cottage, it got the wind just wrong or something, and probably was jerry built as well. He gave me an odd look and said yes. He looked as if he hadn't slept at all; and there was an awful anxiety in his eyes. He hadn't eaten much breakfast; he sat fondling the dogs, and the hand that held his cigarette was trembling. But I wasn't feeling too rested myself after that night.

I pottered around doing nothing much, and Griffiths excused himself and worked awhile in his study. That doesn't matter, I'm making a long tale of this; I'll get on. We drove into the village for a drink that afternoon, and talked of things irrelevant to this story. And came back, and had dinner. The ghost didn't show up; we hadn't wanted to overdo it, you know. That night was as bad as the first—I thought I'd never sleep. First the house, then those damned mice (or rats), and then the dogs, and Griffiths leaving his room to steal downstairs. I finally drifted off, but was wakened again when he came creeping upstairs at dawn. A damned good job he wasn't married, when he kept such hours, I thought savagely.

The whole farce had misfired anyway and I was fed up. He seemed rather relieved when I said I couldn't stay over Sunday. I thought it was no wonder he looked haggard; and perhaps he was having trouble with his work too.

He said again, "It's a nuisance, yes. I should have warned you." He didn't press me to stay. Just as I was leaving something rather queer happened. I put my bag in the car and shook hands with Griffiths, and casually reached to pat the nearest dog—and he pulled the dog out of my way. It was quite unexpected and rude. He recovered himself at once, and we said the right things, and I left.

As far as I was concerned it was a waste of time and energy. I went and told Barlow that, and he was pleased at being right and sorry we hadn't laid a bet. "I told you he wouldn't fall—too downy a bird."

"Well, he certainly suspected a trick right away, by what he said. I felt rather a fool. But at least I've learned why you can't sell that house." And I told him about the noise.

"Green lumber," he said easily. "Newish houses often do that—settling. Well, happy to have been an accomplice, old man. Any time you need a conspirator call on me. Too bad it fizzled out."

I drove over to the place where the others were staying and broke the news to them. "We'd better call it a day," I said. "He was on to it right away, evidently. Didn't turn a hair. At the moment he seems to think it's some of the natives playing a joke, but he isn't much amused and he may set the dogs on the ghost next time."

"Oh, hell," said Bob. "No reaction at all?"

"Oh, I wouldn't say that. I think he may have been startled at first, but he certainly isn't exhibiting panic terror or anything like that. It was a damn fool thing to do anyway—like a bunch of kids."

"But I'll bet we did frighten him a little," said Ruth. "The first time. One of us should have been there to see."

Well, they'd had a nice little holiday and some innocent fun, and we all—I think—felt foolish and just as relieved to forget the whole thing. It hadn't been a very funny practical joke. We came back to town and told Kenny and Neville how it had gone. We were all suffering from reaction (if Griffiths wasn't)—an unpleasant feeling that we'd made fools of ourselves. The sight of each other emphasized it, and we scattered about our own affairs. I didn't see any of them for a week or so.

Until that next Monday. That was the day I had a wire from Barlow: *Can you come some odd developments Griffiths in hospital.*

"Overwork," said Barlow. "That's what the doctor said, anyway. The daily woman found him yesterday morning—in a dead faint at the foot of the stairs, and the front door open, and the dogs going mad shut up in his bedroom. She called the doctor—very sensible woman, didn't lose her head—and they took him off to the hospital."

"But—"

"It couldn't be anything else, could it?" he asked uneasily. "He did rather seem to drive himself. He's all right now; the doctor said he'd be released tomorrow. I went in to see him last night, but he was pretty dead to the world. I just thought somebody who knows him better ought to hear. I expect they'd let you in."

"Yes, I'll go to see him." I had been suffering pangs of conscience all the way from town; what Barlow said only confirmed my suspicion. We had after all played too deep on the nervy little Welshman. He wouldn't admit his fear and it had festered inside until . . . Or was it just overwork as the doctor said? I didn't know; but if our crude tricks had anything to do with Griffiths' illness we had some apologies to make, and would probably lose a friend—as no doubt we richly deserved.

I went to see him at the cottage hospital. He was sitting up in bed, looking thin and ill and bluer-chinned than ever, but in possession of himself; and he didn't look too pleased to see me. I said a few conventional things. He sat there smoking, an odd look in his eyes, and finally interrupted me in his abrupt harsh voice. "Overwork," he said, and laughed. "D'you agree with the doctor then, that's what it was?"

"Well, I don't—"

"Tell me, Alex, it was you, wasn't it?" he asked. "I thought you had some reason for wanting to come here, that time. The ghost—it was your idea, wasn't it? And all the rest of it. But I don't know why. Why did you want to do a thing like that to me, Alex?" He sounded, damn it, like a bewildered child.

And to gain time I asked, "Why should you think I . . . and what was it, after all, put you here? You didn't—"

"You're not a very good liar," he said. "I don't understand it, Alex. How could you *do* such a thing? I thought it was you—you were so interested in my reactions! But why?"

So I told him. I did it badly, because I felt like hell about it then. It had started as a joke, but as a childish joke so often does it turned out cruel, and I was ashamed, and I knew the others would feel that way too, looking at him. I told him how it had all begun, and what fools we felt, and I suppose I made a lame job of apologizing, because a thing like that—to a man like Griffiths—is beyond apology. It was never very funny, and he would not see even the little elementary fun there had been originally.

"Yes, I see," he said. "The eternal savage attacking the rational man. You would never have thought of such a thing if you didn't half believe all the superstitions yourselves." He put a hand to his head as if it ached. He looked as if he might drop off to sleep at any moment; the doctor had said he seemed starved for sleep. I expect they'd given him something.

"There's nothing I can say except I know it was worse than ridiculous. We never thought—we never meant . . ." And what the hell had it done to him, and why? He was himself; his creeds had not toppled; only there was that awful anxiousness in his eyes still. "It was a very childish kind of ghost," I said desperately, "I know."

"Oh—the ghost. That never deceived me. But I don't under-stand—I thought we were friends." As if I needed any more to make me feel the way I was feeling. "I couldn't believe you were *capable* of it," and he leaned back and shut his eyes. He said in a thin dreamy voice, "The ghost," and laughed. "That was childish, yes. It was the rest of it—I couldn't *bear*. Couldn't *bear*. And what was the—the connection, Alex? I don't under-stand—how any sane man—just for a *joke*—"

"What d'you mean, the rest of—"

"I fastened all the windows, and the doors were locked—how did they get in? Perhaps there's a secret way into the house. Barlow would know. That's how you did it, isn't it? Or one . . . one of you. It was a compulsion—terrible—after that first time, when I heard and went to see. I had to go out—try . . . Couldn't sleep, knowing what it *was*. I tried to catch some of them—God, I couldn't bear—try to help them, but . . . It was frightful. Must have been loosed somewhere at the back of the house—running all over . . ."

I can't set down the extraordinary sensation I began to have then, but I managed to ask him very quietly—because he seemed to be drifting off to sleep—"What, Griffiths? What was running all over?"

"Why, the animals," he answered in a tired whisper. "You know. How you *could* . . . All the little animals, all so frightened, and all so terribly hurt. Frantic to get away—frantic with pain. The blood . . . I couldn't bear it—tried to get to them, to help them, but I never could. So I'd have to . . . open the door and wait . . . until they all got out." I thought he had gone to sleep, but after a silence he said drowsily, "All so frightened—so hurt. Just—for—a—joke. I don't understand . . ."

And then I remembered the old lunatic Graves, and his laboratory.

You see the awful dilemma I am in. How can I tell Griffiths he has seen not one ghost but hundreds of them? For he saw *that*—it was real; and yet if he knows, and cannot find a physical explanation, as the man of reason, he is quite likely to have a real nervous breakdown. How can I believe, myself? I never considered myself materialistic—but *I* didn't see. Would I have, if I had got up and looked? Or was it only for him?

But I cannot have Griffiths thinking me a sadist, only in pursuit of a practical joke. What am I going to do about it?

FLASH ATTACHMENT

M ichael Garvan sat by the window in his room, looking out. Nothing much to see but grass in the side yard and the house next door. The bushes were blowing in the wind and it looked as if it might rain any second.

He heard the man walking around in the living room again. He'd sit smoking one cigarette after another, the man named Sammy, and then get up and walk round and round. Mike didn't like him much.

Nothing to do, even if he could go out. The doctor'd said, better not let him out in this cold for another couple of days. She hadn't got the doctor until he said maybe she ought to, he felt so terrible, and then there was a fuss and poor baby, where does it hurt? And the doctor said measles and gave him shots. It had been pretty awful while it lasted, because, of course, like always she said Darling and Honey, but she was out a lot and didn't think about getting him things to eat or clean pajamas and so on when she *was* home, but that was just Mother. He'd managed somehow, getting stuff for himself, and now he was O.K., all the spots gone and everything, except he still felt kind of funny if he stood up too long and like that.

Nothing to do much, inside or out. They'd only been in California a month, and it was Christmas vacation now, and he hadn't got to know any other kids at school here yet. There was a kid he'd seen on this block, looked about ten, just like Mike, but he hadn't got to know him before he began feeling bad with the measles.

The man called Sammy was still walking around in there. Mike didn't like him, but he didn't like a lot of people Mother brought home; that wasn't anything new. Mother, he thought, just didn't have very much sense about people. He supposed it was maybe on account of the stuff she drank all the time. They used to have arguments about it, her and Dad. . . .

There. It had happened. Thinking about Dad again. He tried awful hard not to, because it wasn't any *good*. That judge, something about a thing called custody, and Dad so awful mad, and another man—a lawyer, Dad's lawyer—saying swearwords about damn sentimental judges putting, what he called Pure Womanhood on pedestals. Dad. Dad saying, "You write letters to me, Mike, and I'll write to you, see? We won't lose touch. I'll be working on this, kid, don't you worry. We'll be seeing each other."

Oh, he *hadn't* meant to think about Dad! Mike shut his eyes tight against shameful hot tears. He wasn't a *baby*, he knew why and how it was. It was the money. The money she got from Dad, for him, the support money. Sure, she said Baby and Honey and she kissed and hugged him sometimes, if mostly she did forget all about the laundry or getting stuff to eat at the market and like that. That was how Mother *was*. She wasn't mean or anything like that. You just couldn't *count* on her about anything. She liked playing cards and going to parties or anywhere with a lot of people, and the stuff in bottles that made her act silly and giggly, like a real little girl. So when you looked there wasn't any bread or peanut butter or milk, but if she was there and not gone someplace she'd say, "Oh, honey, isn't there? I'm sorry, you go 'n' get some," and give him the money. Mother was fine, if you just knew how she *was* and expected it.

Sammy'd sat down again. No, he was coming in here. Mike didn't turn from the window, because he didn't want Sammy to see he'd been crying like a baby. Besides, he knew what Sammy looked like. A tall, thin man with black hair, that looked like he'd used shoe polish on it, and little black eyes, and a long nose.

"Look, kid," said Sammy. "You want to go to a nice movie tonight? There's a Western on down the block. I give you the money."

"Thank you," said Mike, polite, "but I'm not s'posed to go out." He didn't want to, much. It wasn't much fun going to a movie alone. Nobody to talk with about it, after. And he didn't know any kids here.

Sammy said a swearword in a funny kind of whisper and went away.

Mike got the handkerchief out of his pajama pocket and blew his nose and wiped his eyes. Hadn't *meant* to think about Dad. It just wasn't any good.

Write to me, Dad had said. He had, and that was the only time he ever remembered Mother getting real mad. Kept asking him what he'd *wrote*, when he got Dad's letter back. And next thing, they'd come clear out here to California where they didn't know anybody, and she said they had a different name here, Robertson, that was her name before she married Dad. He wasn't a *baby;* he knew why he had to be Mike Robertson here. Something about the judge and what laws said. And the money, the money she got for him from Dad. In case Dad could maybe get the judge to say different.

It just wasn't any good thinking about it. Quick, think of something else.

Sammy was walking around again. Living room, kitchen, hall; only not in Mother's room, where the door was shut.

There *would* be something to do, if he had the flash attachment. He sure did want that flash attachment, and when the money came next month, he was going to ask her for it. If he caught her just the right minute, when she was feeling good—that silly, giggling way she got—she'd likely say, "Why, sure, honey, you can have it," and give him the money. Fifteen dollars it was, for the whole thing: the one that fitted his Kodak. Take anything, anywhere, then. Inside, practically in the dark. It was lucky he just had the little Kodak reflex, the attachment for a Leica or Rollei cost a lot more.

Dad didn't like a reflex.

There he was, back at Dad again. Mike went over and lay down on the bed. No *good*. Dad was a long ways off in New York, unless he was on a special assignment somewhere.

Mike's Dad took better pictures than any other pro photographer, news pictures and other kinds. He got prizes for it. He didn't like a reflex camera, on account of the square negative; he said it didn't lend itself to good composition. He used the Graphic mostly. A great big camera, awful heavy, but he was strong, so he lifted it easy, even way over his head sometimes to get a special picture. And he never let *anybody* develop his negs, he always did it himself. To be sure. But he said, about the Kodak, it's a good little baby to start on, Mike, see?

It had been for his eighth birthday present.

Mike figured Dad had meant to give him the flash attachment for his birthday last year. Because he'd said Mike was *coming along*. "That's a pretty damn good shot of the bridge. I guess you inherited an eye for composition, boy!" Only, of course, last birthday had been after the judge and the custody, and Dad hadn't known where to send it. Otherwise he would've.

Well, Mike guessed maybe it was just that he was more *like* Dad—looks, and every other way. Mother meant O.K., but you couldn't count on her at all. He just couldn't see why she couldn't remember they were out of milk, or that he hadn't clean shorts to put on, or like that. He guessed ladies didn't wear shorts and she just never thought. She washed out her stockings every night and hung them on the shower thing.

The clock said almost six. He wasn't awful hungry, but it was time for dinner. Maybe if there was any peanut butter . . . The doctor had said something named beef bouillon. Mike wondered what it tasted like.

You were supposed to have dinner about now.

He got up slowly and went out to the kitchen. He had to go past Mother's bedroom, and it looked funny with the door shut. She never did. It was Sammy shut the door, some reason.

There wasn't any peanut butter, and the bread felt awful hard. Sammy heard him and came in. "What the hell," Sammy said, and then, "Oh, you hungry? Look, you take this, go out 'n' get something, huh?" He offered Mike a dollar. "Hamburger or something. And . . ."

"I'm not s'posed to go out," said Mike.

Sammy got a funny look and said a swearword, but then he said, "Sure, that's right, but see, I fix you a good supper, kid, and doctors don't know everything, see, you feel fine after supper, and you go see that Western tonight. You'll be inside the movie, that's O.K., isn't it? You like Westerns? Sure, all kids like Westerns." He laughed, but he kept looking like he wanted to say swearwords.

Mike sure hoped Mother'd come home pretty soon. Of course, you never knew what Mother'd do, but she'd never done a thing like this before, just go *off* and leave a man like Sammy.

He'd seen Sammy before, of course. A couple of times Sammy'd come home with her and other people; they'd played cards or just sat talking and drinking stuff. She called Sammy Darling, but she called a lot of people Darling.

They didn't really *know* anybody here, just a month, not real good. She always got to know people easy, but it wasn't like people you'd known a long while.

She didn't have an awful lot of sense about people.

Mike wondered anxiously just where she'd gone. It was *like* Mother in a way, just pick up and go off. He could kind of imagine her saying to Sammy, "You look after my li'l honey bug a couple days, see he's O.K. I'll be back Tuesday," or whenever it'd be. That was Mother, though she'd never done it before. But was it anything to do with the judge and the thing called custody? Had she found out about the Letter?

For the hundredth time, Mike told himself she couldn't have. If she had, she'd have set to at him the way she did before, what had he written and so on.

He'd thought a long time about the Letter before he'd written it. Because it kind of scared him to find how *dim* Dad was getting in his mind, that was it. He had to think to figure up how long it'd been: the judge and the custody thing and Dad looking so mad but trying to pretend everything was O.K., and saying about letters. Just before his ninth birthday, and he'd been ten last month. The thing was, if he wrote letters, then Dad knew where to write, and so right off as soon as she knew that, they moved somewhere. Mike didn't like moving around like that. The only time she was ever cross was when he wrote to Dad.

She hadn't remembered his birthday. She wouldn't remember about Christmas either, likely. You couldn't expect Mother to.

That was how come Mike had first understood. Because he knew Dad had remembered. It wasn't a thing he had to wonder about; he just knew. And there hadn't been a present in the mail or anything. So Mike knew she hadn't let Dad know where they were. Maybe the money got paid to a bank or a lawyer or something; anyway she got it without Dad knowing just where.

And now he'd written another Letter, and probably it'd all happen again just like before, her being cross and them moving.

Dad would have sent a birthday present. That wasn't a thing you had to worry about.

It was funny where she could have gone, though. If she didn't know about the Letter, and she didn't or she'd have said something.

He'd remembered Dad saying once, a long while ago, about the *Tribune,* a picture he'd sold to the *Tribune.* That had been in New York, so it'd be the New York *Tribune.* He didn't know where else to send a letter to Dad, now, so he'd sent it there. Somebody sure would know who John J. Garvan was, there, and see he got it.

He hadn't said anything bad about her in the Letter. He hadn't really said anything about her at all. Just, he'd like to see Dad again, and couldn't he come stay with him instead, if Dad got the judge to say it was O.K., and about the picture he'd taken of the swans on a lake there was here, and it was pretty good, even if the drugstore had developed it.

Someday he'd have a darkroom of his own, do it *all*. Dad had let him watch and help, sometimes, at home. Before there had been the judge and the custody thing.

And anyway, even if she knew about the Letter (it'd be just about getting to New York now, he figured, that was last week), why'd she want to go off somewhere about it?"

Sammy fixed fried eggs, and he tried to act friendly and, well, kind of like a kid, making up to Mike. You could tell it was put on. He kept talking about that Western at the movie down the street.

Mike didn't like Sammy much.

It *was* funny, Mother acting that way. You couldn't count on her, but she'd never done a thing like that before.

Eating Sammy's eggs, Mike thought about it. Thursday, it had been, and this was Saturday. Thursday night really, because he'd heard her come home then. He'd taken his bath and noticed the soap was awful thin, so they'd need some more pretty soon, and he'd gone to bed and then they'd come home, her and this Sammy. And a while later, he'd heard them in her bedroom, having a fight. Kind of. Swearwords, and thumps, and thrashing around. Well, Mother had fights like that with a lot of people, and next minute calling them *Darling* again.

She'd gone away somewhere that night. Because next morning there was Sammy, looking awful funny and surprised at Mike, when he came out of his room, and saying, "Uh—your ma, she went off on a little trip an' left me to look after you, kid. Just a day or so. Can you get your own breakfast?" (As if he was a *baby*!)

It couldn't be anything to do with the Letter to Dad. But Mike wondered where she'd gone. You never knew what Mother'd do, of course.

Her bedroom door shut looked funny. She never *did*. Even when she was undressing. Mother was awful pretty, all white and soft and smooth, with her pretty blond hair; she didn't mind you looking at her. Dad had been mad at her, but she never meant anything bad, Mother; you just had to know what she was *like*, and come to know you couldn't *count on her*. Mother was O.K., you just had to know her.

She never remembered to get peanut butter or milk, or send his pajamas and shorts and shirts to the laundry, but Mike felt kind of homesick for her just then (Mother saying *Darling* and *Honey*), and he put his hand on the doorknob of her room, on the way back to his own.

"Get *out!*" said Sammy viciously behind him. "What the hell you after—listen, you little—!" And then pretending to be friendly again. "Look, kid—what's your name? Oh, Mike, sure. Look, Mikie, here's a buck. You go down 'n' see that Western, huh?"

"Thank you, I'm not s'posed to go out," said Mike politely.

Back in his room, he got out the Kodak and thought about that flash attachment. It'd sure be swell to have.

There was Sammy walking around again.

All of a sudden, Mike began to get an awful funny feeling. Not the kind of *soppy* funny feeling about Dad and the Christmas lights downtown and her being gone when he got home from school. A *real* funny feeling, and new. About Sammy, and Mother going off.

It was like handling the Kodak sort of made him think straighter. He hadn't felt much like taking pictures lately, even before the measles, and today was the first day he'd felt really a lot better, like he was all well again. Yesterday, what about yesterday? He'd had the last of the cereal for breakfast and the last of the milk. He'd laid in bed again, looking at magazines, not very interested; Sammy walking or smoking there in the living room. Yesterday was Friday. Thursday night she had gone away somewhere.

Sammy said.

He still hadn't felt so good yesterday. All of a sudden, it seemed to Mike like he hadn't paid *notice* to Sammy much, like he deserved. In a kind of way.

You take one of the kids he'd known back home, Danny Foster or somebody like that, he'd sure think it was awful funny, all of a sudden finding his mother gone and a man he didn't hardly *know* there instead. It *was* sort of funny, but of course Mother wasn't like most other mothers were, Danny's or anybody's. You could always expect Mother to do funny things. And all of a sudden, too.

All the same, though, all the same. . . .

Those little tablets in the bathroom, she took sometimes for a headache and to make her sleep. He couldn't get to sleep last night, and he remembered them, and got up to look for them. It was like he was really remembering it for the first time, right way round like. Sammy looking funny, almost scared, in the sudden bright light, saying, "What the *hell*! What you after? Go back to bed!"

It must have been awful late, but Sammy hadn't got undressed. Maybe he hadn't brought any pajamas with him.

And a while after that, Mike got up to go to the bathroom, and there was a light in Mother's room, and Sammy came out quick, switching off the light, and saying, "What the hell," again and didn't Mike ever stay in bed all night.

A lot of people Mother knew acted funny in all sorts of ways, of course.

It was just that for a minute there Mike saw how *awful* funny it would look to somebody like Danny Foster, and there was a queer hollow feeling in his stomach.

It was a funnier thing than had ever happened before.

Mike sat by the window with the Kodak in his hands, hoping the queer feeling would go away. Almost like being scared of something.

Nothing to be scared of. Tomorrow or next day, Mother'd come back from where she was, and Sammy'd go away. Everything be just like usual, except that by now Dad might have the Letter and know where they were. He might even come, if he hadn't an important assignment somewhere. Maybe a judge out here would say different about the custody thing. Anyway, there was no reason to feel all funny and hollow inside like this right now.

It was getting dark outside. Quick, the way it did out here. One minute it was light, and then all of a sudden dark.

Like Mother. One minute (come to think of it that way) there in the next room talking up sharp to Sammy, and next minute gone off somewhere.

It was funny, too, living in a little house (thought Mike desperately, trying to think of just ordinary things and stop the funny feeling), a house with a yard instead of an apartment. People did a lot out here.

It was nearly all dark outside now. He ought to put on the light.

Sammy put on the light. He said, "Listen, kid, whyn't you go see that movie?"

Mike turned reluctantly to look at him. Sammy stood in the doorway, the light shining on his oiled black hair, on the sweat on his white face.

"I don't guess I want to," said Mike.

"Damn it," said Sammy, "get up, go out 'n' *play* like any kid! Go *somewheres*! I—it ain't *natural,* sit round alla time. A kid . . ."

"I've been kind of sick; the doctor said I'd better not go out."

Sammy wanted him to go out somewhere real bad. The movie, anywhere. Mike started to wonder why.

Because, now he thought about it straight, he could see Sammy'd tried to make him go somewhere last night, too—the movie, the drugstore for a soda, somewhere.

He was saying swearwords over and over now, like he hardly knew he was saying them. The way he looked at Mike, standing there, made the hollow-stomach feeling worse, some way. Like he was blind, the little black eyes staring, blank.

"Look," he said. "Look." It didn't mean anything. He came over and laid a hand on Mike's shoulder, a bony, hard hand. Mike sat very still. "Kid, look, you do me a favor 'n' go out somewheres a couple hours, see? I—I—I got a fellow comin' to see me, talk over some private business, see? That's all. You—you get dressed 'n' go take in that movie."

Slowly Mike got up, and the hand fell away from him. He put the Kodak down and took off his pajama jacket.

Sammy looked relieved, and stepped back away. "That's right," he said. "That's right. I give you the dough." And then his eyes went blank again, and now he *was* scared about something. It was queer. Mike didn't ever remember seeing a grown-up look plain scared before. "But you *seen* me," said Sammy in a whisper. "I shoulda thought. Jesus, I ain't thinking straight. . . . Listen, kid. Listen. I never *meant* to do it. I . . . What the hell'm I goin' to do about you? Oh, damn it . . ." And then he turned and went out into the living room.

Mike put on his shorts and undershirt, the last clean pair he had. He felt a lot better in one way, *steadier* sort of, but another way he was scared too.

There was something wrong about it, about Sammy. If he hadn't been still feeling kind of sick yesterday and not paying notice, he'd have seen it before. Mother, she might do most anything; but if she was going away somewhere, she'd have said so to him, said about Sammy staying.

Just like a baby, like a little kid with no sense, he'd believed what Sammy said. Hadn't *thought* about it.

But now he was. The way Sammy acted a minute ago, what he said. Mike was thinking about it hard and cold.

Sammy wanted him to go away, out of the house. Ever since he was there, Thursday night, he'd wanted Mike to go away. No, only at night. He hadn't tried to get him to go to the movie yesterday afternoon, only at night, last night and this night. There was something bad Sammy wanted to do, in the dark, here. He'd somehow got Mother to go away, or—Mike's stomach lurched as he reached for his best brown pants in the closet—*had he?* Maybe Sammy had Mother all tied up and gagged in the bedroom, like burglars in stories, and that was why he had the door shut.

A *burglar?* But she'd spent most of this month's money, he knew. He remembered her saying it just the other day, "Oh, damn, only the seventeenth and I only got twelve dollars left. Don't know where it goes. . . ."

Well, well, there was the diamond ring she always wore. And her pretty soft fur coat. Anyway, *something* Sammy was after. Way he acted.

And the bedroom door shut.

Mike had forgotten all about the Letter, and the lonely feeling he had, way out here so far from where Dad was and all. He just thought about Mother, who hadn't any sense about people, so she'd taken up with Sammy; and about Sammy, and about why Sammy might want him away somewhere for a while.

A real *gangster* maybe. Mother—maybe right *here* all the time, tied up like they did?

Dad said about not losing your head. Keep sensible, think what's the sensible thing to do.

Mike put on the shirt he'd worn three days already, before he had the measles, but it was the only one he had *to* put on, and the brown jacket over it. He thought of a thing, an idea. He thought of a couple of ideas. He didn't know if Dad would think it awful sensible, but it was all he could think of right then.

Sammy didn't know much about kids. Looked like he thought somebody ten years old was just a *baby,* didn't know anything hardly. And Sammy wanted him out of the way awful bad. As soon as Mike was out of his way, and it being dark now, he'd go on and do whatever bad thing he'd come to do. And run away. And there'd be no way to catch him, unless. . . .

Mike felt his heart pounding and pounding away under the brown jacket. But it was the only thing he could *think* of. And there was Mother.

He picked up the Kodak and went out to the living room. Sammy was sitting there smoking. He jumped up; he gave Mike a big nervous-looking smile. It was cold—he hadn't turned on the wall heater houses had out here—but he was still sweating. "You going out?" he said. "That's swell. That's right. You go to that movie, huh? I'll give you the dough. . . ."

"No, sir," said Mike. He tried to make his voice sound like

always, but it didn't; it sounded funny and squeaky, but Sammy didn't seem to notice. "I—I thought I'd like maybe to go down and get my Christmas present, see. Mother said I could have it for Christmas, and I could pick it out myself, account of I know what kind to get. The flash attachment for my camera, it is. She said I could have it, even if it is fifteen dollars. Did she—did she leave the money with you, maybe, sir? She *said* I could get it. For Christmas. It was all I asked for. It's almost Christmas—day after tomorrow—and she said . . ."

"Oh," said Sammy. He probably didn't even know what a flash attachment was. "Fifteen bucks. Gee, that's a lot just for a kid. . . ." But he wasn't really thinking about the fifteen dollars; he was thinking of Mike being out of the way. Mike felt his heart pounding like one of those drills they used on the street. Sammy was reaching into his pocket. "Sure she did, kid. She left it for you. Here you are." Three five-dollar bills.

"Thank you very much," said Mike. His heart seemed to have got up into his throat, somehow, now, pounding and pounding. It was like he kept hearing Dad's deep calm voice saying about not losing your head—whatever happened.

You could say it was all Mother's fault, because she hadn't *any* sense about people; but all the same, she was Mother. Even if she forgot things and lost things and got silly and giggly from the stuff in the bottles.

"I—I guess I'll go to the bathroom again before I go," said Mike. Just, he had to *know*. For sure. On account, it *was* Mother.

He went into the hall and opened the bathroom door, making it noisy. He took two steps and very careful, very quiet, he eased open Mother's bedroom door. The bathroom light was on, he wouldn't have to turn on the bedroom light.

It was like somebody hitting him, hard and hurting. Time didn't mean anything anymore, he didn't know anything else just a minute—only Sammy, the flash, and Dad saying *sensible*. . . . And then somehow he was in the bathroom, leaning against the tub, pushing down the toilet flush.

Everything was just nightmare, but you had to *try*.

□ □ □

The feeling was kind of like four-five-six days ago, when he'd been real bad with the measles and her not home, and he'd got up to get a glass of water. Like he'd fall down any minute. He'd hung on to the bureau and the door and the icebox and been O.K., but it was a funny feeling. Only now he mustn't hang on to anything. He had to look just like usual. On account . . .

He got back down the hall and across the living room. He didn't look at Sammy at all, wherever he was. He just went out, into the cold black night, and he began to run. He ran toward the main street, a block up, the lights and people and noise, and he kept his free hand curled tight around the money in his pocket.

"Th-that one," he said. "For the Kodak reflex. And a—and a six-twenty film."

The clerk looked at him. "That comes to fifteen sixty-five, son. You got the cash?"

"Yes, sir. Right here." It was lucky he had some change left, from last week's lunches at school. He'd forgot about the tax on it. "I—I—I—please give it to me. . . ." He had to hurry.

"O.K. Take it easy, you'll get it—s' long as it's cash." The clerk had to write in a book. It took a long time, and Mike stood there, shaking all over inside himself. Not thinking about anything, not daring to think, just *waiting*.

But they gave it to him in the end, all wrapped up in brown paper.

He got out of the store, crowded with people shopping for Christmas. The music all over from loudspeakers, "Hark, the Herald Angels Sing." Out in the dark, up the side street.

He sat down on the curb and tore off the brown paper, and loaded the camera. You could do that easy by feel. Under a street light, careful, he turned the neg up to where it said 1; screwed the thread of the cord into the synchro-flash hole in the Kodak's side.

Sammy thought he was just a *baby*, didn't know anything.

The flashbulb didn't want to go in straight, but he persuaded it, finally. He got up and walked on up the block toward the house. Most houses dark or dim-lighted. He came to the one he was just learning to call home, not really home. Just where you lived now.

He didn't go in. He went around, very careful and quiet, around the side to the back yard. There was grass, he knew, a tree, flowers.

It was like something was telling him what to do. Maybe Dad.

He waited, a long while; the shutter lever cocked on the Kodak, and his finger on the release.

Like a half-remembered dream, Dad saying, "You never know when the big shot'll turn up. You've just got to be ready for it."

And after a while—after a long while, it seemed—there was a little noise: the back door opening. And slamming. Not loud, but loud enough.

Mike sat up a little straighter, where he knelt alongside the bush. The bush had some kind of flower on it, even at Christmas time, in California, and it smelled beautiful, warm and sweet and like heaven might smell.

Another noise, pretty near. Steps on the grass down from the back door. It was awful hard to tell just where to point the lens; you kind of had to guess by the sound. He'd done what Dad called *gone by the book,* set it at f/4.5 and 1/50th second, with the number-six flash. You had to kind of guess. And hope.

It went off like a bomb, only no noise; but that *kind* of feeling, one great big blinding flash.

1/50th second. And Mike was on his feet, the next fiftieth second, and running.

One big blinding flash. Just that instant of time, lighting up everything. Sharp black-and-white. Shocking and clear.

Sammy there, bending, with the limp, slender body over his shoulder, the long blond hair hanging down over his chest. Sammy, his eyes and mouth three dark O's in the night. The shovel there on the ground in front of him.

You were supposed to turn the film right away, in case you forgot and made a double exposure. But Mike's hands were shaking so, he didn't think he could, even if he didn't have to run.

He ran, holding the Kodak and the new flash attachment against his chest, hard and safe and precious. He ran up the block toward the lights and the open stores full of Christmas shoppers and the tan-uniformed policeman on the corner. And the funniest way, it seemed he wasn't really running toward all that at all; he was running toward Dad, looking for him and finding him.